# Praise for Maria Grace

"I've loved every book I've read so far by Maria Grace, and her latest *Pride and Prejudice* variation, *Fine Eyes & Pert Opinions*, was no exception." **Diary of an Eccentric**

"Maria Grace is stunning and emotional, and readers will be blown away by the uniqueness of her plot and characterization" **Savvy Wit and Verse**

"Maria Grace has once again brought to her readers a delightful, entertaining and sweetly romantic story while using Austen's characters as a launching point for the tale." **Calico Critic**

"I believe that this is what Maria Grace does best, blend old and new together to create a story that has the framework of Austen and her characters, but contains enough new and exciting content to keep me turning the pages. ... Grace's style is not to be missed." **From the desk of Kimberly Denny-Ryder**

# Fine Eyes & Pert Opinions

*Maria Grace*

White Soup Press

Published by: White Soup Press

For information, address
author.MariaGrace@gmail.com

ISBN-13: 978-0-9997984-1-6 (White Soup Press)

Author's Website: RandomBitsofFaascination.com
Email address: Author.MariaGrace@gmail.com

# Dedication

For my husband and sons.
You have always believed in me.

# ❧Chapter 1

*My mind was more agreeably engaged. I have been meditating on the very great pleasure which a pair of fine eyes in the face of a pretty woman can bestow.*
  ~ *Jane Austen,* **Pride and Prejudice**

Most days, Elizabeth could keep herself occupied and remind herself of the blessings she and her family enjoyed. But days like today reminded her far too much of what had been lost—and almost lost—since autumn cast its bony grip upon the vicarage. Best not dwell upon those grey thoughts. They were too quick to make themselves at home in one's mind, only to overstay their welcome.

She made her way along the dirty village street, the skirts of her dusky pink walking dress picking up a coating of dust as they swished around her legs. Spring, with its fresh smells and gentle warm breezes, had finally come to the little hamlet of Lambton, driving away the vestiges of a long, dark winter. Bits of new green—a very particular shade, quite different from the old established green of hardy plants— dotted the edges of the road. Birds chirped and twittered from unseen perches, their songs dappling the fresh afternoon air with musical notes unique to the season. Reminders that life continued on were a good thing.

Finished with her morning calls, she left the cobblestone street in favor of the dirt footpath that led into Pemberley's woods. The deep shade of arching hardwoods embraced her. The loam's perfume and the insects' twitters soon screened out all traces of Lambton. Yes, this was what she needed.

The ladies she had called upon had been kind when they remembered Mama—and well they should be, for she had been a gentle, kind, and gracious soul—but the pain of loss was still so fresh.

Still, today was the start of the seventh month since her passing, a time to set mourning aside. So many memories floated too close to the surface, though. The day would be better spent keeping to herself, quietly remembering … and grieving.

Mama would not have approved, insisting it was more important to celebrate with the living than to consider the dead. What better way to honor her memory than to do just that? At least, that was what Papa had said.

If only her feelings would cooperate with those directions. Would it be so bad to take a respite here in the woods that always soothed her soul?

Perhaps she should try to appear active. Some moments to practice her archery might suit. If questioned, she could explain that she was honoring Uncle and Aunt Gardiner's gift of a membership to the Derbyshire Archery Club by preparing for their next meeting. That might be just the thing.

The footpath forked; the right side led to Pemberley, the left toward the vicarage. A familiar tall dark form approached from the right. Long purposeful strides, brow furrowed, mouth drawn into something most mistook as a frown. Something troubled Mr. Darcy.

"Good day, Miss Elizabeth." He tipped his hat and bowed from his shoulders—an odd mix of formal and familiar.

He had been calling her Miss Elizabeth from the moment they had met—what was it, ten years ago now?—when Father had taken the living at Kympton. He would hardly call her anything else now.

She curtsied. "Good day, Mr. Darcy."

"Am I intruding? You are walking alone. I know, sometimes …"

"It is six months to the day of my mother's passing."

"Forgive me, I should have recalled. I must be intruding, so I will go. You cannot want company now." He was always so polite, so proper, but his deep brown eyes seemed crestfallen.

"Pray, do not. I think perhaps—perhaps too much solitude might not be a good thing for me today. I am walking to the vicarage—"

"Might I walk with you then?" They set off together down the left-hand path, their steps falling into a comfortable harmony as they often did when they walked together.

"It seems you have something on your mind. Pray tell, would you like to talk about it?"

He clasped his hands behind his back and stared at the path they walked. A sunbeam filtered through the canopy, highlighting his classically handsome profile. She was right; something weighed on him. "It has been a long time since you have called upon Georgiana."

"I am sorry for that, but we have been in mourning—"

"I meant no criticism. You have had other concerns. In that time, though, she has quarreled with Mrs. Younge. The situation escalated to the point where I was forced to dismiss her. Georgiana is without a companion at present. This is the third—no, the fourth companion—who has quit or had to be dismissed in eighteen months."

Actually, it was the fifth, but Mrs. Allen had only remained for a week and a day. No point in reminding him of that.

"She needs another companion, but I am at a loss how to find one suitable. I had hoped to ask your assistance."

"I should think that one of your aunts might be a far more appropriate source of help. Their connections in good society might be very useful."

"They supplied the last three companions."

She gripped her hands behind her back. That should help conceal her true thoughts. "So, you want to seek help from another quarter?"

"Do not toy with me, I know that tone of your voice. You do not approve." Did he just roll his eyes at her? "If you do not want to help me, I will find other means. You need only say so."

"Do you really want to hear another one of my pert opinions, as you called them the last time that I offered a sentiment you did not like?"

"It was not that I did not like it. I thought—and still do think—you were in error."

Stubborn, arrogant man. Just because he had attended university did not mean he knew everything! "If you take the time to do some reading on the matter, you will find I am correct. Those creatures we saw in the garden last summer were indeed moths—hawk-moths to be precise—not humming birds."

"You are quite mistaken. I am entirely certain—"

"You are an expert in all the natural sciences?"

"I am not accustomed to arguing such matters with young ladies."

"Because most are too stupid or insipid to hold on to a controversial point of view." Her fists clenched—now was not the time to reiterate her arguments.

"Another of your pert opinions." He glanced at her, just a hint of amusement in his eyes, a tiny dimple forming on his left cheek. "Tell me your views on acquiring another companion for my sister."

Why did he have to ask that? "Miss Darcy has had a long history of difficulty with governesses and companions."

"And school masters, do not forget those."

"Those as well. To have so many unfortunate experiences at just sixteen, that is very difficult for a girl."

"It is not easy on those around her, either." He harrumphed. "To have her tutors call her stupid and willful was no easy thing. Had my father been alive—enough to say it would not have been pretty."

She lifted an open hand. There was no need to discuss what Old Mr. Darcy's reaction might have been. "It is a mercy for all of you that he did not live to see it happen. I am certain Miss Darcy is acutely aware of how he would have been disappointed in her and how disappointed you are in her."

"Do I not have a right?"

"Knowing one has let down her family is—" Did she really want to reveal so much? She worked her tongue along the roof of her mouth. "It is a difficult burden to bear. I cannot blame her for not wanting to bring in yet another person to remind her of her failures."

"Then what do you suggest?" He kicked a rock aside with more force than necessary.

"Go without a companion for a little while. Invite some of your cousins or close friends to visit. Give her a little taste of what society might be like when she comes out. Provide an environment where she might succeed and look forward to more successes."

He stopped short and gaped at her. "It sounds like you want me to reward her bad behavior."

"Think carefully, I did not say that."

"What you suggest is ludicrous."

"You are entitled to that opinion, as I am to mine. I remind you, though, you asked me what I thought."

"Yes, I did ask." His brow knotted, and he got that dark look that usually presaged him saying something regrettable. "But I assumed you would offer me the sound advice I expect from you, not merely another one of your brash opinions."

Not today, absolutely not today. "Then I strongly

suggest you seek out someone whose advice will please you more. Good day." She curtsied and marched off.

A fortnight later, Darcy leaned back into the leather wingchair that had been Father's and scrubbed his face with his hands. The first rays of sunset cast a golden glow on his study. Was he doing the right thing?

He stared at the bookshelves that lined the wall behind his desk. Row upon neat row of books in matching black leather bindings, an enviable collection of wisdom, none of which held the answers he needed.

Everything in his neatly ordered office pointed to doing the same thing he had before: find a new companion and put Georgiana in her care. But after four—no, it was five—failures, trying something else made sense. But such a thing to try.

It grated against everything he had been taught, everything that Father demanded of him.

*"You must protect your sister." Father gripped Darcy's forearm hard, drawing him close, the stench of infection and decaying flesh almost overwhelming.*

*"I will. You can trust me," Darcy whispered in his ear, only barely managing not to gag over the foul air.*

*"That remains to be seen; you have never cared for another person, only yourself. I know you are a selfish being, though I suppose your mother and I are to blame. But you cannot be so now. Richard will help you—"*

*"You do not need to appoint a second guardian."* Wounded
pride stung as much as Father's cane.
*"I do. Trust me, I do."*

Father had been right. Though he disagreed with
Richard more frequently than they agreed, having
someone to share the responsibility with had proven
welcome.

Richard's agreement with Miss Elizabeth's suggestion came as a surprise, but having asked his opinion,
Darcy was all but committed to following through on
the notion.

Her ridiculous, preposterous, absurd idea.

But she had proven herself so flawless in her
judgments—there was a reason he turned to her time
after time for advice. He would be a fool to ignore
her now even if Richard had hinted more than once
Miss Elizabeth was really below his notice.

A soft knock at his door and Georgiana peeked in.
"You wished to see me?"

He beckoned her in. "We need to discuss the matter of your companion."

"What do you mean? She is gone, what more need
be said." She stopped an arm's length from him, fury
rolling off her in waves.

She looked so much like their mother when she
was angry: green eyes flashing, color high on her
porcelain cheeks, her shoulders pulled back in her
white sprigged muslin as straight and elegant as a
marble statue. None could fault her beauty nor mistake her displeasure.

Darcy drew a deep breath and counted to sixteen—one for each year of her life. Hopefully he
would not have to do this much longer or the pauses

could grow extremely awkward. "You should have a companion."

"I suppose you have hired another—without even telling me? Why would you care what I think?" She stamped, but the rich carpet muffled the sound.

He stood and gripped the back of the chair—control, he must remain in control. "You will not take that tone with me."

She wrapped her arms around her waist and glowered. "Fine then. Just tell me what I must next endure, and send me away."

One, two, three, four, five long steps took him behind his desk. He riffled through the tidy stack of papers on his desk. "I have a surprise that may please you."

She lifted her head and stared at him with innocent eyes that reminded him so much of their mother's. Jaw dropping, her defiance fell away like a forgotten shawl. "I am not going to have a new companion?"

"We will take some time to consider options, and perhaps give you some new opportunities, new experiences in the meantime."

"What kind of new experiences? You have already sent me to school once, and I will not go again." Her jaw trembled.

Pray, no tears, not now.

"I have received the final letters confirming it all just this afternoon." He tapped the pages in his hand. "We shall be hosting a house party next month. I have invited Bingley and his sister. Ccousins Anne and Fitzwilliam, as well. He invited his friend Sir Alexander—"

"The new baronet?"

MARIA GRACE

"Yes, as well as his sister. I expect them to stay the month complete."

"Pemberley is hosting a house party?" She bounced slightly on her toes. "Pray, say that I will be included, too, even though I am not yet out." She bit her lower lip and stared at him pleadingly.

"On Miss Elizabeth's recommendation, you will be part of the party. You will have a small taste of polite society and see what it requires. Provided of course that you conduct yourself accordingly, you will be included in all our activities."

"Oh, I will, I will. I am so excited! Perhaps we might introduce Mr. Bingley to Miss Elizabeth. He might do very well—"

He dragged his hand down his face, in part to cover the tiny smile trying to make its way across his lips. What was it about introducing men and women that was so fascinating to young ladies? "No matchmaking; do not cross me, or you will be excluded from all company. I shall make introductions if they desire them, but I will not interfere with my friends' lives in such a way."

"Yes, sir." She clasped her hands before her and looked down, a mite deflated.

"I would like you to plan a small affair for our guests. It will be good practice for you. What say you about a picnic? Just after they arrive might be an excellent time, and you may invite the Bennets to attend if you like."

"I can plan it?" Wide eyes and an even wider smile barely contained her excitement.

"Yes, every detail. Work with Mrs. Reynolds and heed her advice throughout."

"I will, I will." Her eyes sparkled.

"Now off with you, go to your planning. There is work I must yet finish."

"Yes, sir. Thank you." She dashed off, as though he might change his mind if she lingered.

Her enthusiasm should please him, but it was a mite disconcerting. He had never seen her respond that way to any of his suggestions. But it was better than the vapors and near hysteria that had preceded Mrs. Younge's arrival, so perhaps it was an improvement.

Cool late afternoon breezes blew across Elizabeth's shoulders, rustling knee high stalks of faintly violet-pink mayflowers into her pale green skirt. She tucked several stalks of mayflowers and a few of yellow cowslip into her basket. They would be pretty on the dinner table tonight. The afternoon warmth would only be with her an hour or two more before sunset laid its golden glow across the garden. So restful and calm—but she really should not remain here while there were still tasks left undone in the house.

"Miss Elizabeth! Miss Elizabeth!" That shout could only belong to Miss Darcy. Her disposition had been so unpredictable recently.

Elizabeth arranged her features into what was hopefully a pleasant order.

A flurry of white muslin and ribbons ran toward her. A young maid hurried to keep up—not Miss Darcy's companion. Interesting, no companion. Could that be the very point of the call?

Had Mr. Darcy listened to her advice after all? She covered her mouth with hand—that probably should not be as pleasing as it was. But it was a great compliment, especially when he had initially thought it ridiculous.

Miss Darcy reached her side, panting and gasping for breath. "I am so very glad to have found you."

"You will forgive me if I hardly consider that a noteworthy achievement. You do it so regularly, I would think it something taken for granted." Elizabeth cocked her head and lifted her eyebrow.

"How can you be a wit at a time like this? I am in such a state, and you see fit to make jokes?" Miss Darcy's eyes bulged, and her cheeks puffed out just a bit. If she had any idea of how like a pug that expression made her look, the poor girl would be certain never to do it again.

Elizabeth pressed her lips together hard, now was not the time to laugh—it would certainly be misunderstood. She looped her arm into Miss Darcy's and looked at the young maid. "Go to the kitchen and take a rest there. The cook will give you something to eat."

"Thank you, madam." The girl scurried off, head down, as quickly as she could without earning an admonition not to run. Miss Darcy must have been in high dudgeon, taking it out on the unfortunate servant all the way to the vicarage.

"Come now, you know I always improve your spirits. Let us stroll in the woods. One can hardly hold on to an ill-temper there." She encouraged Miss Darcy along a graveled path that circled the kitchen and flower gardens. Mr. Darcy had added the gravel just a few months ago when it became so muddy it was difficult for Papa to walk it.

"I am not ill-tempered. I am at sixes and sevens."

Pebbles crunched and crackled as they gave way under Miss Darcy's heavy footfalls. "I know I shall remain so if you do not help me."

Elizabeth pointed to the white painted bench with rough roses carved in the back that sat under the shade of a cluster of oaks and beckoned Miss Darcy to sit with her.

Two songbirds began a conversation in the treetops overhead. They scanned the branches for the songsters, but the musical parties remained hidden in the leaves.

"Fitzwilliam has done it again." Miss Darcy slumped and let her head hang, chin to chest.

"He has hired another companion?"

"No, no. It is much worse than that." Miss Darcy's penchant for finding something to be unhappy about—well it was not her most endearing trait.

"You will have to explain."

"He has planned a house party. I am not only to attend, but to help entertain our guests. He wants me to plan a picnic. A picnic!"

"That sounds like a very good thing.? I am surprised you are not more pleased." Elizabeth bit her bottom lip. Had she been so mistaken?

"I do not know how to do such a thing. You of all people should know that. Fitzwilliam wants me to be an accomplished young lady so he can marry me off and be rid of me. But I am ... am ... just a disappointment to him." Miss Darcy jumped up and stalked along the length of the bench. "Look at me. I am nearly sixteen years old, and I can hardly read. I have had teachers and masters. Not one of them has made the letters stay on the page any better than the next."

"You play beautifully on the pianoforte, and you sing—"

"It is not good enough—not for my brother."

"Your French is so good; everyone who has heard you believes you a native speaker."

Miss Darcy extended open hands, silently demanding answers no one had. "Only until they write something for me to translate for them or ask me to read them some French poetry. Then they call me willful and stubborn—"

"I am sure that cannot happen often."

"Then you are surely wrong. Only this morning Fitzwilliam demanded I read to him in French—in the morning room, no less! He wanted me to practice reading for our guests—according to him, my voice is so pretty it will surely entertain them. It was only by a stroke of great luck that he turned to a piece I memorized long ago. I recited it to him—I thought he would have been pleased. You would have expected that, no?"

Elizabeth nodded, though her gut knotted. Knowing Mr. Darcy, there was only one way this would end.

"Can you imagine—it only made him angry. Angry! He thinks I am headstrong or stupid—I do not know which—simply because I cannot always render so flawless a performance. You see, even when I do something correctly, it is not enough for him. It never will be."

"I am so sorry." Elizabeth pulled a handkerchief from her sleeve and pressed it into Miss Darcy's hand. "Your memory is so good; I can hardly think of a time you have had to work to commit something to memory. Surely that must count for something."

"Nothing pleases my brother."

"I know this is difficult to believe, but this house party may turn into something very good indeed."

"And how do you see my brother's high-handedness being so very good?" Tears trickled down Miss Darcy's cheeks.

"I have every faith that you can do what he has asked of you and do it very well. When you see that you can succeed—I am sure it will make a great deal of difference in so many things."

"How can I possibly plan anything? I cannot write, and I know lists will need to be made. I cannot even read receipts to select the food for the picnic." Her words trailed off in a sob.

"Have you spoken to Mrs. Reynolds?"

"So that she can know how stupid I am? Of course not."

Elizabeth pinched the bridge of her nose. She was only sixteen; allowances must be made. "Her role as housekeeper is to assist you and make certain you succeed. She was a great help to your mother, especially when her ... eyes were too tired to read or write. I recall Mrs. Reynolds often writing what your mother dictated, even reading to her at times. I have no doubt she will be ready to help you as well."

Miss Darcy peeked up over the handkerchief, eyes wide with surprise, or was it disbelief? "I had no idea she did those things for my mother."

"You are not nearly as alone as you like to believe yourself to be."

"I am afraid I might do this wrong. What will happen if it is a disaster?" She squeezed her eyes shut, tears leaking down her cheeks.

Elizabeth rolled her eyes. It was only a picnic. Just

how much could go wrong with a picnic? "I am certain—"

"I know it will be well if you help me. Will you
help me? Pray, say you will. I know I can do it if you
are there with me, advising me like you do with
Fitzwilliam." She caught Elizabeth's hand and tugged
at it.

"I do not advise your brother."

"He trusts your judgment more than anyone else's.
So do I. Pray help me as you help him, and I know all
will be well."

"I cannot neglect my duties at home, but—"
Hopefully, she would not regret this. "—I will help
you as much as I can."

## ❧ Chapter 2

A remarkable three weeks passed. Darcy peeked into the music room. Light, lilting strains poured through the open door. His mother had designed the room with balance and harmony in mind, but recent years rarely saw much peace here, filled instead with Georgiana's unpredictable moods and tempers.

The last few weeks had changed that. Now the pale-yellow walls—populated with landscapes and floral nature studies—and the teal-upholstered furnishings radiated the peace of a summer's day. Either the harp in the right-hand corner near the windows or the pianoforte on the left were in nearly constant use, offering soothing melodies to whomever walked past.

This morning, Georgiana sat at the pianoforte, eyes closed, shoulders swaying in time with the music, a faint smile playing at her lips. Was that a new piece?

No wait, Miss Mary Bennet had played that refrain, though not nearly so pleasingly, a week before when the Bennets visited for supper and cards. How did Georgiana manage to play so well with no music and only hearing the melody once? If only she could learn other things so easily.

Clearly, she was not stupid. But willful? Perhaps.

Why did she simply not do what she was asked, when she was asked, in the way she was asked?

He clenched one fist behind his back. There was a way that things should be done—was that really so hard to accept? Fine hairs on the back of his neck prickled. Miss Elizabeth insisted that methods which worked constituted the "right way" to do something. It was an annoying notion, but perhaps it applied now. The prickly sensation eased a bit.

As long as Georgiana continued on her path to improvement, he would hold his peace. This boded very well for the house party.

He turned away and continued down the corridor. Their guests were to arrive today, assuming their travels proceeded as planned. Pray Miss Elizabeth was right and the experience inspired Georgiana toward further improvement.

The butler approached. "Sir, you requested to be notified when the carriages were seen on the lane."

"Very good. Tell Mrs. Reynolds to lay refreshments in the blue parlor rather than the drawing room."

The butler bowed and hurried off. Darcy strode to the large window at the end of the corridor. Several carriages trundled up the road. The leading one bore the Fitzwilliam family crest. Perhaps he would have a few moments to familiarize Richard with the news of

Georgiana. He would be pleased to hear of her progress.

A few minutes later, the butler announced, "Colonel Fitzwilliam and Miss de Bourgh."

Darcy froze where he stood, stomach threatening to drop into his shoes. The de Bourgh name did that. Pray, let not Aunt Catherine have decided to accompany Anne. He squeezed his eyes shut and pinched his temples. It was just the sort of thing Aunt Catherine was apt to do, especially when the house party offered a most tempting opportunity to "manage family business."

A brisk walk to the blue parlor sloughed away a bit of the tension, but not enough.

His mother had decorated this parlor in defiance of her sister's wishes and tastes. According to Aunt Catherine, it was too small and too bright. Sky blue was a dreadfully blue sort of color for a room—honestly, what logic offered such a critique? The furniture was too small and friendly, lacking the grandeur such a room should have. On and on she would go at how insufficient, informal, and inappropriate the room was. On that recommendation alone, Darcy would never see it altered. And it was good reason to use it to receive his guests now.

Richard ushered Anne into the parlor, both a little dusty, but seemingly in good spirits. Anne wore the vaguely disdainful expression she usually wore, but it appeared more habitual than meaningful. After all, Pemberley offered exactly the type of accommodations and appointments to which she was accustomed.

Richard still had shadows around his eyes—an unchanging feature ever since his return from France.

Even his retirement from the army had not altered them. Despite his ready, if somewhat forced smile, they remained.

"Are you going to greet us?" Anne's voice was pleasant—for the moment—with only the barest edge of ire.

Darcy bowed toward her. "Of course, you are welcome, Anne. I was just wondering what you might need for your comfort after your long journey."

"You kill me with your solicitude, cousin. Tell me, how do you plan for us to make merry whilst we are here?" Anne tossed her head and minced her way to an open armchair. So, she was trying on her mother's persona today. Hopefully the whim would pass soon.

Though her health had improved, she was still unattractive: thin and pale. Prominent collarbones demonstrated her frailty while the blue veins that stood out on her thin skin harkened back to the sickroom. One was afraid to cough in her direction, lest she take ill.

Anne ran her hand along the edge of a chair and sat down. "These are very dated—utterly out of fashion now. At the very least, you ought to have them recovered. What will your other guests say?"

Richard dropped heavily onto the settee and slumped like a feed sack against a barn wall. "That they are grateful for the invitation and find everything entirely to their liking. To do otherwise would be entirely rude."

"Yes, yes, but what would they be thinking? Surely you must be concerned with their good opinion." Anne's eyes narrowed—no doubt she was formulating a way to correct Richard for his posture.

"If their good opinion is lost because of my furnishings, then it was not worth having in the first place," Darcy muttered through gritted teeth.

"That only shows how little you understand of people's opinions and whose is worth the earning. I grant you the current party—that Bingley fellow and his sister, if I recall correctly—may not be the most fashionable of company. Their judgments may be of little consequence. But one never knows when someone might come into a place whose impressions do matter. If I were mistress here—"

Darcy jumped and all but ran toward the sideboard, laden with covered dishes. "Do you care for refreshments? I imagine you must be ready for proper food after having taken your meals at inns the last three days."

"Yes, that is a lovely idea." Anne excused herself to the side board.

Darcy edged to Richard's side and whispered, "Is Aunt Catherine following?"

Richard made that face he had used since childhood to express extreme disdain. It had been uproariously funny at age ten, but not since. "No, but not because she did not suggest it would be a good idea. I fear I had to argue that if Anne spent time alone in your company, it might make you more sympathetic in taking Anne—"

"Not that again! How could you have placed those expectations on me?"

"It slipped out in a moment of weakness, after a third glass of port. I was desperate. It seemed less bad than having our aunt join us."

Darcy rubbed the back of his neck. "Perhaps it is a very good thing for England you are no longer in the service of the King."

"It is a very good thing for me." A savage look filled his eyes, but fled almost as quickly as it came. "Besides, with your other guests, there will be sufficient distraction for Anne to forget about her mission of marriage."

Anne forget her lifelong motivation? "I think that hardly likely."

"No coconut macaroons, Darcy? I should have though you would have remembered those were my favorite." Anne flounced back to her seat, a little pout on her lips.

Richard cleared his throat—a warning sound Anne would probably ignore.

"I shall have Mrs. Reynolds place an order with the confectioner."

"Our French chef prepares them himself." Anne's eyebrows rose and she peered down her prominent Fitzwilliam nose.

"My English cook does not." Darcy ground his teeth lest he say anything to further this conversation.

"And that is why you must bring on a French chef. You know, I could help you manage all these details…"

"Excuse me. I will speak to Mrs. Reynolds." He walked out in slow, measured steps. Running was undignified.

Thankfully, once promised her macaroons, Anne was easily persuaded to retire to her rooms and rest from her travels. Through not as delicate as she once was, she still had little stamina. Just as well—Darcy preferred to greet his other guests without her insinuating herself at his side. No one would benefit from the misguided idea that she might be hostess at Pemberley.

Richard drained the last of his beer and set his glass aside. "Do not allow her to get under your skin. Anne has had no better example to learn from than her mother. Now that her health has improved, you will see. She will develop a whole new set of irritating habits from the ladies of the *ton*. On the bright side, her dowry will attract enough attention that you will no longer be her primary aim."

"I fear Georgiana will learn from her."

"When she is not trying to win your attentions—and Pemberley as her mother demands—she really is not a bad sort."

"Have you considered trying to keep Rosings in the Fitzwilliam family?"

Richard chuckled. "I said she is not a bad sort, not that she is of stern enough stuff to tolerate a crusty old soldier like me."

The butler entered. "Sir Alexander Garland and Miss Garland."

Richard rose and bowed. "How good to see you Garland, Miss Garland. May I introduce my cousin, Fitzwilliam Darcy."

"Pleased to make your acquaintance." Darcy bowed. Neither of his two newest guests bore any resemblance to his expectations.

Garland was by far the largest man he had ever seen—not the tallest, but the most heavily muscled. Impeccably proportioned, he resembled nothing so much as a larger-than-life marble statue with all aspects chiseled and carved to perfection. Jealousy might be a reasonable response, except that Garland provided a most worthy target for Anne's attentions, making him exactly the sort of man Darcy wanted at Pemberley now.

Valkyrie. That was the only word to describe the woman beside Garland. Darcy swallowed hard, sweat prickling his upper lip. Her face—quite handsome— was the feminine form of her brother's. She was easily as tall as Darcy himself. Her expression was impossible to read. Neither pleasure nor censure read in her brilliant, glittering icy blue eyes.

"It was very good of you to invite us on the strength of Fitzwilliam's suggestion alone." Garland glanced at Richard. "Though I am left wondering what precisely he told you, and how Blanche and I are to live up to it."

Miss Garland lifted an arched eyebrow ever so slightly. A painter ought to capture that expression on canvas.

"Be at ease, I have said nothing that was not entirely true." Richard gestured for them to sit.

"Please help yourself to some refreshments before you make yourselves comfortable." Darcy cast a sideways glare. This was not Richard's home, after all.

"Thank you, I am a mite peckish." Garland approached the sideboard, his sister close behind.

Her every movement was elegant, graceful, like a dancer's and as effortless as the morning breeze.

"Darce, you are staring." Richard elbowed him.

Darcy shook his head and blinked.

"Watch yourself—she hates being stared at."

Darcy cleared his throat and looked away. Heat crept along his jaw. Perhaps a house party was not as good an idea as he had originally thought.

The Garlands arranged themselves—she on the fainting couch, he in the largest chair in the room.

"Had you a pleasant journey?" Darcy forced himself not to notice the utterly improper but graceful way Miss Garland draped herself on the sinuously curved seat.

"It was as pleasant as one might hope." Garland shrugged and popped a cucumber sandwich into his mouth.

"Is traveling not just a series of inconveniences that string together two distant locations?" Miss Garland said, her voice sensuous as silk.

"I take it you do not like to travel?" Darcy glanced toward her, taking care not to stare. It should not be so difficult.

"I enjoy being in new places and experiencing all a lovely locale has to offer." The corner of her lips turned up in an expression that might have been suggestive on a woman less refined. "It is the act of getting there and back again which often proves disagreeable."

"Which is why we have a new, well-sprung traveling coach." Garland raised his glass toward her. "I enjoy the entire adventure, beginning to end."

"And because you do not like traveling alone. Really Alexander, you must get yourself a suitable wife soon so you can stop dragging me about from place to place." The corner of her lips lifted and dimpled her perfect cheek.

Darcy and Richard traded glances.

"You know someone?" Miss Garland seemed very interested.

"Our cousin, Miss Anne de Bourgh. She is resting from her own journey at the moment, but you will meet her at dinner." Richard winked at Garland.

"How very promising. You must take pains to

meet her, Alexander. I give you leave to like her very much, provided she does not object to traveling."

"I shall inquire after her preferences at the earliest opportunity." He bowed from his shoulders.

The butler entered. "Mr. and Miss Bingley, sir."

Darcy rose. "I am pleased you have joined us. Sir Alexander, Miss Garland, Colonel Fitzwilliam, may I present Mr. and Miss Bingley."

Bingley bowed, grinning a bit like Darcy's favorite retriever. "So pleased to make your acquaintance."

"Indeed," Miss Bingley made a very proper curtsey. If one were to write a handbook on the curtsey, it might well be illustrated by drawings of Miss Bingley.

Everything about her was proper and formal and ordinary. She possessed enough accomplishments for three women, though she never seemed to make any profitable use of them. Whereas Miss Elizabeth could manage to keep an agreeable conversation alive in a room of dissenting opinions, Miss Bingley only repeated phrases from some young woman's conversation manual with no regard as to whom was present.

"Please, take some refreshment, and join us." Darcy beckoned them in.

"Very thoughtful of you, Darcy—thank you. Those last ten miles of road! I say they must be some of the worst we have traversed." Bingley walked toward the sideboard while looking over his shoulder and talking. He was apt to walk into furniture that way. It had happened more than once.

"You came from Derby?" Sir Alexander leaned forward, elbows on his knees.

"You know the road, then?" Bingley lifted his glass.

"Enough that we traveled a full day extra to avoid it! My sister ...."

"She is fortunate to have a brother so considerate." Miss Bingley's voice had a sour note as she cast a sidelong glance at Bingley.

"But the means are worth the ends, are they not?" Bingley said. "Pemberley is as lovely as I remember it."

"Are you still looking to purchase an estate?" Darcy asked.

"Yes, he is." Miss Bingley stopped just shy of batting her eyes at Darcy.

"You answer most decidedly." *For one not asked—* Miss Garland did not say it, but the words were clearly carried by the tilt of her head.

Miss Bingley started.

"Caroline well knows my desire. I have just not found one entirely suitable, yet." Bingley layered a slice of cold meat over buttered bread.

"Do not mind my sister. She is peevish when she travels," Garland said.

"Peevish, you say? If my company is so disagreeable, I think it best if I were to rest and collect myself before dinner." Though she smiled and made all the right gestures, something about her speech felt like the bitter aftertaste of a fruit gone off.

"Yes, do. We shall all be better off if you find something with which to soothe your temper. You sound as though you have a headache coming on." Garland waved his sister off.

"I shall have my housekeeper show you to your room." Darcy preceded her to the door.

"I think I shall excuse myself as well, if you do not object, Charles." Miss Bingley turned her back on her brother.

The two ladies met Darcy at the door. Miss Bingley, though generally considered tall and handsome, seemed diminutive and unfinished beside Miss Garland. He called for Mrs. Reynolds and watched their retreat. What would Georgiana think of their company?

Later that evening, Darcy paced the length of the blue parlor. The furniture had been rearranged for the comfort of his guests. The large chair that fitted Garland had been moved closer to the couch and chairs. The fainting couch —on Mrs. Reynolds' advice—had been placed near Darcy's preferred seat. Yes, Richard would doubtlessly harass him for it, but when Mrs. Reynolds spoke, it was wise to listen.

Anne would still complain the furnishings were dated and the floral carpet was hopelessly out of fashion. The color was drab, according to her—Darcy found it soothing. The gold curtains were too heavy, as were the sideboards and the carved oak tea table that had been his mother's favorite piece in the room. No matter what Anne believed, she would never be the woman whose taste governed Pemberley.

Or his own dress. He tugged his sleeves more from habit than from need. It had been a long time since he had taken such care dressing for dinner. The navy-blue jacket was new—although not purchased for this event, he was not the sort of man who would do that—and it fitted very well.

Tonight's company was far more distinguished than what he usually kept in Derbyshire. But more importantly, he did not wish to be found wanting in the eyes of Anne or Miss Garland. The former because she would not hesitate to make her opinion known before his guests, and the latter ... just because he did not.

Georgiana entered, her eyes glittering and her cheeks glowing. This was her first time joining such a party for dinner. Her pristine white gown of fine muslin struck just the right balance for a girl who was not yet out, but was enjoying company in her own home.

"Will you wish me to play tonight?" Georgiana glanced at the pianoforte, at him, and back again.

"I believe our guests would find it very entertaining. Perhaps the new piece I heard you practicing?"

"Yes, I think I am ready to perform that one. I have two other new pieces ready as well."

"Indeed? I look forward to hearing them."

"To hearing what?" Richard strode in with large purposeful steps as though master of all he surveyed.

He was a guest at Pemberley and should—somehow—demonstrate he understood and appreciated the hospitality. Proper guests behaved that way. But then, Uncle Matlock had never been as concerned for propriety as Father had. Perhaps no one had ever been as concerned for such things as Father had.

"Georgiana will play for us tonight—new music she has just perfected," Darcy said.

"Excellent." Richard rubbed his hands together. "I love a good musical exhibition."

"Music? Did I hear you say music?" Miss Garland swept in wearing a gown of blue so pale it was almost white. Ethereal. The shimmering fabric carried the glint of fresh cut ice, bringing a chill to the air as she breezed past. "I adore anything musical."

"Miss Garland, this is my sister, Miss Georgiana Darcy." Darcy gestured toward Georgiana, and the ladies curtsied.

"Do you play, Miss Garland?" Georgiana's voice was soft and demure, exactly as it should have been.

Garland burst in, booming, "She plays and sings marvelously well—pianoforte and harp—one of the loveliest voices I have heard."

Darcy winced. Surely, he could moderate his tone. "May I present—"

"Your sister? So, I heard." Garland took her hand and bowed over it. "Very charmed, Miss Darcy."

Georgiana blushed a most becoming color and curtsied—thank heavens she did not giggle. "I am pleased to make your acquaintance, Sir Alexander."

"I have long hated the name Alexander, but it sounds something quite distinguished from your lips. Perhaps I shall rethink it now." He smiled broadly and stepped a little closer to her.

Georgiana giggled.

Darcy winced.

"You say the most absurd things," Miss Garland rolled her eyes. "Please do excuse him. He is always rather cakey in the presence of a pretty young thing."

Garland laughed, a deep-bellied rumble that rattled the windows and Darcy's nerves. How could Garland accept such treatment from his sister?

"You are a fine one, putting on airs, Blanche. You have just proven yourself every bit as improper as I am with your remark." He winked.

Instead of being cowed by her brother's remonstrations, she laughed—laughed!—with him. Pray Georgiana did not mimic their behavior.

"I suppose I have been too long in your company,

brother, and have begun taking after you." Miss Garland fluttered her eyelashes three times, just enough to make her point.

"Then by all means, seek other company—is that not what we are here for?"

"I believe I shall." She tossed her head with an affected huff and left the room.

A chill silence fell. Darcy glanced at Richard who had the good grace to display some alarm.

But Garland rolled his eyes and offered Georgiana his arm. "Why do you not show me about the room?"

Georgiana took his arm and headed toward a glass case of garniture their mother had collected.

"What do you think—" Miss Garland breezed in with Anne and Miss Bingley on her arms. Bingley followed a step behind. "Have I sufficiently obeyed your command? I believe I have located quite suitable alternative company."

"Did you hear that, Richard? I have been deemed suitable company." Anne pressed her hand to her chest. She might be smiling, but clearly, she was not amused.

"Do not worry, dear," Richard's eyebrows flashed up. "Miss Garland will learn the truth soon enough."

Georgiana snickered from the far side of the room. Darcy glowered. She wilted like a cut flower in the sun.

How could his sister learn how to act in proper society with examples such as these? Miss Bingley had the grace to look affronted. Why the Bennets, every one of them, showed far better manners!

"Do not listen to him." Miss Garland's eyes admonished Richard. "The men in one's family are often one's harshest critics. Is that not true, Miss Bingley?"

Miss Bingley's cheeks colored to match the deep rose of her gown. She felt the impropriety of it, too. How odd to find himself of the same mind as she.

"Let us proceed to dinner." Darcy gestured toward the door.

Miss Garland appeared at his arm as though claiming her right of his escort. She dropped her fingers onto his elbow and looked him in the eye. How odd not to have to lower his gaze to a lady. They led the others to the small dining room.

"It seems I have offended you," she said softly. Not a whisper that might have softened her position, but a quiet voice that left none of her assurance behind.

"I am not accustomed to siblings taking such liberties with one another." No, that probably was not the most proper answer, but how else could one answer such a direct question?

"No surprise. Your sister, and I imagine much of your family, are entirely intimidated by you."

"She is twelve years my junior. I am more father to her than brother."

"Still, you might find your desires are better met with a bit less pride and a bit more privilege." Judgment lingered in her tone.

"You have decided opinions on the raising of young ladies."

"I was one not so long ago, sir. Perhaps I know of what I speak." Her lips pulled into a tight expression that was anything but a smile.

Darcy would have pulled at his collar had it not been unseemly.

"Not all young ladies are empty-headed flibberti-gibbets. Many of us are capable of quite rational thought and enjoy company that would treat us so. Some of us have improved our minds by extensive reading."

"My sister reads very little, Miss Garland. I fear her opinions are not so well-informed as yours."

"And you do not approve? You prefer well-informed company?" He eyebrow arched.

It would be far easier to remain annoyed with her had she not been so beautiful … and so right.

"Do not be so hard on her. I think there is a great deal more to her than you give her credit for." She turned just enough to catch a glimpse of Georgiana over her shoulder.

"She is an excellent musician when she puts forth the effort to learn." Somehow that sounded like very faint praise.

"I am pleased to hear she is in possession of some redeeming qualities."

Thankfully, he was able to seat Miss Garland at the table rather than respond.

Anne's lip curled back as she entered the small dining room. Obviously, she would rather have sat in the great dining hall. She might not have minded the way the chamber echoed when only eight sat at the table, but he did. Even this room was hardly full, as the table sat twelve easily. With this small a party, they could sit closer to one another and enjoy far broader conversations than the great hall would permit.

Many candles lit the room, shimmering off four large mirrors, two on either of the long walls and smaller ones that flanked the fireplace on the short wall. The Darcy family china lined the walnut table: a white background with a dark blue stripe that matched the small dining room walls, with a lozenge containing a gold script "D." A similar initial topped the silverware alongside the plates.

He rang the crystal bell, and Mrs. Reynolds orchestrated the parade of serving dishes to the table. Yes, he could have had the table set before they were seated, but there was something pleasing in the precise and ordered display of his household's efficiency.

Mrs. Reynolds introduced the dishes, and he rose to carve the fragrant roast beef joint.

"Do you care for beef, Miss Garland?" He gestured toward her plate.

"Thank you, no. I prefer fish."

Of course, she did, vexing woman. "Miss Bingley?"

"Yes, please." She smiled, just a hint of appreciation in her tone. Much more agreeable.

Agreeable? What was he thinking? When had he ever found Miss Bingley agreeable?

"So, Miss Bingley," Miss Garland's eyes did not rise from her plate. "I have heard you are quite musical."

"I am not sure from where you may have heard that." Miss Bingley turned her face aside demurely.

"Do not be so modest. I have been to several drawing rooms in London where I have heard mention of your skill. You must play for us this evening."

"Oh, yes," Georgiana said. "My brother has already asked me to play, and I should prefer not to be the only one."

"I shall be pleased to oblige." Miss Bingley seemed to speak directly to Georgiana.

"Excellent." Miss Garland's smile seemed genuine,

but if she was as skilled as her brother insisted, why had she not offered to play herself? A woman who did not push forward her own accomplishments was an interesting creature.

Intriguing, with effortless manners, well-informed, if decided, opinions. She was everything a woman should be and more. Fascinating, but yet unsettling.

"Tell me, Darcy, what does one do at Pemberley? We are so far from the diversions of society." Garland heaped a thick slab of meat on his plate.

"Shooting season has already begun. So, we may hunt or fish or ride," Richard said.

"How gracious of you to offer birds not your own." Miss Garland tsk-tsked under her breath.

Richard laughed. Loudly.

"I had planned for hunting parties." Darcy glanced at Georgiana and nodded.

"My brother has permitted me to plan a picnic— tomorrow if the weather agrees. I have invited the vicar's family to join us as well." Her voice squeaked, and she stammered just a mite. Though that would be viewed unfavorably when she came out, it was oddly appropriate right now.

"Vicar? Do not tell me he is a stodgy old killjoy who quashes the enjoyment from everything," Miss Garland said.

"He is not at all stodgy. His daughters are most amiable. They have promised they would come." Georgiana's gaze shifted between Miss Garland and Darcy.

"Daughters you say—how many has he? Are they sensible girls?" Miss Garland's eyes twinkled, almost mischievously.

"The eldest two are steady, well-bred young ladies

whose company I encourage my sister to keep." Hopefully that would end this line of conversation.

Silence. Heavy and prickly. Somehow it was almost worse than the conversation had been.

"I love a good picnic." Bless Bingley's artless enthusiasm.

"Do you now, sir?" Miss Garland leaned toward him. "Why do you find it so amusing when being ordered outside can be so very inconvenient?"

"I know of no place I like better. None at all. How could it be inconvenient to enjoy grounds as lovely as Pemberley?" Bingley raised his glass.

"How indeed sir—"

"Picnicking is not like traveling, Blanche. It is a very civilized pastime—a most agreeable way to spend an afternoon." Garland cast a sidelong look at Georgiana then frowned at his sister.

They locked eyes for a long, breath-stealing moment.

Finally, she dropped her gaze just enough. "Forgive me, I am a dreadful tease. I did not mean to offend, Miss Darcy, merely incite interesting conversation. I look forward to anything you have so graciously planned for us."

"Did any of you attend the theater this Season?" Garland asked.

"We did, as a matter of fact." Bingley set down his wineglass. "We had a lovely box at Drury Lane."

"Mr. Darcy joined us several times," Miss Bingley said.

"I should like very much to go to the theater." Georgiana spoke so softly they almost could not hear her.

Garland gasped. "You have not been?"

"Not yet. I am not out."

"But you will be soon. I promise you next Season, I shall escort you to every play in London." Richard should not promise such things.

"You will not." Darcy harrumphed. "There are quite a number of plays I do not find fitting for a young woman."

Georgiana sighed.

Sir Alexander leaned a little closer to her. "I am afraid he is correct. There are some utterly scandalous theatricals performed."

Richard swallowed a large gulp of wine. "Very well, I shall take you to every one your brother approves."

Darcy glanced around the table. Thankfully, no one appeared interested in any more food. "Shall we adjourn to the drawing room?"

Anne rolled her eyes and shook her head.

# Chapter 3

Darcy rose. Brandy and manly company would have to wait for another day. Was that a good thing or not? Garland might be even more unpredictable given enough libation.

He led his guests to the drawing room. It still smelt vaguely of furniture polish—a testament to Mrs. Reynolds' thoroughness. Formal and regular and proper, it was easily his favorite public room in the house. While the furniture was elegant and understated and the burgundy drapes and upholstery to his tastes, he was most comforted by knowing the rules that governed the room and the company in it. Regular and predictable—how much more could one ask?

"I should like some music very much." Richard sauntered past the couch and matching chairs and the card table, to the far side of the room, opened the pianoforte, and dusted the keys with his handkerchief—not that Mrs. Reynolds would have permitted any dust on them to begin with. "We have had promise of such delightful entertainments. The question is, whom shall we have to begin? Anne, why not you?"

Good idea. Appeasing her pride and getting the inevitable unpleasantness over with as quickly as possible could harm no one. "Do favor us with a song. Georgiana may accompany you."

Georgiana hid her face from his view. Was she about to turn missish? "Perhaps Anne knows that folk song I practiced yesterday. It is such a lovely light piece to start an evening."

She rifled through the music laying atop the pianoforte and handed a sheet of music to Anne.

Anne snatched it from her hand and harrumphed. "Very well."

Georgiana looked over her shoulder at her. "You choose the tempo, and I shall follow?"

Anne adjusted her posture, drew a deep breath and sang the first line.

Darcy grimaced. How many verses would they have to endure? Anne's voice had all the appeal of a hound baying at a cornered fox.

Richard pressed his lips into a hard line and shared an aggrieved glance with Darcy. Even Georgiana's deft playing did not do much to assuage their suffering. But she was a clever girl and began the closing measure before Anne could draw breath for a third verse. Georgiana's final note rang out to soft, polite applause.

"Perhaps, Miss Bingley should regale us next." Richard gestured to Miss Bingley before Anne could comment.

Darcy braced himself for an acerbic remark, but

Anne demurred gracefully and sat in one of the arm-chairs beside Garland on the couch. Ah, now it made sense.

Miss Bingley replaced Georgiana at the pianoforte. Georgiana took her place near Bingley, sitting at the nearby card table.

"Miss de Bourgh does not entertain company often?" Miss Garland asked.

Darcy started. How could Anne's performance have distracted him from the woman on his arm?

"No, she does not. Lady Catherine has deemed her health too fragile to permit her much opportunity to do so."

"I thought as much. You look quite surprised. Do not tell me you failed to think the same thing." She looked up at him, one eyebrow cocked.

"I am not in the habit of commenting on a lady's performance." The muscles between his shoulders grew tight.

"Then you have no opinion?"

"Whatever opinion I have is not necessary to share."

Miss Garland snickered and peeked at Anne. "You keep your opinions under perfect regulation, then?"

"It is not proper—"

"Not everything in life is about propriety and control, Mr. Darcy. One must allow for a proper amount of abandon in one's life." The corners of her mouth lifted slightly as though daring him to disagree.

"Abandon? I see no need. It is control that is required. It is the core of civilized society, of every virtue—"

"And very, very dull indeed, sir." Miss Garland applauded Miss Bingley's performance and moved to take her place at the pianoforte.

Garland leaned back in his seat and folded his arms across his chest, all but ignoring Anne who seemed insistent on garnering his attention.

"May I find some music for you?" Georgiana asked.

"Thank you, no, my dear, for I mean to make a point here." She caught Darcy's gaze. "Miss Bingley delighted us with as fine an example of precision and control as I can remember hearing." She applauded softly at Miss Bingley standing just behind her. "However, I wish to demonstrate that there is equal appeal in spontaneity and abandon. I will begin to play, and any who dare may join with me."

"But what are you going to play?" Bingley leaned on his elbow, toward the pianoforte.

She lifted a graceful arm with a flourish. "I have no idea. We shall see when I begin." She played a sweet chord. "Is that key agreeable?"

"What nonsense." Anne snorted and ambled toward the book shelf, filled with books she would never read.

Garland sauntered toward the pianoforte. "You are performing on our first night here, Blanche?" He leaned his elbow on the instrument.

"I have a point to make, and I will not be deterred." She pounded out another chord, paused, closed her eyes, and danced her fingers across the keyboard.

Haltingly at first, the notes picked up speed and rhythm as she went, weaving into a pleasing melody. Richard, grinning as though he had too much wine, added a clapped counterpoint from Darcy's side of the room. Sharp staccato beats accented the rhythm—at least most of the time.

Miss Garland glanced over her shoulder at Richard and graced him with such a smile.

Garland winked at Richard and added his striking baritone to the mix—snippets of words here and there, but mostly just pleasing notes that fit Miss Garland's lead. Bingley tapped his foot and bobbed his head in time while his sister barely concealed her frown.

The music was pleasing to the ear, but lacked the structure and order needed to truly make it soothing. He wanted to like it—clearly everyone else in the room did, but something grated on him, ever so slightly, like a pin left in a shirt.

Georgiana glanced at Miss Garland who shifted over just slightly. What was she doing? Dear heavens, she was sitting at the instrument, too! What was she thinking?

Miss Garland nodded, and Georgiana began to play with just her right hand. Timid, quiet notes grew in confidence until she added her left hand as well. The two women locked eyes, heads swaying in tandem.

The simple melodies turned far more complex and intriguing. Sill, their raw, unpolished quality nettled Darcy's nerves. Had they only taken time to plan or practice, this might have been truly remarkable.

Georgiana's eyes sparkled, and her cheeks flushed. Had she ever looked so happy?

"I think it quite unseemly." Anne whispered at his shoulder—when had she approached? "How indecorous to leave us out."

"You may join if you wish. You might sing as Sir Alexander is doing." It must be Richard's influence that he said such a thing.

Anne pursed her lips.

He should not feel so satisfied. Touching her vanity was perhaps very low, but better that than have her clinging to his side.

"I should add a bit of decorum to this display." She moved to Sir Alexander's side, and after failing a few notes, hummed along with the musicians.

Alone on his side of the room, Darcy wavered between loneliness and contentment. What would it be like to not be an observer, but a participant?

Miss Garland and Georgiana's hands tangled on the keyboard and the music dissolved into mirth.

"I say, excellent, most excellent." Bingley clapped with the same enthusiasm he showed at the pugilism matches.

Darcy clutched his forehead. What was his drawing room becoming?

"He is right. That was a memorable performance," Richard elbowed him sharply.

"It was most … unique."

"You must learn to relax and enjoy yourself, man."

"I did enjoy it."

"Even if it left you wanting to crawl out of your skin." Richard laughed.

Of course, he would not understand. He never had.

"If you cannot enjoy it for your own sake, do so for Georgiana's. Look how well she is doing in the company of a baronet, no less." Richard pointed with his chin. "It seems that Miss Garland's company has set her at ease."

The two had not left the pianoforte, their spirits and color high, still gushing and laughing over their musical adventure. Miss Bingley, though, stood apart from them, a deep "'v'" forming between her brows.

Richard nodded firmly. "This is excellent preparation for her coming out next Season."

"I do not like the way they exclude—"

"The Bingley woman? Look—"

Miss Garland beckoned Miss Bingley to the piano and slid close to Georgiana. She said words he could not hear to Miss Bingley who began to play a piece she clearly knew well. A few measures later, Miss Garland added her own improvisational lines around Miss Bingley's melodies. Georgiana added hers.

Like the previous performance, it was not without merit, but still uncomfortable. Perhaps less so, though, being built upon an underlying foundation.

"See there, is not that the very example of gently bred civility and decorum?" Richard nodded toward the ladies.

Darcy grunted.

Richard leaned closer and whispered, "So what do you think of her, Darce?"

"Who, Miss Bingley?"

"Surely not. You are not in need of an heiress as I am. Miss Garland—what do you think of her?"

"I have had less than twelve hours' acquaintance with her." Darcy clasped his hands behind his back.

"I did not ask for a definitive sketch of her character, only your impressions. Or is that asking too much spontaneity from you?"

"I hardly think it fair—" Darcy turned aside.

"Do you find her pretty?"

"She is a very striking woman."

"What of her manners, are they pleasing?" Richard pressed his shoulder to Darcy's.

"Her knowledge of the forms of etiquette seems adequate, though her conversation—"

"Can be quite shocking, I know. Delightful, is it not?"

"Disconcerting, I would say."

Richard snickered. "You would. But I would say it is utterly delightful to meet a woman with clear and considered opinions and the spine to express them."

"I am not sure I share your enthusiasm."

"Blast and botheration! Are you going to let this opportunity slip through your fingers?"

"What opportunity?"

"I bring you the most eligible, sought-after woman in our circles, and you ask me what opportunity?" Richard slapped his forehead.

"Excuse me?"

"Every second son in the peerage, and a number of heirs as well, seek her attentions and count themselves fortunate to receive even three words together from her, much less a complete sentence. You have been the recipient of her fixed attention all evening and hardly sensible to the honor paid you!"

"Surely, you exaggerate." No, he should not roll his eyes, but the expression was growing harder to contain by the moment.

"Not at all. She turned away no less than four of my friends who sought her attentions just this past winter. The rumor is she will settle for no less than the perfect man. So naturally, I thought of you."

Richard knew him too well to be using those words by chance. "You have taken to playing match-maker now?"

"Not at all. Only offering you the opportunity to meet a very eligible lady in the most comfortable circumstances for you." Richard stepped between Darcy and the rest of the room. "I am entirely aware of your discomfiture in the ball room, or in any kind of a crowd."

"My behavior—"

"Is not what I am talking about. That is always completely and utterly perfect. You are well-known for your excellent manners, perfect comportment, and entirely boring company."

"If you intend merely to insult—"

"That is no insult, just a statement of unfortunate truth. Talking with you can be like conversing with a rock. Your opinions are correct, your information is correct, everything about you is correct."

"What is wrong with that?" Darcy retreated a step. This was not the first time he had endured this sort of lecture.

"Nothing. But some of us mere mortals also like a spot of enjoyment in our drab lives as well. However—" He huffed out a long breath. "It does not appear mere mortals are capable of drawing the interest of the ethereal Miss Garland. Thus, I brought her to you."

Miss Garland left the pianoforte, Georgiana in tow and joined her brother and Anne at a card table.

"I think you two would be a splendid match. You are equal in consequence, and you would balance one another exceedingly well. Do not waste this opportunity. In Town, you stand little chance of getting near enough to say good day to her—she is so surrounded by admirers."

"I do not think she has much interest," Darcy muttered.

"You might think so, but I have caught her looking at you numerous times this evening, and that look in her eyes I have only known to mean one thing."

"That being?"

"A few compliments on her eyes and her dress, some walks in Pemberley's gardens and a ride on the grounds, and I have reason to believe she will be quite interested in furthering her acquaintance with you."

The next morning, Elizabeth unplaited her hair, sidling between the end of her bed and the dressing table, trying not to catch her skirts on the rough edge of the footboard. There would be no time to mend a torn hem today. So many things to do before Pemberley's picnic, best get to them quickly.

A crisp breeze slipped through the open window on the adjacent wall, fluttering the pale-yellow curtains against the old oak chest of drawers wedged between the window and the corner. The cool morning boded well for the afternoon; it should be comfortably warm, but not hot.

She picked up her brush; it had been Mama's—one of the few things she had of Mama's. Papa had assured them each would have an equal share in what had been Mama's—but he was talking about monies to fund their dowries, not of the small personal things a daughter, even a less favored one, might treasure.

Jane and Lydia, Mama's favorites, had received most of mother's legacy. Jane had even hinted at wanting the hairbrush because of all the fond memories associated with it. How stupid it was that Elizabeth felt guilty for denying it to Jane every time she brushed her hair.

Perhaps she was just being petty and jealous and should give it to Jane.

As if that would prove the bishop wrong. She braced her elbows on the dressing table and pushed her face into her hands.

How long ago had it been? Papa and the bishop had gone into his study to talk in private. No doubt they would have never spoken so if they had known she were there. But she was, tucked in the spot behind the large chair. The morning sun there was ideal for reading, which was precisely what she was doing.

It was wrong to eavesdrop, and she had managed to ignore them until the bishop said her name.

*"...Elizabeth?"*

*"She is very well, thank you."*

*"You have an unfortunate number of daughters, it seems. It is fortunate she is a prettyish sort of girl. Though she cannot compare to her sister, Jane."*

*"We try not to speak of it lest we encourage Jane to vanity."*

*"Or Elizabeth to jealousy."*

Elizabeth had clapped her hands over her mouth at that remark. How hard it had been to remain silent.

*"Elizabeth has too many fine qualities to be jealous of her sister."* Father's voice had been firm. *"She is quick to learn and has a very keen mind."*

*"That is a dubious asset for a woman. With their weak moral constitution, it is more apt to lead them into sin than produce any real good."*

*Papa slapped something; she could not tell what. "How can you say that? My Lizzy is a very good girl. She is the first to see a need in the parish and quick to find a way to help."*

*"It might seem that way now, but you must watch her very carefully."*

*"Watch her for what?"*

*The bishop cleared his throat. "Cleverness brings corruption in women, all forms of vice: vanity, jealousy, bitterness, conniving. She is the very kind who is apt to do the greatest evil, tempting men of high standing with her ready opinions and fine eyes. She must not set her sights outside her sphere—in fact, I would urge you to make sure she marries humbly. She needs hard work to ensure her character does not become dissolute."*

*"Her mother and I—"*

*"Are doing your best to shape her. I know, I know. But look how easily she laughs—a disgusting display of passion and frivolity."*

*"She is a sweet-tempered girl who delights us with—"*

*A chair creaked—it must have been the bishop leaning forward. "Do not indulge such a child, Mr. Bennet. I implore you. Has God himself not declared his disfavor upon you by giving you only daughters? Do you wish to further tempt the Almighty's wrath by—"*

*"That is entirely enough."*

*"Cultivate her character by good works, not her mind. Her cleverness will be her downfall, mark my words."*

A sharp knock at her door—she jumped and nearly dropped the hairbrush.

The maid peeked in. "Miss Darcy is come to call upon you, Miss."

"Please, show her up." What could bring Miss Darcy here so early? Pray she did not have another falling out with her brother.

She closed her eyes and drew a deep breath. Mr. Darcy had his sister's—and everyone's really—best interests in mind, but he could be just so abrasive and high-handed in the way he did the right things. A little gentleness would go a long way in his dealing with most anyone.

Still though, being the son of a man like Old Mr. Darcy, he deserved a little mercy. The old man had been kind to her family, but his standards for his son had been impossibly high.

The maid showed Miss Darcy in. Her color was high, standing out in sharp contrast to her white, sprigged muslin gown, and sweat glistened on her brow. Had she run all the way from Pemberley?

"Please, sit." Elizabeth rose and pushed her chair toward Miss Darcy. "Would you care for something to drink? You are here so early. Is something wrong?"

Miss Darcy started to sit, but fluttered up again, a nervous butterfly flitting from the chair to the bed, to the bedside table and back again. "I do hope I have not troubled you too early."

"Not at all—I am nearly ready to go below stairs." This was not the time to touch upon Miss Darcy's social faux pas. "But do tell me what has you so animated."

"The picnic. It is today—my very first social event. I am so anxious."

Elizabeth perched on the foot of her bed. "Surely there is help for you amongst your party. Is not your cousin Miss de Bourgh—"

"Anne?" Miss Darcy laughed a derisive little sound. "Heavens no! I mean, yes, she is at Pemberley, but dear me, she knows even less about nearly everything than I."

"That is an unkind judgment."

"But it is entirely and completely true! She does nothing at Rosings Park, goes nowhere, knows no one, all the while declaring she should have been a proficient had she only learnt."

Elizabeth fought unsuccessfully to hide a snicker.

"At least she had the good graces to sing one song in the drawing room last night. I would rather step on a cat's tail and listen to the screams than endure Anne's singing."

"Do stop pacing. That is your third time about the room. I cannot keep up with you."

Miss Darcy clasped her hands tight before her chest. "Pray, Miss Elizabeth, come back to the house with me. I know it is early, but I need your help to ensure everything is in readiness and … and …." She stopped in the center of the room, covered her face with her hands, and choked back a sob.

Elizabeth laid her arm over Miss Darcy's shoulder and guided her to sit on the bed.

"I do not wish to make a fool of myself in front of *him*."

"Who?"

"Richard's friend, Sir Alexander."

So, that was the trouble. And trouble this could indeed become.

"Do not look like that. Sir Alexander is a baronet and very refined and proper …."

"And well-looking?" Elizabeth's eyebrow rose.

"Yes, that too—but there is something more. He and his sister are so … so easy. Last night, we all played music together as I never have before." She peeked up. Through the tears, there was a different sort of look in Miss Darcy's eye, one very grown up and sensible.

"Tell me more."

"I think his sister was trying to perform for

Fitzwilliam—to show him something. I do not know how she managed—but she followed no music at all. She just improvised. Then she invited me to join her, and Sir Alexander sang. There was no right nor wrong way. It was all so very freeing and beautiful."

"How intriguing." And unsettling, especially for an ordered man like Mr. Darcy. What kind of people were these?

"You must join us some afternoon or even for dinner to hear—" Miss Darcy sighed at the ceiling. "It was astonishing!"

"So, you like this Sir Alexander very much after only one evening?"

"Do not look at me that way! It is only that I would like to come to know him better. I ... I think he might be the sort of man who might ... might not look down upon me for not being able to do things the way everyone else does. He might accept me as I am, for all my oddities and strangeness."

"I must say, I can think of no better reason to want improve your acquaintance with him and his sister."

"Truly, then you will help me?"

"Allow me to get my bonnet and shawl and tell Jane. Then, we shall be off." Was Mr. Darcy aware of her feelings? He ought to be.

In the short walk to Pemberley, Miss Darcy related all her plans for the picnic, the amusements, the food, the location, and all the things she feared might go dreadfully wrong with each, including the weather turning hot, cold, windy, or rainy. If the current fine weather was not going to encourage her, what could Elizabeth possibly say for reassurance?

"Now what say you of that spot over there, near the little gazebo, for our repast?" Miss Darcy shaded her eyes from the sun and pointed to a shady stand of trees near the lawn at the back of the manor.

"Fresh and inviting. It is an excellent spot and very convenient for the servants, too. A very sensible choice." Mr. Darcy rode past the white domed gazebo, cutting a fine figure on his favorite riding horse. "What thinks your brother of your company?"

"He is mostly annoyed that Anne is here. He tries to avoid her, you know, because Aunt Catherine wishes him to marry Anne. He enjoys Mr. Bingley's company—" Miss Darcy gasped and covered her mouth with her hands. "Oh, Mr. Bingley—I forgot all about that!"

"About what?"

She grabbed Elizabeth's hands. "I do so want you to meet Mr. Bingley. He is handsome, and good-natured. His father was in trade, but he is quite gentleman-like, nonetheless. Honestly, he is so pleasant—I do not quite make out how he is Fitzwilliam's great friend."

"Do not be so unkind."

"I am sorry. Still though, I think you will like him very well, and he you."

"You are not considering matchmaking, are you?"

"No, certainly not. My brother warned me ever so harshly about such things. But it would be a splendid thing if you were to marry a friend of Fitzwilliam's. Then I know we would often be together."

"Then why not marry me to your brother and ensure I am part of the family instead?" Elizabeth bit her lip. Merciful heavens! If she did not better manage her clever remarks, she would surely embarrass the Darcys in front of their company.

"What an intriguing thought."

"I was merely joking. Do not for a moment—"

Miss Darcy laughed. One note in the melody felt off, though. "I would not match you with my brother! He is so grumpy and cross all the time. You are far too good and kind. You must have someone of a far gentler disposition."

"I am glad you think so. But whatever disposition my husband need have, be assured, he will not be your brother."

"Why? He is not a bad sort of man."

"No, he is good and attentive and thoughtful and kind. But I am not the kind of woman a man like Mr. Darcy notices—nor should he. He is as entirely outside my sphere as I am outside of his. I have no fortune, no connections. My father is but a vicar who does not pursue position or power. I am not nearly proper enough for him and never shall be."

"I am not sure anyone is."

"Shall we go and consult with Mrs. Reynolds now? The time for the picnic will be here before you know." Elizabeth looped her arm in Miss Darcy's and encouraged her toward the house and away from this uncomfortable conversation.

## ❧Chapter 4

Darcy slowly descended the grand stairs to meet with the rest of the party in the blue parlor. What joy would be the inevitably awkward moments when everyone stood about stupidly, waiting for someone to begin a conversation. A great deal of conversation was not required, just enough to fill the empty space. But what exactly did one say in such circumstances?

Still, Georgiana deserved the sacrifice. She had worked diligently to plan this picnic—the first social event of her making—and Mrs. Reynolds had assured him she had done well. Thank heavens for that. It would be well. It would be well.

He tugged his jacket straighter and dusted off his sleeves. With a deep breath, he plunged into the parlor. He paused just inside the doorway, allowing his eyes to adjust to the sunlight from the open windows in the room.

His mother's presence lingered in the room, steady and calming, residing in the little portraits she had painted, hanging on the far wall, and in the stool she had embroidered with sweet williams the Christmastide before her passing. Usually, it was enough to soothe his nerves. But today, there were too many uncontrolled possibilities for him to feel at ease. He scanned the company already present.

No! Botheration! The Bennets—all of them, mostly on chairs pulled from the tea table—sat between the Garlands—he in his large chair and she on the fainting couch—and Georgiana on the settee. What would the Garlands—Miss Garland—think of them and of him for permitting their invitation? Certainly, they could not be the sort of company Miss Garland usually kept.

"Mr. Darcy!" Mr. Bennet grabbed his cane and slowly rose from an open arm chair. "Thank you for your generous invitation." Though grey-headed and a bit stooped with age, his voice was strong and compelling.

All five Bennet daughters rose and curtsied almost as one. How did the vicar manage five young ladies in a household when just one threatened to drive Darcy barking mad?

"Come and sit with us." Georgiana patted the space beside her on the settee she shared with Miss Elizabeth.

Usually relaxed with a ready smile and good humor in her eyes, Miss Elizabeth seemed uncomfortable. Was Georgiana's anxiety affecting her so? Darcy sat beside Georgiana.

"Your sister was just telling us of all she had planned for today," Mr. Bingley said.

Darcy started. How had he missed Bingley sitting beside the eldest Miss Bennet? "Do not let me stop you."

Georgiana clasped her hands tightly in her lap. "Well, before we eat, I thought we might have a go at some archery."

"Do you shoot, Miss Elizabeth?" Miss Garland leaned forward slightly, her bodice struggling to contain her assets.

"Oh, she is very good indeed." Miss Kitty said from Bingley's other side. "She could probably hunt very well should it take her fancy."

"Kitty!" Miss Elizabeth glowered at her.

"Our uncle and aunt support her membership in the Derbyshire Archery Society," Miss Lydia added.

He had several friends in that society. Why had she never mentioned she enjoyed shooting? It was the sort of thing he should know.

"I am all anticipation." Miss Garland relaxed into the fainting couch as though modeling for a portrait.

Garland chuckled and crossed his ankles as he leaned back. "Indeed? My sister has quite a penchant for the bow. Generally, she has had very little competition to test her skill. She is a member of the British Amazons and won several prizes when we were last in London."

"I hope she is a gracious loser." Miss Lydia giggled as her shoulders turned this way and that.

"Lydia!" Bennet rarely sounded so sharp.

"I do not mind." Miss Garland laughed. "I find it rather endearing that they would be so supportive of an elder sister."

"They are very generous in their support, but I am sure I shall learn a great deal from you." The warning

warning glance Miss Elizabeth shot at her youngest sisters! They would be fools to ignore it.

"Do the rest of you shoot?" Garland asked, looking at Miss Bennet.

"Only a little and very ill indeed," Miss Bennet said.

"But we dearly love a good game of rounders." Miss Lydia bounced a little in her seat.

Darcy opened his mouth, but Miss Garland cut him off. "I have not played that in years. What a jolly good idea."

No, it was not. The impropriety of ladies running!

"Did I hear something about rounders?" Richard led Anne and Miss Bingley into the room.

"Indeed, you did." Garland stood and offered a small bow from his shoulders. "Right after we observe a most intriguing archery competition."

"Indeed, sir." Anne batted her eyes. "With whom will you be competing?"

Oh, that was an unpleasant expression. Pray let her stop soon.

"Now that is an interesting notion." Garland raise his brows at his sister and clucked his tongue.

She nodded.

"I believe I shall shoot against the winner of the contest between my sister and Miss Elizabeth."

"Miss Elizabeth?" Richard's eyebrows rose high. "No offense, madam, but in all fairness, you should know of the longstanding rivalry—and accuracy—of these two. He is a champion among the Kentish Bowmen." He leaned against the mantlepiece.

"Do you wish release from the contest?" Miss Garland extended an open hand. "I shall not be offended if you so choose."

Miss Elizabeth smiled her enigmatic smile. "My courage only rises with each attempt to intimidate me."

Miss Mary clapped softly.

"Lead us onward, Miss Darcy. I am anxious for the challenge." Garland offered Georgiana his arm.

The dappled shade of the far lawn offered the ideal spot for archery. Georgiana had chosen well.

Targets had been placed about twenty-five yards from a shooting line, carefully set so the sun would be at the archers' backs and the targets were lightly shaded. A pleasant breeze whispered across the tables that held the requisite equipment. Chairs and blankets on the lawn invited the audience to take their leisure.

"Do you shoot, Miss Darcy?" Garland asked.

"Only a little." She bit her lower lip and gazed up at him.

"What? Richard has not taught you?"

Richard snorted. "I have, but she is not proficient."

"To be proficient, one must practice, and practice you shall! Let us have you and Miss Bingley shoot first." Garland gestured toward them.

"I do not know how." Miss Bingley said, looking at Darcy.

"Bingley may assist you." Darcy shook his head vigorously. He would do nothing to raise Miss Bingley's sights to him. He suppressed a shudder. Fine manners, fine dowry, but good at finding fault with others. Not the sort of woman he needed running his home and trying to run him.

"I will instruct you." Richard beckoned her toward the tables.

Georgiana fastened the protective leather brace to her forearm and slipped on the shooting glove while Richard instructed Miss Bingley on how to do the same.

Two arrows launched, neither hitting their mark; one did not even make it to the target. Georgiana and Miss Bingley tittered. Two more flew with no success.

Georgiana's face formed into a familiar frustrated scowl. No doubt a show of her temper would be soon to come. Botheration! Everything had been going so well.

Miss Elizabeth hurried to the shooting line, and he exhaled a little of the breath he had been holding. "I think I see your trouble." She stood behind Georgiana, back straight and shoulders level, covering Georgiana's hands with hers. "Here, you must line up the arrow with the mark on the bow and your target. Now hold this arm very straight and just release your fingers gently."

*Thunk.*

The arrow quivered in the outer ring of the target.

"Well done, Miss Darcy. Miss Elizabeth, you make a fine teacher." Garland crossed his arms and nodded.

Miss Elizabeth blushed and turned away from him.

Strange. She rarely retreated from conversation.

"May I try again?" Georgiana reached for another arrow.

Garland stepped back. She let fly another arrow that landed at the very edge of the target. "Well done, Miss Darcy. Let us see what your pupil can do, Fitz."

Miss Bingley missed again, her face tightening into something very sour.

"Perhaps Miss Elizabeth's guidance might help." Miss Garland suggested.

"Thank you, no. I believe I shall keep to the piano-forte." Miss Bingley handed the bow back to Richard, stripped off glove and brace, and stepped away from the firing line.

"Do you wish to shoot again?" Garland asked.

Georgiana turned to Miss Elizabeth. "No, I would like to see Miss Elizabeth and Miss Garland. I did not know Miss Elizabeth was so adept, and I want to see more."

"As do I." He handed the bow to Miss Elizabeth.

So did Darcy. Archery was a very attractive sport.

Miss Elizabeth smiled at Garland, but it was forced. Still, she was pretty when she smiled.

"Will you go first, Miss Garland?" Miss Elizabeth gestured at her.

"Sizing up the competition? Very shrewd of you" Miss Garland raised her bow.

Valkyrie, definitely a Valkyrie.

Five arrows flew, each landing in the center rings of the target. Applause rose from the spectators.

"She will be a challenge for you, Lizzy," Miss Lydia called.

"Excellently done, Miss Garland." Miss Elizabeth never hesitated to offer praise. She lifted her bow. Her arrows flew as true as Miss Garland's, filling the center of the target.

Garland applauded. "At last, you will have to work for your victory, dear sister."

"I suppose I shall. Well done, Miss Elizabeth. Shall we increase the challenge? Fifty yards should do nicely." Miss Garland glanced at her brother.

"Come help me, Fitz. The fair maidens have spoken." Garland strode toward the targets.

Richard trotted after him. "More Amazon than maiden, it seems."

"Do you not know better than to tease an armed woman?" Garland chuckled and winked over his shoulder at his sister.

"Are you saying we are too unsteady to be trusted with so dangerous an object in our hands?" Miss Garland nudged Miss Elizabeth with her elbow.

"Not at all, my dear. I only suggest such an intriguing creature should be appreciated, venerated…."

"Feel free to ignore my brother, Miss Elizabeth. He fancies he inherited wit along with his title."

The younger Bennet sisters tittered behind them.

Miss Elizabeth cheeks flushed. Did the levity embarrass her as much as it did him?

Richard and Garland returned to the shooting line.

"Is that to your satisfaction? Garland handed arrows to his sister.

Miss Garland tipped her head. "You should shoot first this time, Miss Elizabeth."

"As you will, Miss Garland." She raised her bow and released five arrows, one after the other, with silent grace.

If Miss Garland was a Valkyrie, Miss Bennet might well be Artemis, her posture and her stance—and her profile—as perfect as a classical statue.

Miss Garland filled the target with her own arrows. "I believe we are evenly matched."

"Wait, wait," Garland called. "I believe there is one of yours just outside the third ring. Let me see." He ran to the target and pulled out the arrow in question and peered at the hole it left. He retrieved the remainder of the arrows. "Miss Elizabeth has bested you." He presented her with an arrow. "This one has betrayed you my dear."

She curtsied to him and handed him her bow. "Do not gloat. You may yet find yourself humbled."

"Do you care to put a small wager on that, Blanche?"

Did no one notice the displeased expression Miss Elizabeth wore?

"Indeed, if Miss Elizabeth loses to you, I shall play my pianoforte composition for the company. But, when she bests you, as I know she shall, you shall share with us your new play and allow us to perform it here, among our party!"

"You know very well I do not allow anyone to see my unfinished work."

"Then concede defeat to Miss Elizabeth now and declare her your superior." Miss Garland folded her arms across her waist and waited.

"I shall look forward to hearing your new piece tonight." He turned to Miss Elizabeth. "Shall we make this a touch more interesting? I shall shoot first. You place your arrow next to mine, then I next to you. Whoever remains truest to the line shall be declared the winner."

"As you say, sir."

"Now that is a good sport!" Bingley, Anne, and Miss Bingley whispered among themselves.

Garland let the first shot fly. "Set the line Miss Elizabeth."

Darcy peered at the target, jumping only slightly when her shot landed a finger width from the first arrow.

Garland's brows shot up, but he should not be surprised her near-perfect form should produce such results. He fitted his bow again.

Her own shot quickly followed until a nearly straight line of arrows stood quivering in the target.

Richard nudged Darcy with his elbow. "Help me bring the target in."

They brought the target near the firing line.

"You have an outlier, Garland!" Richard pointed to the errant arrow and chuckled.

Miss Garland applauded. "I told you, Alex. You should never have doubted. Brava, Miss Elizabeth you have brought my brother to a much-needed place of humility."

Garland bowed deeply. "Congratulations, Miss Elizabeth. I shall bear my defeat graciously, I assure you."

Miss Elizabeth's face flushed, and she looked everywhere but at Garland. "Perhaps we should find another amusement? Lawn Bowling, perhaps? Or shall we eat, Miss Darcy?"

Miss Garland took Miss Elizabeth's arm. "No need for such modesty, my dear. He is not nearly so stricken as he would seem, for now he has captive players and an audience for his new work. It will give him a rare opportunity to refine his offering before presenting it to the theatre company next Season."

"What?" Darcy sputtered.

Richard elbowed him hard and hissed in his ear. "If you had objections, why did you not speak out earlier?"

"I did not consider it possible he would lose the bet."

"You cannot forbid it now—it would be entirely unseemly of you."

Garland gestured toward the vicar. "Assuming of course, you, Mr. Bennet, do not object to your daughters participating in a home theatrical."

Bennet heaved himself up from the chair with the aid of his cane. He took several deliberate steps toward Garland. "In principle I have no objections, sir, but I must be concerned with the specifics of the play. Is your work of good moral character? What values do you espouse? Is evil venerated and allowed to triumph, as occurs in some modern works?"

"Although it is yet unfinished, I would call it a cautionary tale against vice and excess."

"Oh, now that sounds very dull indeed." Miss Garland flicked her hand. "Perhaps it is not worth performing at all."

"She does have a point. Too much moralizing is not healthy for the soul, sir." Bennet wagged a finger at him.

Garland threw his head back and laughed. "I have indeed been caught! Remind me not to practice my theater tricks with you. I think you will find it far more entertaining than mere moralizing, and my heroine shall, in the end, make the right choice."

"Who shall play your heroine?" Miss Lydia sounded wistful.

"There is only one appropriate to ask." He bowed before Georgiana. "Our most gracious hostess. Will you take the role?"

"I ... I ...."

"Go ahead, Georgiana." Richard winked at her.

"I ..." Darcy grumbled under his breath. Richard stepped on his foot. Bother! "If my vicar approves, I can hardly do otherwise."

Elizabeth looked from Mr. Darcy to Miss Darcy and back again. Which of the two was more distraught?

Miss Darcy's panicked gaze fastened on Elizabeth, like a drowning girl clutching a rope. "Pray, Miss Elizabeth, say you will help me."

Poor dear. This was Elizabeth's fault. Had her pride not demanded she win the bet with Sir Alexander, Miss Darcy would not be in this situation. "Very well, I will help."

"Thank you! And thank you, Sir Alexander, for the honor." Miss Darcy clasped her hands before her chest. Was it for relief or for joy? There was no telling.

Sir Alexander beamed. Yes, the expression was too unrestrained for good taste, but he was rendered more handsome when he did it. "Excellent. I have roles for five ladies—no, six, and four gentlemen. Perhaps we may discuss it all at length over our picnic."

"Do let us go to the gazebo." Georgiana pointed across the lawn.

"Capital notion. Sounds like quite the diversion. Caroline, you might make use of all your elocution lessons from your school days." Bingley offered Jane his arm.

Miss Bingley's eyes narrowed as she fell into step beside her brother, effectively ignoring Jane all together. "If I am asked, I shall be most pleased to offer what service I may."

"Do not ask me. I will not take part. You have more than enough ladies from whom to choose," Miss Garland said.

Sir Alexander waved her off and offered Miss Darcy his arm. They sauntered off toward the heavily-laden tables set up in the shade of the gazebo.

Elizabeth lingered behind.

"Will you join us?"

She jumped.

Mr. Darcy stood closer than she expected, regarding her with a somber expression of concern, or discomfort. It was difficult to discern which. His usual poised mask seemed askew on his face.

"Please forgive my forwardness, but it is...that it seems you are displeased with this turn of events."

He nodded ever so slightly. "I am sorry to have been so obvious."

She dropped her gaze to the toes of her half boots peeking out from beneath her pale blue skirts. "Forgive me. I was out of place to allow things to have happened so."

"You believe you should have permitted him to best you, although you had the power to do otherwise?"

"It would have been far more proper and would have lessened your discomfort." Ladies did not best gentlemen in sport; it was just not done.

"I hardly think so. It seems clear to me that this theatrical scheme would have hatched sooner or later. Better have it done with earlier." He tapped his foot on the soft lawn. "Besides, seeing anyone pretend to be less than they are disturbs me. It is too like disguise which I abhor. I would not ask that of –"

"Come along, Darcy. It looks like you are off sulking." Colonel Fitzwilliam slapped Mr. Darcy's shoulder. "Thank you for keeping him from storming off entirely." He offered his arm to Elizabeth. "Permit me to escort you to our repast."

Colonel Fitzwilliam released her just outside the gazebo and strode in to take a place near her younger sisters. He must be amused by silly company—or perhaps he enjoyed the way they doted on him, lingeringly calling him "'colonel" as often as they could. They were so unruly in Papa's absence. Where had he gone? Was it possible he sought Mrs. Reynolds for a cup of mint tea for his stomach?

Miss Garland claimed Elizabeth's arm. "Come sit beside me. Tell me, where ever did you learn to shoot?"

All manner of cold delicacies lay expertly arranged before them: cold ham and chicken, pickles—at least three varieties—biscuits and jam, a pigeon pie, a cold salad, a pyramid of fruits, a blancmange, and several jellies.

"It is of very little interest, I assure you."

"How can you say that, Lizzy?" Lydia looked up from her plate. "It is a very amusing story, very much like what happened today."

"Indeed, I am all agog—do tell." Was that genuine interest or an affectation? Miss Garland seemed accomplished enough an actress for either to be true.

"Lydia, please, say no more. It is of no import."

"La!" Lydia rolled her eyes and dabbed the corners of her mouth with her napkin. "Our cousin, William, came to visit one summer. Dreadfully freckled little thing he was, just older than Lizzy, but younger than Jane. He told Lizzy he thought girls too stupid to be bothered with and that he was quite put out to be sent to a house full of them."

"I do believe there is an age at which all young men say such things." Miss Garland winked at Elizabeth, a hint of conspiracy in her eye.

"Well, Lizzy did not take very well to his highhandedness," Kitty said more loudly than necessary.

"Lydia, Kitty, stop! It is not a flattering tale and if you persist, I shall—"

"Do what? What shall you do to me?" Lydia's eyes flashed.

"I shall go home as I do not wish to be party to this conversation. You may explain the reason to Papa." Elizabeth rose.

"You will only punish yourself and miss all the good fun," Lydia said.

Kitty and Mary had the good grace to look a bit more concerned, but they remained silent. That was nothing unusual.

"There is little pleasure to be had in company whose chiefest pleasure is embarrassing me. Excuse me, Miss Garland." Elizabeth curtsied and turned away.

Where was the quickest path out of public view?

A small clump of trees marked the start of the footpath to the parsonage. She paused in the cool, deep shade when the gazebo was out of sight.

Why must Lydia delight in embarrassing her? She wrapped her arms tightly around her waist. When in company, it was Lydia and Jane who were always in great demand. Few seemed to care whether or not

Elizabeth was there, unless an obscure fact needed recalling or a conversation needed starting ... then she was useful—like a counting horse or intellectual pig. Something one brought out for the sake of show and novelty.

What an imprudent move to agree to shoot today. She should have demurred modestly and allowed the Garlands to enjoy each other's competition. What a fool she was! What good were all the skills, facts and information the world had to offer if she could not somehow put them into proper use?

She dragged the back of her hand across her eyes. No, she was not going to seal all that thoughtlessness with tears. Not today.

"Miss Elizabeth?"

She looked up into Mr. Darcy's disturbed eyes. When had he left the picnic—or had he even sat down?

"Miss Elizabeth? Are you unwell? Why have you left—"

She turned from him. "Forgive me. I must return to the parsonage."

"What has happened?" He matched his paced to hers.

"I fear my youngest sister—she is high-spirited and sometimes becomes insensitive to the feelings of others."

"I understand." How kind he seemed; in this moment, it felt like that was his true character. Her heart did a tiny butterfly flutter. Oh, he was handsome.

"I am sorry that you do." Somehow, the thought of someone vexing him the way Lydia vexed her drove a sharp stab into her heart. "If I may be so bold, you do look quite displeased. Is there something I might offer for your relief?"

He blinked at her, indecipherable thoughts flashing behind his expressive eyes. "What do you think of this home theatrical notion?"

"You are uncomfortable with it?"

"Exceedingly." Dry leaves and small twigs crunched under his feet. "There is nothing intrinsically wrong with it, I grant you; it is a commonly done thing. As your father noted, there are plays enough that have redeeming value. Those I would not repine seeing Georgiana take part in."

"But Sir Alexander's work is an untested quantity? You do not know what he considers appropriate?"

He paused and caught her gaze. "You have seen it, too, then?"

"I would not presume to criticize your guests and your friends." She stepped around him to continue walking.

"I did not mean to imply anything improper toward yourself." He lengthened his stride to catch up to her. "Pray tell me your thoughts."

"I have noticed a liberality in his manner that is quite different to your attention to all forms of pro-priety. It seems you might be best served to rescind your permission—say that you have reconsidered."

"Though sorely tempted, I fear to do so would provide great offense to my guests, my sister, and even your good father."

"Papa is not apt to take offense, you know. He says offense only allows our offender to live without rent in your heart and continue to grieve you."

"He is very wise and a very worthy man if he is able to accomplish that feat." Mr. Darcy chuckled softly. It was a pleasant sound that no one heard enough of. "I fear for Georgiana. She is not even out. I did not anticipate a house party might lead to her performing to an audience."

"It certainly was not in my mind when I suggested it, either. Perhaps Miss de Bourgh might be able to step in and ensure—"

"Suffice to say, I have little faith in Anne's ability to set aside her own interests to protect my sister's."

"And Miss Bingley?"

"Is entirely focused on making connections and furthering her own position in the marriage mart. Like Anne, she is too preoccupied. Besides, my sister does not hold them in high regard. She does not value their understanding, not as she does yours." He stopped and studied her. "She has nothing but praise to offer for your good sense."

"I am flattered she might regard me thus." Why did he have to look at her that way? Her cheeks burned.

"Were you serious when you offered assistance?"

"I am not in the habit of saying things I do not mean."

"Then would you consider an invitation to Pemberley, to join our house party? I know your regard for my sister. I trust you to guard her delicacy and alert me of anything untoward."

"I will not be your spy. I am her friend and will not violate her confidence in me." She pulled her shoulders back.

"I would not ask you to do so. I need only be involved if you foresee any danger to her. Under the guise of helping her learn her part, as you already promised to do, it should be easy enough. Perhaps you would be more comfortable if Miss Bennet is also included? We might then say it is for the sake of the theatrical, that all may be available here to practice and prepare at a moment's notice. My good will as a host is evidenced, and none need be the wiser about the particular service you are rendering my sister."

"I thank you for your confidence. I do not take it lightly. If my father permits it, then you have my agreement." She curtsied and turned away.

"I shall approach him straight away. Will you not return to the picnic?"

"I think not." Pray he keep any remarks about the fragility of her constitution to himself.

"I have been told on rather good authority that my glower is entirely effective at intimidating others into silence. Perhaps I might use it on your behalf, should you choose to return with me." Was that a hint of mirth lurking in his dimple?

Her heart fluttered. "I suppose then, under such a promise, I might be persuaded."

They returned to the gazebo in companionable silence.

"Lizzy!" Papa clambered up from his seat at the table. "My dear, I have been concerned. No one knew where you had gone."

"Lydia was well aware." Elizabeth turned over her shoulder to gaze at her sister, laughing in the company of Colonel Fitzwilliam.

His face grew dark. "I am sorry. She knows better."

"It makes little difference to her behavior."

"Then I shall see her home and discuss the matter with her." From the look in his eye, the discussion would be rather one-sided. "I think she shall not participate in this theatrical project, either."

"She will be very disappointed."

"As am I in her. I have spoken with her on the matter before. Several times. She needs to feel the weight of her choices. Excuse me."

"Sir, before you go." Mr. Darcy stepped forward. "May I request that Miss Bennet and Miss Elizabeth join our house party, for the sake of the theatrical? Miss Elizabeth promised Georgiana she would help her learn her lines. I know she will want to practice a great deal. It should be easier for all involved if Miss Elizabeth is here."

"How do you feel about this, Lizzy?" Papa studied her face.

There was no point in trying to hide anything from him—he always knew. "I do feel responsible for her dilemma."

"You feel responsible for foul weather on a day I wish for fine. You take far too much on yourself." He turned to Mr. Darcy. "Have you suggested ...."

"No, sir, Miss Elizabeth is not responsible for any of this. It is all my doing and mine alone."

Papa grumbled something indecipherable. "As long as that is entirely understood. My question remains. What do you wish for, Lizzy?"

"I am concerned you will need Jane and me at home."

"Mary and Kitty, and Lydia too, can very well step up—it would do them good to rise to the challenge. But that tells me nothing of your wishes." He took her hand. "It is entirely acceptable for you to indulge in something for your own pleasure, my dear. Not everything must be done in the service of others. You must refresh yourself, too—an empty well cannot provide refreshment for anyone." He stepped a little closer and whispered in her ear. "You are a good girl, my dear. I would be pleased for you and Jane to have a bit of a holiday. It is not as if you would be so very far from home. Should there be any real need, we can send for you directly."

"I would like to visit Pemberley."

Papa squeezed her hand. "You and Jane have my permission. Mr. Darcy, I charge you to protect them in my stead. I expect you to be a direct participant in this theatrical so that you may observe it all first-hand and ensure nothing untoward is asked of my daughters."

The panicked look she had seen in Georgiana's eyes appeared in Mr. Darcy's. Papa recognized it, too, but remained unmoved. How unlike him not to have compassion on another's discomfiture. He cocked his head and tapped his foot.

"Very well, sir. I shall do as you ask."

"Then I shall trust you with that which is most precious to me. Shall we return to the party? I believe you have some news for Jane, and I for Lydia." Papa set off ahead of them.

## Chapter 5

Why had he capitulated to Bennet's terms? Darcy resisted the urge to clutch his temples and groan as he trudged back to the picnic. Few demands were worse than performing in company. It was a very high price to pay for Georgiana's safety.

At least, this once, Georgiana was delighted at his efforts on her behalf, squealing and clutching Miss Elizabeth's hands before she hurried off to inform Mrs. Reynolds of the new plans.

Miss Elizabeth then followed her father, pulling Miss Lydia and the rest of her sisters into the gazebo. Thankfully, he had the decorum to manage the matter in relative privacy.

Anne and Richard approached, looking back and forth from him to the Bennets.

"So, we are to have more company?" Anne rolled her eyes and leaned heavily on Richard's arm. "Do you not think people of their class very tiresome?"

"Why must you find fault in everything?" Richard's lip curled back just a mite. "Everything is one shade of disagreeable or another in your eyes. You really must learn to see the advantages in a situation, not just the flaws."

"But to add two more ladies—and I use the word only in the most general of ways— to the party. We are now so unbalanced."

"The Bennets are agreeable company." Richard released Anne's arm and stepped back. "If the elder had more of a dowry, I'd pursue her myself. Her temperament is as lovely as her face. And Miss Elizabeth, if she were not so poor, I think she might have made a match for you, Darce."

Darcy snorted and glowered. The Bennets were from a completely different social sphere—Richard should not even joke about becoming affiliated with them. Those sorts of remarks tended to be overheard, repeated, and the source of no end of trouble.

"Heavens, no!" Anne clutched her chest. "Even if she were high enough to be suitable, she is neither pretty enough for you nor … well, she is lacking in the proper deference to male judgment, in my opinion."

"You think Miss Garland a better choice for him?" Richard snickered into his hand.

"Her wealth and connections certainly are. She is far better looking than that upstart."

Darcy schooled his features into something properly neutral. No doubt Anne thought herself a better match for him. That was certainly what her mother had raised her to believe. Hopefully, unlike Aunt Catherine, Anne would be well-mannered enough not to bring it up directly.

"But her deference to Darcy is certainly not as favorable as you suggest it ought to be," Richard said.

"I was not intimating that she would be at all suitable for Darcy." Anne tucked her hand into the crook of Darcy's arm. "Only more suitable than Miss Elizabeth."

"I will thank you both to cease your speculations. I am in no need of a matchmaker." How could he disengage himself from Anne without creating greater problems?

"I beg to differ, Cousin. I think you are in great need, and you should listen to my advice. Miss Garland is an excellent foil to your stuffiness. Under her guidance, you might well become acceptable in society."

"Richard! How can you say such a thing? Do not listen to him. He only means to provoke." Anne batted her eyes at Darcy.

He cringed and removed his arm from her grasp. Damn the consequences. "Excuse me." He stalked away.

Was no one but Miss Elizabeth on his side today?

That evening, Bennet, Miss Bennet, and Miss Elizabeth joined them for dinner. Whether encouraged by Miss Elizabeth's presence, or cowed by Anne's badgering, Georgiana suggested the ladies withdraw after dinner and leave the gentlemen to their port. A most gratifying turn of events considering Anne had placed herself next to him during the meal, and all sensible conversation seemed to be taking place at the other end of the table. What a relief to enjoy a few moments of good port and conversation where he might relax just a bit.

The servants cleared the tablecloth away, revealing the brightly polished walnut tabletop that reflected the flickering candles nearly as well as the wall mirrors. How much easier his breath came with the clutter cleared. He poured the rich burgundy port and distributed the crystal wine glasses.

Bennet savored a long sip. "Mr. Darcy, your taste is impeccable."

"Indeed, it is." Garland raised his glass. "You are a most gracious host. Particularly in indulging my sister's desire to flaunt my humble theatrical work before all of you."

"You are not keen to have it performed?" Bingley asked.

"Of course, I am. There is little to compare with seeing your works come to life on a stage. But this work is still quite rough."

"What do you mean by 'rough'?" Bennet resettled himself in his seat with a pleasing parental air.

"Nothing untoward, to be sure. I just have not quite worked out all my characters, their motives—"

"You do not know how it ends, do you?" Richard chuckled and took a long draw of his port.

"Not precisely." Garland drew his fist along his chin.

Bennet grumbled. Good, perhaps he could raise an objection that might bring a halt to this scheme. "I thought you told me—"

"I did, and I have purposed that virtue will indeed triumph in the end. But I am at a loss as to why or how."

"I do not follow." Bennet's shaggy brows drew tight.

"Neither do I," Richard said.

"Are you not the master of your pen?" Bingley asked. "Do you not hold the fate of your stage-world in your hands, your players doing as you direct?"

"Would that were true! A common misconception, indeed. I am in no more control of my characters than our host Darcy here is in control of the seasons. Like him, I can only try my best to predict their direction and do my best to stave off disaster when the unexpected comes."

What melodrama! Darcy fought not to roll his eyes. "Surely you jest. You do not know at the beginning what the end will be?"

"I try to, most diligently I do. And sometimes my characters are most cooperative with me. They obey my command and speak the very words I intend for them. Well-behaved children who honor their father. But then others are as headstrong as—well, as my sister. They take on their own notions, speak words I did not expect of them—even march from the room when I would command them to stay."

"Balderdash! You speak of them as though they were alive and willful beings," Darcy muttered.

"Does your harvest, do your flocks, always follow your commands? Are you ever in perfect control over all that surrounds you?" Garland shrugged almost apologetically.

"By no means, only one who believes himself the Almighty could make such a claim." Darcy turned to Bennet who frowned just a bit.

"And I am certainly not He, sir, merely a mortal man. So why should I be able to exert more control over my world than you can yours?"

"Because mine is real, tangible, substantive. Yours is of your own making. If you are unable to order what is of your own creation, then what are you able to manage?"

"According to Blanche, very little." Garland raised his glass to them and took a gulp.

Bingley laughed. "Your sister and mine seem to have much in common."

"She is not actually my sister."

"Indeed?" Bennet set his glass down. Hard. "How then do you come to pass her as your sister?"

"Do not think ill of me, for I do regard her as my sister. She is my cousin, daughter to my father's elder brother, who originally held the title of baronet. He and his wife were struck by small pox. She was sent to us for her protection and then stayed when her parents succumbed to the infection. Since Blanche was their only child, the title passed to my father, and thus to myself. She and I grew up together as brother and sister might, so I count her as a sister. I fancy being the sister of a baronet is preferable to being the cousin of one—I hope I do not cast her in a bad light if I suggest that she likes the distinction and connections it affords."

Interesting. Darcy chewed his cheek. It should not matter that she was not so closely related to the baronet, but it did. Miss Garland might be no more like him than Georgiana was like Richard. Her peculiarities could be only an affectation due to her current association with him, but not native to herself.

After all, Georgiana did pick up characteristics of the Fitzwilliams when she visited. Interesting.

"...so then, tell me of what you have crafted thus far in your play. I am less convinced than ever that my daughters should be involved."

"Oh, pish posh. Show me a little good faith. It is called *The Appearance of Goodness*. It is the story of a young woman of good fortune and good breeding who is faced with two suitors. Both rich and handsome men."

Richard sniffed and waved off the notion. "No wonder you are having difficulty—could you not find something of more interest to write on? That is the gossip every young woman of the *ton* desires to be the center of."

"And no man wants to have a part in." Bingley elbowed Richard.

"On first glance, it would appear so. But bear with me, the story goes much deeper. No one—well almost no one—is as they first seem. Before we can resolve the apparent conflict of who will marry whom, we must come to know each character's secrets."

"Secrets?" Darcy ran his fingers under the edge of the table. Secrets were rarely a good thing and never a safe thing.

"Yes, secrets. Everyone has them—even you, Mr. Bennet." Garland studied Bennet.

"What secrets do you believe a widowed old vicar with five daughters would keep?" Bingley snickered.

Garland studied Bennet, tapping his fist on his lips. "A colder man would speculate that you secretly wished they were all sons—but that is far too obvious—and obvious does not make for good drama.

No, for that it must be something entirely unexpected."

"So, he is a vital member in a secret tea smuggling operation and uses the follies of Pemberley as stations for the transfer of the illegal stuff?" Richard asked.

"And unbeknownst to his fellow smugglers, he is actually an agent to the crown setting them up for capture," Bingley added.

Bennet's eyebrow arched. "Thank you for redeeming my character. For that you may have permission to converse with either of my daughters freely tonight."

Bingley smiled sheepishly. "I count myself honored."

"While that plot device is certainly unexpected, it perhaps goes so far afield as to be unpalatable to my audience. No, a secret must be both unexpected and acceptable to the ones to whom it is revealed."

Darcy bit his upper lip. Pompous nonsense.

"So, then what do you propose?" Richard leaned back and crossed his arms.

Garland stared at the ceiling, a range of nameless expressions passing over his face, like a man trying on hats for fit and style. "You are difficult to make out, sir, for your character is good at keeping secrets. I think—if I were writing your character, your secret would not be so dark as smuggling but rather something inconsistent with the man we commonly see. I might suggest you would have a truly shocking temper and live in fear and dread of ever being found out. So, you portray yourself as kind and moderate all the while a tempest seethes within."

"Which becomes the source of your conflict?" Bennet asked.

Why was he playing along, encouraging this non-sense?

"Indeed. What happens when his secret is exposed—will he rise above his weakness or fall as a tragic hero? Sometimes, I do not know until the very end. Such is my dilemma with the two suitors now. They do not readily confess to me, so I do not quite know what they are about. They both appear good, but father and sister favor one, mother and brother and friend another. My poor heroine does not know whom to believe."

What utter hogwash.

Bennet stroked his chin. "That is a very realistic di-lemma, for who can know a man's heart? Do you not worry that perhaps it is too close to truth for your audience to appreciate?"

"Another very good question for which I have no equal answer. I had thought at first this was to be a farce, a comedic romp in the ridiculous, but it has turned far more serious than that. Yet, it still retains too much good humor to be a tragedy."

"I do not envy your dilemma." Richard swirled his glass. "I have no desire to play maker, even in a world of my own creation."

"Perhaps that is why Blanche contrived this theat-rical as a means of helping me past this impasse. She has always been the most considerate of souls."

The ladies paraded in a loose group to the drawing room through a long, dimly lit corridor populated by an array of portraits and landscapes of country houses, enough to inhabit an entire county. Elizabeth lingered behind the rest.

Miss Bingley and Miss de Bourgh's conversation offered little pleasure. How did Jane managed to tolerate it with such equanimity? Miss Garland's seemed better, but only a little. Though she did not engage in the same sorts of talk, her facial expressions spoke volumes, most of it rather caustic.

Odd that no one else seemed to notice. But even if they did, what could come of it? No doubt someone would come to her with the observation, and she would be put in the position of having to defend Miss Garland. Not an ideal circumstance by any reckoning.

Miss Darcy dawdled at the doorway and took Elizabeth's arm as she entered the drawing room, holding her back. "Do you think I chose rightly, Miss Elizabeth? Withdrawing with the ladies?"

"I am quite sure no one will fault you for following established convention." Elizabeth patted her hand as she scanned the room, heady with the fragrance of beeswax and a veritable garden of ladies' perfumes.

The burgundy and ivory of the drawing room lent a formality to the space that was just the slightest bit strict and demanding—reminiscent of the way Pemberley felt when the two elder Darcys were alive. Mrs. Darcy, gentle, but formidable, somehow mediated the elder Mr. Darcy's harshness, but it always lingered in the air. It was difficult not to walk gingerly and look over one's shoulder in their company. Only in the late Mr. Darcy's waning years did she understand what drove him to demand so much of his son. Not that it excused the pain he inflicted, but at least it made sense.

Miss Darcy shook her arm. "Are you well?"

"Yes, yes, I am sorry. I was distracted for a moment. Have you rearranged the furniture in the room? I do not remember the chairs being so near the cabinet."

"I did, just a little. But that is not why I am worried. I do not wish to embarrass myself or my brother." Miss Darcy bit her lip and stared at her guests, gathered at the far side of the room, admiring a tall curiosity cabinet.

How kind of Miss Garland to illuminate the other ladies about the collection of shells that Mr. Darcy had acquired from the Indies.

"I have every faith in you. Do not fear. Your company wants to see you succeed. They will be gracious to you."

"How can you be so certain?"

Miss Garland peeked over her shoulder at them, eyebrow raised.

"They all desire your brother's good opinion and are wise enough to realize they cannot obtain it if they are critical of you in any way. So, they will convince themselves that whatever you do is right and proper. Even if you were to dance upon the pianoforte, they would create some excellent reason for it being the right and proper thing to do. They might even join you there. Perhaps not Miss de Bourgh and Miss Bingley, but Miss Garland would likely dance with you and defy any who dare call it peculiar."

Miss Darcy tittered behind her hand. "You say that to humor me."

"Miss Bingley might placate you, but when have you ever known me to speak words I do not mean?"

"Or not to know exactly what you are talking about." Miss Darcy sighed. "You probably would like to go over there and correct Miss Garland's description of my brother's favorite shell. Even I know she is entirely wrong. It is a cowrie, not a conch."

"I noticed. But there is little harm in the error. Few people appreciate being corrected over something so minor."

Miss Darcy chewed her fingernail. "How do you always seem to know what to say and when to say it? I wish I had your confidence."

Miss Garland approached them, a living marble statue in a gown of icy blue. "Pray do come in and join us. One might wonder if you were the hostess here at all." She took Miss Darcy's arm. "Pray come, none of us here are nearly so frightening as Miss Elizabeth must be making us out to be." Her laugh held just the barest trace of vitriol, her pupils oddly narrow for a candlelit room.

"Mrs. Reynolds has provided us a lovely selection of coffee, tea, and biscuits." Miss Darcy stammered as Miss Garland led her into the room.

"How lovely to have the drawing room to ourselves even for just a few moments." Miss Garland arranged herself on the fainting couch and folded her arms over the side. She rested her chin on her hands and sighed. Had she learned that posture from a portrait? "They can be such taxing company."

Miss Darcy pulled an armless gold-painted chair near the tea table, and the other ladies selected seats near her. Elizabeth sat beside Jane.

"I have no idea how you could call such a party of gentlemen trying." Miss de Bourgh sniffed, primly folding her hands in her lap.

Sister to a baronet on one side, granddaughter of an earl, daughter of a knight on the other—so much grandeur, how might a common gentlewoman bear it? To be fair though, Miss Garland carried her greatness much more tolerably than Miss de Bourgh.

"They are very pleasing company." Miss Bingley glanced from one grand lady to the other, ignoring the mere gentlewomen who sat between. Apparently, she had chosen sides in the war of the great ladies. Siding with the Pemberley bloodline was probably a good choice.

"All their attempts at genteel conversation when they want nothing more than to talk of the land, hunting, and racing? They could not find an interesting topic among them if it were to bite them on the nose, and they had a quizzing glass in hand." Miss Garland flicked her hand toward the dining room.

"That is very harsh, I think." Jane's brows knit as they always did when fault-finding began.

"I grant you, Miss Bennet, your partner for dinner is far more amiable a conversationalist than any of the rest—no, no, I must stand corrected. Your dear father is quite capable of interesting conversation and has quite developed the skill of listening rather than merely waiting his turn to talk. I pronounce him very good company, indeed." Thankfully Miss Garland's eyes twinkled with sincerity.

"I am sure he will be grateful for your approbation," Elizabeth said. How ironic as Papa rarely cared for such opinions one way or another. She pressed her hands on the seat of her chair and clutched the wine-colored floral upholstery. It helped to control one's tongue.

"But the rest—oh! I am quite certain they are as relieved for some distance from us as we are from them."

"I do not find the loss of their company desirable at all." Miss Bingley nodded at Miss de Bourgh. It seemed she believed the enemy of her enemy was her friend. "I thought Sir Alexander's comments on the last Season's theater offerings to be uncommonly insightful."

"Indeed," Miss de Bourgh said, a bit too enthusiastically. "His opinions were quite well informed and very pleasing."

Miss Garland snickered. "I am quite intrigued you would say so. Miss Bennet, what say you on the matter?"

Poor Jane colored. "I … I found him well-spoken."

Elizabeth knew very well what her opinion must be, but those were not remarks Jane was likely to make in company, if at all.

Miss Garland's lips twitched as though trying not to smile. "And you, Miss Elizabeth, surely you had an opinion of my brother."

At least she was sparing Jane further questioning. That was some mercy. "He is a very clever man, I am sure—and well attuned to dramatic devices. No doubt he was quite intentional in his use of irony, stating the opinion of the theater critics from *The Morning Herald* and *The British Press* as his own when he is known for his rather colorful disagreement with both of them."

The look of—what did one call it?—that crept across Miss Bingley's face would have fueled a dozen of Sir Alexander's characters. Miss de Bourgh veiled her contempt a little more effectively—only a little.

Miss Garland, though, she smiled with the cold look of a satisfied predator. "Irony indeed. He will be gratified to know someone other than myself made the same observation. Do you often find yourself in agreement with those critics, or do you, like my brother, find them tiresome and dreary?"

"I … I do not know. We are rarely in Town. I have had little opportunity to have seen the works they critique."

"But surely you visit the local theater company?"

"Once or twice a year, we are privileged to attend." Elizabeth glanced at Jane who seemed relieved not to be part of the conversation.

"Then you can hardly consider yourself a patron of the theater arts." Miss Bingley all but pounced with glee.

"I never called myself that."

"Indeed? With all your knowledge of critics and their commentaries, I was certain you had." Miss Bingley raised her brows over a little glare. "My brother and I regularly attend the theater when we are in Town. And you, Miss de Bourgh?"

"I think music would be in order now—what do you think, Miss Darcy?" Elizabeth stood.

Miss Darcy jumped up. "An excellent idea. Who would care to begin?"

"Miss Bingley is quite the proficient—please would you play for us?' Miss Garland gestured toward her.

Miss Bingley fluffed her feathers and smiled sweetly. Surely, she did not believe in the flattery that had just been dealt her, did she? Her posture as she sauntered to the polished pianoforte suggested she just might.

The first notes of a complicated concerto resounded through the drawing room. Ah, she was that kind of player. Well, that was fortunate. Neither she nor Jane would be able to offer any real competition to her—the way Miss Bingley would prefer, no doubt.

Miss Garland extended her hand as she rose, graceful and poised. "Come, Miss Elizabeth, take a turn about the room with me. It is so refreshing!" She took Elizabeth's arm and veritably dragged her to the far side of the room.

Near the bookcases on the wall farthest from the pianoforte, away from the fireplace and candlesticks, shadows enveloped them.

"Thank heavens she is so easily distracted and that her playing is not as dreadful to listen to as her opinions." Miss Garland pressed a hand to her ample chest. "You hardly think differently, I am sure. You are just too well-mannered to give voice to what is going on in your quick mind."

Somehow that did not quite sound like a compliment. Elizabeth avoided making eye contact. "I often find it the wisest course of action to refrain from saying what is uppermost in my thoughts."

"And thus, the world is deprived of a truly sparkling wit and conversation."

"I hardly think it fitting to declare brash and outspoken words clever conversation."

"Perhaps, but you must agree with me as to how much more interesting a conversation would we have if you actually gave voice to everything you were thinking." Miss Garland blinked a little faster, just short of batting her eyes.

"Pray do not put words in my mouth."

"Only if you will agree to speak more freely in my company. I long for intelligent, well-informed conversation. Not the vapid dwelling upon fluff and trivialities that passes for acceptable in the drawing room."

"Are you not being harsh upon our sex?"

"I think perhaps you enjoy a rarified environment here in countryside. No offense intended, but I believe I have kept company in far more drawing rooms than you and know of what I speak."

"Still, I think it wise and proper to maintain conversation in such a way that all may be able to participate and enjoy. It is the very height of rudeness to flaunt one's information."

"I suppose that is true, but quite dull indeed. What think you of Miss Bingley and Miss de Bourgh?" Miss Garland peeked over her shoulder at the ladies in question.

"I think you are trying to encourage me to say something unkind."

"Nothing of the sort. If you are unable to find something kind to say of them, then that onus is entirely upon you."

"True enough. I shall only say this: I find them very unlike their relations whose company we are enjoying." Pray that would satisfy her.

"Indeed? The dissimilarity is clear enough with Mr. Bingley, who is quite the gentleman, despite his almost insipid mildness. But you think Miss de Bourgh that different from Mr. Darcy?"

"You think them the same?"

"Do you not see in them both a rather droll need for propriety in all things, little humor and no appreciation for the colorful or creative?"

Elizabeth chewed her lower lip. "One might be persuaded to characterize Miss de Bourgh that way, but certainly not Mr. Darcy. And perhaps on further acquaintance, not even Miss de Bourgh."

"I am all agog. You must tell me more. What is the nature of your further acquaintance with Mr. Darcy?"

A true lady would ignore the hint of suggestion in Miss Garland's question. Tonight, she would be a true lady. "He has been my father's patron for these ten years, and we have had many dealings with him. He is a fair and generous master to his servants, a kind landlord to his tenants, and most attentive to those in his care."

"But he is always so stiff and proper."

"Propriety for him does not appear to be so much a matter of pride as a way by which to order and understand the world. I have never seen him dismiss and despise those around him as Miss de Bourgh appears to do. He is the soul of consideration and generosity."

"How interesting. I would not have guessed that on my own observations. I shall endeavor to revise my opinions of him. And look, there—he arrives. You will excuse me." Miss Garland slipped away.

Mr. Darcy greeted Miss Garland with a rare soft smile and genuine warmth in his eyes.

Elizabeth swallowed back a sigh. She might have just conversed with Pemberley's future mistress. With her quick wit and lively mind, they might even find genuine happiness together.

Her stomach churned as she swallowed back a vague bitterness. Perhaps the fish at dinner tonight disagreed with her.

## Chapter 6

The first rays of sunrise teased Elizabeth awake. Why was the light coming from the wrong direction and why did sleep not easily slough away? She stretched and glanced about. Elegant oak furnishings not her own surrounded her. The bed linens—so fine—and the mattresses—so soft—Pemberley. She was in a guest room at Pemberley.

She pushed herself up to sit. How late had she come to bed last night? Certainly, far later than she was accustomed to. How odd yesterday had been. All things considered, though, all company considered, it was probably best that there was someone dedicated to look after Miss Darcy's welfare.

She swung her feet out of bed and yawned—so many cobwebs in her head this morning. Fresh air—a walk, that was what she needed to clear her mind. Yes, mornings always agreed with her, beckoning her to come out and take part in the day before it became full of too many other people.

A simple morning gown would do—one that would likely earn Miss Bingley's censure for its drab color and lack of ornamentation—but no one would see her, so it would suffice. She tied on her half boots and bonnet and slipped outside into the morning.

Was there any fragrance so pleasing as dew upon the grass? Any song so soothing as that of distant sheep bleating, making a counterpoint to the twittering songbirds? Why would anyone trade such pleasures for the dismal confines of London and its dreary, dirty demands?

It seemed most of Pemberley's current occupants, save Mr. Darcy himself, found London the center of great delight. For Sir Alexander, it made sense. Where else might he find such attention for his works? But the balls and parties and society the rest found such a draw—

Her lip curled and she shuddered. No, that was no place for her. The wild countryside of Derbyshire was much more to her tastes. She paused to look up into the leafy canopy of old hardwoods that enveloped her along the footpath. The woods called her deeper into their shade, and she obeyed, old leaves and deadfall crunching underfoot.

Jane might be able to navigate that sphere of society. She fitted in so well with the Bingleys—Mr. Bingley had paid her many attentions last night. Perhaps that life might suit her well.

It would be lonely without Jane. But if it meant she were well-settled and Papa might stop worrying for all their futures, it would be worth it. If it all came to pass, how fitting that Mr. Darcy would be responsible for that benefit as well.

"My goodness, that is a most thoughtful look on your face, Miss Elizabeth. What heavy considerations might you be weighing at so early an hour?" Sir Alexander jumped down from a large branch of the tree directly beside her.

Elizabeth gasped and jumped back. "My goodness, sir! Do you make a habit of lying in wait in the tree tops for unsuspecting prey like some jungle cat?"

He threw back his head and laughed, a full-bodied sound that must have started somewhere near his toes and worked its way up to his throat. His hazel eyes twinkled like the sun through the trees, matched by his ready smile. For all her prejudices, he really was as well-looking a man as everyone said. "I have at times been thought a predator, but never a jungle cat. Should I consider that a compliment or censure?"

"Neither, I think."

"You are not accustomed to men falling at your feet?"

"Hardly." She folded her arms across her waist.

"Well, that is a pity. You should be accustomed to it." He gestured toward the path ahead with a grand flourish. "Do not beautiful women desire to be fought for, fought over, by gallant men who would throw themselves at their feet?"

"I would not know." He already knew that.

"Do not tell me you do not have scores of gentlemen suitors crowding your father's door for merely a glimpse of you?" He stepped very close, too close.

She edged back to a more comfortable distance. "You confuse me with my sister, Jane."

"Modest, beautiful, and my sister tells me, far

more informed and intelligent than most men." He stared intently into her eyes. Caroline Bingley would probably be happy to receive such a look from him.

"Pray do not flatter me."

"Then what am I to do with you, Miss Elizabeth?" Could he make her name sound any more indecent? "Tell me what am I to do with you if I am not to compliment or flatter. It seems you neither desire my falling at your feet nor even asking you questions. What does that leave me to do?" His eyes—no one, no man, had ever looked at her that way: the way men looked at Jane or Miss Garland. He closed the distance between them again. "You seem so startled. Have you never been appreciated by a man before?"

"You well know the answer."

"Such pert opinions! Now that is a charm. It is quite endearing." His cheeks dimpled as he smiled. "Especially with such beauty to appreciate."

"Are these words your own, or are you trying on a speech for one of your stage rogues who will shock and delight your audience?"

Again, that whole-body laugh that tried to reach in and coax her soul to join. "You are preternaturally perceptive. For I am in all my characters, and they are all in me. But truly, I am a harmless fellow. You have nothing to fear from me."

"I do not fear you." She lifted her chin and met his gaze.

"But you are discomposed by me."

"You have been difficult to understand."

"And what you do not understand, you do not trust." He circled her, lazily, predatorially. "I think there is little you do not understand. The sensation must be very unusual for you."

Why did words fail her now?

"And perhaps invigorating?" There he was again too near—so near the heat of his breath played on her skin.

Every nerve awakened, standing at the ready to catch and act upon whatever might next stimulate it. Her breath came more rapidly, and her chest ached.

"I think I will—" he whispered, "—kiss you…"

"No." She jumped back into a long shadow. "Mr. Darcy!"

Two long steps brought him to stand between her and Sir Alexander. "Good morning, Garland. I did not know you to be fond of an early walk."

Sir Alexander smiled oddly and tipped his hat. "I keep rather unusual hours—I sleep very little, you see. Blanche will vouch for me—she finds me pacing the halls and grounds at all hours—tormented by my muse who calls and demands obedience. If you will excuse me." He bowed and sauntered into the trees.

Mr. Darcy watched until he disappeared, eyes narrow, lips drawn tight. "Are you well? You seem distressed."

"I … I hardly know what to say. I came upon him so unexpectedly; he jumped out of a tree at my feet. It was rather—disquieting."

His eyebrows flashed up, then knotted into something that might have been fearsome had she not seen it accompany deep thought before. "What is your opinion of him?"

"I find him difficult to make out." That was the kindest thing she could say.

Mr. Darcy offered his arm. Was it silly to feel safe and protected with him? Probably, but it did not change the fact that she did. They walked in the opposite direction to Sir Alexander's retreat.

"You know that I find your insight quite keen. May I ask you a rather difficult question?" How vulnerable he sounded. "Few are honest with me, especially to the degree which I can count on you to be."

"I am not sure if that is a commendation or a condemnation."

"Truly, you do not know?" He paused and searched her face. "I mean it as a compliment."

Something about the intensity of his gaze—her face flushed hot, nearly burning.

Thankfully, he began to walk again. "You are quite perceptive, particularly where my sister is concerned. Do you believe Garland harmful company for her?"

"I understand he is a great friend of Colonel Fitzwilliam."

"The acquaintance is not of long standing. They met shortly before Garland inherited the baronetcy. As I understand, he was the heir presumptive. Miss Garland's father was the previous baronet."

"They are not brother and sister as they portray themselves to be? I confess that is odd, but he treats her very well for a cousin. That speaks well of him, I suppose." Better than others of his actions.

"Do you think he would trifle with Georgiana?"

Heat crept up her face. Would Sir Alexander dare speak to Miss Darcy as he had just spoken to her? "I do not know, sir. But I believe his open nature, excellent appearance, and dramatic flair might easily be misinterpreted. It might do to caution Miss Darcy with respect to his impulsive speeches. She might easily be swayed to believe he means something that he does not."

"You would give the same caution to your father?"

"I would advise Lydia be kept well away from him, though Kitty and Mary could be in his company far more safely. Lydia is not the kind who thinks through her actions nor is she able to fathom what consequences there may be."

"I have the same concern for Georgiana."

"Miss Darcy is very clever. I understand why at times it may be difficult to have faith in it, but I have no doubt of her understanding. She is very much like your mother."

He nodded, that deep somber nod that made her believe he was actually listening, not merely absently responding for politeness' sake.

"Miss Garland seems very fond of Miss Darcy. As well as Sir Alexander treats his cousin, I hope he would not interfere with one of her friends."

"She and Georgiana played together very well last night. It was a very different sort of music though—made up as they went. I cannot fault the pleasure they found in playing or say listening was in any way unpleasant ...."

"But the lack of order detracted from your enjoyment?" There really was no need to ask. "I have never heard anything like it."

"None of us has, I think."

"You approve of Miss Garland's friendship with your sister?"

"Georgiana does not often take to a person so quickly or easily. That speaks well of her." Mr. Darcy closed his eyes and turned his face toward the sky. "She is a unique woman. Entirely striking. Utterly so. I have never seen her equal."

"It is difficult to imagine anyone who would not

pale in her company." Those words should not have been so difficult to say.

"That is true, but I believe she has suffered much for it. Few women are easy in the company of one so superior to them."

He was right, she probably was very lonely if the glares and glowers of Miss Bingley and Miss de Bourgh were an indication. Sympathy for Miss Garland would be appropriate, but it was just out of reach.

"Miss Garland spoke very highly of you in your absence after the picnic. I think she was pleased that you accepted the invitation to stay at Pemberley."

"I am flattered." Hopefully her voice did not sound as flat to him as it did to her.

"Do you think Miss Garland misses London very much? Will the amusements of the country be sufficient for her?" He bent his head, thoughtful, perhaps even worried.

"I hardly know. It appears she is able to enjoy the pleasures of wherever she is, city or country, with equal aplomb." How tempting it was to speculate on exactly the nature of those pleasures, but it would not do to be simultaneously unladylike and uncharitable.

Again, his nod. What was he considering beneath that furrowed brow? Probably Miss Garland, and what kind of social asset she might be.

Her belly churned again. Indeed, those fish must still be disagreeing with her.


Elizabeth walked with Darcy back to the house where breakfast had already been set out in the morning parlor. If only she could take to her rooms, but no, she had best join the party lest Jane worry.

Sir Alexander noted her entrance with an upraised eyebrow and something that very much resembled a smirk. Was he proud of disquieting her so early in the day? Or did he merely dislike kippers with his morning meal? It was possible.

Either way, he would not have the satisfaction of her acknowledgement. Elizabeth helped herself to a Bath bun—whose fragrance was too tempting to ignore—and tea from the marble-topped mahogany sideboard and took a seat by the window, near Jane. The morning sun embraced that side of the wide, round table, perfect for driving out the last vestiges of the damp chill of her walk—and Sir Alexander's attentions.

Jane greeted Elizabeth with a nod and a smile and returned to her conversation with Miss Bingley. Perhaps she need not be here at all.

Mr. Darcy seated himself at his customary place near the door, marked by his newspaper and coffee. Beside him, Colonel Fitzwilliam made a show of trying to take the newspaper before Mr. Darcy read it. Though Mr. Darcy appeared rather annoyed, it seemed more the pleasant exchange of brothers rather than a genuine disagreement.

Miss Garland, in a posture that could only be described as draped over her chair, seemed to enjoy observing one and all, well out of the morning sun that might have deleterious effects on her complexion. She spent a great deal of time studying Mr. Darcy.

Miss Darcy sat between the two Garlands, half-whispering lines to Sir Alexander while Miss Garland occasionally whispered bits of acting advice. Elizabeth swallowed hard. In her white muslin gown trimmed with pink bows, Miss Darcy looked like such a child between the worldly, wise, and wealthy Garlands. Perhaps suggesting that she be allowed to participate in the house party had not been wise.

The following day the house party, save Garland, assembled in the morning room to repeat their performance of the day before. Darcy took his seat. Everyone else sat in the same places. The sun lit the same spots on the floor and table. The furniture, polished and dusted until the graceful mahogany lines shone, sat in precisely the same places: neat, regular, and soothing.

The only material difference: there were Chelsea buns, not Bath buns, on the platter on the sideboard. Darcy preferred Bath buns.

After they had finished their breakfast, Sir Alexander presented himself in the morning room, hair disheveled, cravat half-tied and dark circles under his eyes. Had he even slept? How dare he appear in such disarray?

"At last! I have done it!" Garland brandished at least a quire of foolscap at the room.

"Done what?" Miss Garland, elegant in a pale-yellow muslin gown with tiny white flowers embroidered at her throat, rolled her eyes and glanced at Georgiana who giggled.

"Finished the play, or at least the first draft of it, you ninny." He dropped into a chair beside her, manuscript still clutched in hand.

"Well, congratulations. That is an accomplishment. The country air must suit you very well. You have labored only a month on that last bit."

"You know, I have you and your foolish little wager to thank for it." He tapped Miss Garland's shoulder with the papers. "So now you shall have the honor of helping me assign the players."

"Now that sounds like great fun." She rose and leaned on his shoulder. "Now you must all ask me very prettily for the part you most desire."

"Tell us our choices." Bingley leaned forward on his elbows.

Garland flipped through the pages, though clearly it was just for show. "Ah yes, for the gentlemen we have four roles. The suitor, thought to be a gentleman, the suitor thought to be a rake, the father, and the elder brother."

Miss Garland circled the table to stand behind Bingley. "I think you well prepared to be a suitor. So, which are you, rake or gentleman?" Her eyebrows arched.

Bingley glanced around the room, eyes lingering on Jane. "I fancy myself a gentleman."

"Then gentleman you shall be. But that leaves us in need of a rake." She continued her circuit around the table. "Mr. Darcy, you would never do for that role."

Darcy snorted. How could she even suggest it, especially when it would be acted with his sister?

"And Colonel, while I expect you could make a fine rake, it would not do to play that toward a girl in your guardianship. You see, Mr. Darcy, I do have some finer sensibilities." She batted her eyes toward him.

Miss Elizabeth pinched the bridge of her nose and squirmed in her seat.

"So, Alexander, the role must fall to you."

"If I must, I must." He executed the deepest, most theatrical bow possible from his seated position.

"That leaves the role of brother for you, Colonel, and Mr. Darcy as father. Are those to your liking?"

If he had to be a part of this endeavor, he could tolerate such a role. Darcy nodded slowly.

"Splendid, though I am not certain our heroine will be able to discern when Darcy and I are acting and when we are not." Richard chuckled and took a long sip of coffee.

"The best actors are those who can live their roles," Garland said.

"And the ladies." Miss Garland paced behind the ladies' seats, the sunbeam playing off her golden curls. "Our heroine, Miss Darcy, has been chosen, so I have roles now for a mother, companion, a sister, and a friend.

Neither of the Miss Bennets met Miss Garland's gaze while Anne and Miss Bingley sat very straight. If Miss Garland did not choose well, the remainder of the house party might become very unpleasant indeed.

He balled a fist under the table. Why had he ever agreed to this scheme?

"Miss de Bourgh, as her cousin you are closest to being a sister, you shall have that role. Miss Bingley shall be her dear friend."

Darcy released his tension in a slow measured breath.

"Mother must go to Miss Bennet, who is all gentle sweetness." Miss Garland rested her hand on the back of Miss Bennet's chair.

Miss Elizabeth smiled at that. Her solicitude toward her elder sister was pleasing, especially when many might have been jealous.

Miss Elizabeth jumped to her feet and looked Miss Garland in the eye. "And you must be the companion, a voice of wisdom and sure advice."

"I have no intention of acting." Miss Garland skittered back half a step.

"Have you no confidence your brother's work?"

"I have said no such thing!" Miss Garland glanced back at Garland who seemed to be enjoying the exchange far too much.

"An actress is expected to be quite beautiful in all her bearing. You are far better qualified in all ways. So, you must take the part." Miss Elizabeth nodded at Miss Bingley and Miss de Bourgh who added their support.

A slow, crooked smile crept across Garland's face. "Ah, Blanche, I believe you have been out-foxed. Your loyalty will not permit you to deny me, and your vanity will not permit you to deny her." His deep laugh rang off the morning parlor's ivory walls. "Miss Elizabeth, I promote you to director's assistant. You will be my right hand in all matters. I shall seek your advice in all things."

Miss Elizabeth winced ever so slightly. "I had thought to assist Miss Darcy with her role."

"And indeed, you shall. But you are eminently capable and shall have no trouble accomplishing both, I am sure."

Color rose on her neck and touched her jaw. Her

profile was very pretty in this light. Still nothing to Miss Garland's, but pretty nonetheless.

"Please, Lizzy. You know we cannot do this without you." Miss Bennet turned to take Miss Elizabeth's hand.

Beside her Georgiana nodded vigorously. "I could not bear knowing that you would be left out."

Somehow, Miss Elizabeth's expression suggested that was exactly what she most wanted. "Very well, I shall offer you what assistance I can, after I have done whatever Miss Darcy requires."

Garland applauded. "Then let us begin at the beginning. I shall read you the play from start to finish—not a word or question until I am through. Then we may discuss all things, sets, costumes, characters, and make our plans. Are we agreed?"

Darcy grunted—agree or not, there was little choice.

Miss Garland sat beside him, eyes on her brother, and whispered, "I can see the scheme is not entirely to your liking."

"I prefer not to act."

"I tried to give you the part in which you would be most comfortable." Her chin wrinkled in a tiny pout.

"I do appreciate the effort." What was Garland saying? It was difficult to pay attention to him and Miss Garland at the same time.

"I appreciate the length to which you are willing to go to accommodate the amusement of your guests. Not like Miss Elizabeth, with whom I am exceedingly put out." She folded her arms over her chest and narrowed her eyes toward Miss Elizabeth. "I do not appreciate her machinations."

Darcy turned his face to look directly at her. "Do

not judge her so harshly; it is done in the service of my sister. She promised to assist Georgiana in learning her lines."

"So, I have already heard. Still, it does not signify. I could have done that—really how much difficulty might there be?"

Darcy pressed his lips together and glanced at Georgiana. She sat in rapt attention to Garland as he read his work. The girl veritably hung on his every word. Who knew she might enjoy theater so much? He would definitely have to arrange for a box next Season.

"Have you so little faith in the intelligence of ladies that you would—"

"No, that is not at all the case." His voice must have been very sharp indeed considering her withdrawal. Though intelligent, he must remember—and put into practice the knowledge—that ladies did require softer treatment. "My sister's confidence is somewhat lacking. Whilst I have faith in her success, I do not wish her to give up before she finds it."

"And you consider only Miss Elizabeth appropriate to bolster you sister?"

"She has proven to be a faithful friend to her."

"Though decidedly below her station." Miss Garland lifted her chin a mite and offered him a view of her elegant profile. "How very liberal-minded to promote such a friend for your sister. I would have not thought it of you."

"You do not approve?"

"Miss Elizabeth holds you in high regard and has defended your character most assiduously. I believe I have seen a glimpse of why." She rose and made her

way to Georgiana and Miss Elizabeth, every movement easy and graceful and assured.

She seemed so at home with Georgiana. Perhaps
that was a very good thing. How kind of Miss Elizabeth to have spoken well of him.

But why had she needed to?

# Chapter 7

A fortnight passed, occupied in the initial flurry that went hand-in-hand with any new undertaking. Miss Darcy required near-constant attention—she insisted Elizabeth read her lines to her over and over again, until Miss Darcy had committed them to memory. Though Miss Garland had promised to help Miss Darcy, the fulfillment was yet to be realized, so often did she keep to her chambers with a headache. Moreover, with each script change—and Sir Alexander seemed to write them daily—the process had to be repeated.

At least the theatrical exceeded expectations. For all Sir Alexander's flourish and frivolity, he instilled his characters with tantalizing depth and complexity. And he would settle for little less than perfection in their portrayal.

Sir Alexander paced across the music room—the

only room in which Mr. Darcy would consent to house the home theatrical—moving in and out of the sunbeams pouring through three large windows along the longest wall. "The room is too long and narrow for a theater. You must persuade Darcy to allow us to use the drawing room."

Elizabeth drew two long breaths and set down a blue and white porcelain vase on a bench pressed into service holding similar objects. That particular article had been removed from the blue parlor to dress the set which they were building along the narrow wall farthest from the doorway. The graceful ivory-painted tables which had once flanked the fireplace had been crowded against the opposite wall in an ungainly, haphazard sort of way, near the pianoforte's new home, piquing Mr. Darcy's ire each time he visited the music room.

"Once he has made a decision, Mr. Darcy will not be persuaded of anything. If we move the harp to the same corner as the pianoforte, this room will do very well. A scenery board to cover the fireplace is all that is needed, and the stage will be entirely suitable."

"Oh, very well. I insist upon the use of the stool in the blue parlor, though. It is well suited for me to stand upon whilst—"

"That is out of the question. The late Mrs. Darcy embroidered that the year she died. He will not see it moved from the parlor." Was he trying to find the most precise means by which to upset Mr. Darcy's equanimity?

"Do be reasonable. It is just a piece of furniture." Sir Alexander gesticulated widely.

"If that is so, then I am sure something else suitable might be found."

"It would serve the intractable lord of the manor right if I wrote him out of the play all together."

Mr. Darcy—who was in fact an excellent actor despite his dislike of performing to others—had already been relegated to a minimally important character who only had speeches in two scenes. It would take little to remove him all together. Moreover, Mr. Darcy would probably appreciate it. Greatly.

Sir Alexander need not know that.

But perhaps she should mention that some rehearsals, particularly those scenes with him and Miss Darcy, danced along the line of impropriety as though it were as inconsequential as a chalked decoration on a ballroom floor, to be brushed away and disappear by the end of the evening without any care at all to its removal.

Elizabeth wrestled a scenery board that had been leaning against the long wall opposite the windows into view. "Does this sketch satisfy the need, now?"

He stomped to her side. "It is better, not perfect, but better. The barn in the distance is still all wrong. Hand me the pencil." He scribbled over her drawing. "More like that. And change that tree. It is too much in the center. I do not like it."

Had he not told her to put it exactly there the second time she had redrawn this background? Was this his natural way of being, or was he doing it simply to make a show of vexing her? "I will work on it this afternoon."

"See that you do—we will need it for our rehearsals immediately." He turned his back and stormed to the other side of the room.

Miss Garland swept in on a breeze of rose and lilac. "Is he being a tyrant again?"

Sir Alexander snorted. "What is tyrannical about wanting to see the play that you insisted we perform shown to its best?"

"You must learn to ignore him dear, really. He is far too full of himself. It will do him good to have someone stand up to his demands." Miss Garland stood between her and Sir Alexander.

"As though you do not manage that enough on your own. Really, Blanche, one would think you do not want the performance to go on for all the support you have offered."

"Acting the part of your heroine's companion in your theatrical is not sufficient support?"

"No. Support would be convincing Darcy to permit the neighborhood to attend the presentation."

"It would not be fitting for Miss Darcy to perform if a large audience observes." Elizabeth slipped out of Miss Garland's shadow. "She is not out yet—"

"Blast and botheration!" Sir Alexander growled.

"Perhaps you should let me see to him. He can be such a beast when in a temper." Miss Garland pointed to the door.

Elizabeth hurried out and shut the door behind her.

Miss Garland's voice filtered through the door. "Calm yourself, Alexander, really. Can you not see she is in agreement with Mr. Darcy? You cannot expect her to change his mind. Trust me with the task. ..."

Deceitful, wretched woman!

Quiet, she needed quiet lest the pounding in the back of her head blossom into a full-blown headache to rival any of Miss Garland's. But where? Yes, the gallery, the most tranquil place in the manor. She rushed for that sanctuary.

The long, dim room—the curtains were drawn to protect the art—felt cooler than the rest of the house. It was difficult to know if it was actually so or just seemed that way because of the coolness of her marble companions. Just enough light filtered around the drapes' edges to allow her to move about. The room smelt of stone and the vague memory of linseed oil paint.

The line of portrait faces staring down at her, from the deep red walls were familiar and some felt like very good friends. Years ago, Mrs. Darcy had toured the gallery with her, telling her about the portraits as if she had personally known every Darcy ancestor. That afternoon had changed Pemberley from a frighteningly huge and fancy house, to a comfortable abode with amusing, if obscure, denizens. She had once told the late Mr. Darcy of her observations while reading to him. He had laughed at the notion and encouraged her to help Mrs. Darcy pen a volume of genealogy, just for family consumption, of course—a project which they undertook with great relish. He had enjoyed it so when Elizabeth read it to him during the last weeks of his life.

Was Mr. Darcy even aware of that venture and how it resided in the drawer of the large bombé chest beneath his mother's portrait? Would he find it as amusing as his father had? His sense of humor was so difficult to predict.

It might be years, even decades before anyone came across it.

Elizabeth sank into a hall chair near the chest and rubbed her temples. Oh, for the company of the elder Darcys or their ancestors! The Garlands' personalities overwhelmed nearly every interaction. Was she the only one who felt it?

Quite possibly.

Jane appeared too well-pleased with Mr. Bingley's company, and he with hers, to take much notice of the Garlands. Though Miss Darcy had made efforts to push Mr. Bingley toward Elizabeth, his temper was much better suited to Jane.

A marble bust stared blankly at her—a familiar enough expression. It was the same sort of look most people offered if she diverged from the typical insipid conversational topics to anything remotely interesting. The same expression Mr. Bingley had offered her last night in the drawing room just before Miss de Bourgh's suggestion that Elizabeth's decidedly "intelligent" conversation might be more fitting for a courtesan than a lady. Miss Bingley had tried to play it off as though it were only a tease, but the words struck their mark as surely as Elizabeth's arrows had found theirs.

Tension crept up the back of her neck, shooting pain up to her temples. It was time to share her concerns for Miss Darcy with her brother and take leave of the house party.

Darcy stopped in the doorway of the gallery. What was Miss Elizabeth doing here, silhouetted in the stray sunbeams that peeked around the curtains? So opposite to Miss Garland, dark and petite, her profile was quite striking, though.

What a shame her future held such limited prospects, especially in the countryside. Perhaps, when they went to London for their next Season, Georgiana might wish for Miss Elizabeth's company as she did with the house party.

While certainly not suitable for their circles, there were always a few men, of Bingley's sort in particular, who might find Miss Elizabeth very acceptable. Not to mention the vicars and barristers and a physician or two within his circle of acquaintance—some of them favored intelligent women.

And Miss Elizabeth certainly was that. Though some did not appreciate it, what was there not to admire in a woman with a well-informed opinion, ready to debate it in an intellectual and civilized manner? That trait in particular made her a very good friend.

Neither Bingley nor Garland admired it as much as he did, though. Then again, neither of them was Miss Elizabeth's intellectual equal. It would be a shame to see her tied to a stupider man. Care would have to be taken in making introductions for her. Her fine eyes and pert opinions might draw the wrong sorts of men to her. And they would definitely not do—but he could, he would, protect her from that.

Yes, if Georgiana wished for the company—and he might even go so far as to suggest to her that she did—they would bring Miss Elizabeth to London for the Season. She deserved a decent match.

"There you are, Darcy!" Bingley clapped his shoulder.

Darcy jumped. How had he sneaked up like that?

"Your sister has been looking for you. She has declared it is time for us to play that game of pall-mall we skipped in favor of rehearsals a few days ago. She insists that you join us."

He groaned. Pall-mall was a frightfully silly, pointless game.

"She insists, and I will not disappoint my hostess." He shouldered past Darcy, into the gallery. "Miss Elizabeth …"

Of course, the ladies would be included in the play. Lovely. He pinched the bridge of his nose. What an opportunity to make a spectacle of himself—and be the object of laughter for it. Exactly the way he most wished to spend an afternoon. Gah.

"Come along, Darcy." Bingley led the way out of the gallery, Miss Elizabeth on his arm.

Darcy was the last one to join those gathered on the lawn around the immaculately groomed grassy mall. A gentle breeze blew, carrying a light perfume from the garden, as if to make him a peace offering. Hoops were already set in the ground, balls and mallets in a neat rack along with a few chairs in the shade of the nearby arbor. It might have been picturesque if he did not dislike the activity.

Garland stood in the shadow of the manor between Georgiana and Miss Elizabeth, smiling and chatting away like a magpie. Did he ever stop talking? At least Georgiana did not seem to mind, but Miss Elizabeth's expression seemed strained, though. Something definitely bothered her.

Bingley fluttered around Miss Bennet, another one of his "angels," no doubt. His trifling infatuations never lasted very long. In fact, this one had already lasted longer than most, perhaps all. Miss Bennet was difficult to make out—very prim and proper. But was she actually touched?

He dare not judge that. In any case, if something

were to come of it, they were not an unsuitable match. Though Bingley would be better off with a woman worth more than just a thousand pounds, at least she was a gentleman's daughter.

"Mr. Darcy—" Miss Bingley and Anne approached from the mall, arm in arm, wearing walking dresses in similar shades of green.

Oh, merciful heavens!

"You must instruct me in how to play." Anne simpered as she slipped her arm into his. "I have never done so."

"And I, too," Miss Bingley echoed.

"Really now," Miss Garland appeared at his other side, a Valkyrie in a vivid blue muslin, the striking color its only decoration, charging to his rescue. "What you demand is too much for any man. Colonel, come now, do be a dear and take charge of Miss Bingley. Teach her the game, for she is entirely without understanding."

Richard sauntered up. "Did I hear my name called?"

"Indeed, you did. Miss Bingley is in need of instruction, and you are just the man to give her what she needs." Miss Garland guided Miss Bingley away from Darcy.

Did she just wink at Richard?

"I would be pleased to assist you, Miss Bingley." Richard bowed.

Miss Bingley smiled, but it was thin—like a child taking second place in a contest. She took his arm and allowed him to lead her away.

"Do you play, Miss Garland?" Anne asked through her teeth.

"I do. My father found it a very acceptable pastime

and had several malls maintained on his property. I am surprised you are not familiar with the game."

"My mother does not think highly of outdoor games for ladies. She believes they ruin the complexion and encourage unladylike behavior."

"Indeed? Then I am surprised you should wish to learn, given your mother's objections." Miss Garland cocked her head just so.

Anne's face turned red, and she stammered a bit. "I am willing to concede that my mother's views might not always be correct."

Darcy's jaw dropped. Perhaps Richard's assessment of Anne had been correct.

"How very independent of you. I dare say you shall find the pastime quite as diverting as I do. Might I offer you some instruction?" Miss Garland looped her arm in Anne's.

"My cousin—"

Darcy stepped back half a step. "No, no, I insist. Accept Miss Garland's generous offer. I am not the least bit put out."

Anne huffed just a little as Miss Garland directed her to the far end of the mall where she retrieved a mallet and ball and demonstrated for Anne.

The view was inspiring. Despite her decidedly unfeminine height, Miss Garland was everything Anne was not: strong, graceful, assured in every movement. Miss Garland swung her mallet and the ball sailed across the lawn in a perfect ballet of strength and control. Her lovely bosom heaved just slightly, enough to heat his blood and direct his thoughts toward base pursuits.

MARIA GRACE

"Mr. Darcy, would you be so good as to return our ball so Miss de Bourgh may try?" How could something so mundane sound suggestive?

"Of course." He trotted down the mall.

*Thwack.*

Crunch.

Pain—searing, blinding pain, felled him to the lawn with an undignified shout.

"Mr. Darcy!" He opened his eyes to Miss Elizabeth's face occupying all his vision, her dark eyes trained on him. "Are you hurt beyond your ankle? Did you strike your head?"

He rolled to his side, propped on his elbow. "No, I do not think so." He pulled his knees up and touched his foot to the lawn. Stomach-churning pain coursed in waves. Terrible, terrible idea. He groaned, fighting off rising nausea.

"Colonel Fitzwilliam, Mr. Bingley, please, help him inside." Miss Elizabeth waved them over. "He must not place any weight on his ankle."

Strong arms pulled him upright, supporting his arms over their shoulders. Miss Elizabeth ran ahead.

When had the distance from the lawn to the house been so great?

Miss Elizabeth met them at the door and directed them to the blue parlor where Mrs. Reynolds was waiting. They arranged him on the fainting couch.

Darcy clutched at the upholstery, panting until he no longer saw stars.

"We need to get your shoe off, Darce." Richard crouched beside the fainting couch.

"He is right." Miss Elizabeth handed him a folded towel. "Bite down on this as they remove it."

He took the towel. How utterly humiliating. Where was his valet?

Richard took hold of the shoe and slowly, steadily, agonizingly removed it.

He groaned; his shoulders knotted as tightly as his fists. Shoe removed, he fell back into the fainting couch, sweating and stomach roiling. A gentle hand dabbed sweat from his brow. A whiff of lavender—Miss Elizabeth remained near. Why was she still here? Would she stay?

His valet arrived and conferred with Mrs. Reynolds and Miss Elizabeth.

"The surgeon should be called," Miss Elizabeth said.

"I will not be bled or purged for a bloody injured ankle." He growled for good measure. People obeyed when he did that.

"I doubt Mr. Langley would recommend either of those remedies as efficacious under these circumstances." There was an irritatingly patient note in Miss Elizabeth's voice.

"Just as well since I will not accept them."

"That has little to do with your need to consult a surgeon." Miss Elizabeth skirted around the fainting couch to look him in the eye.

"What will he do that my valet cannot?"

"He will be able to assess the severity of your injuries."

"I do not wish to see him."

"And you would endanger yourself and by extension your sister because of your stubbornness." She folded her arms over her chest.

"I am bruised and nothing more."

"How do you know that? Or does the master of

Pemberley lay claim to that area of expertise as well?" Why did her expression remind him of his mother when she scolded?

"What leads you to think it is more serious?"

"In the absence of a mistress at Pemberley, your people often sought out my mother for assistance in such matters. Now they come to Jane and me. I have tended broken bones, often in the company of Mr. Langley, and as a result, I am concerned for the extent of your injury."

Damn it all. Why could she not have a reason he could argue with? "Then you tend me."

Her eyes went wide, and she edged back, losing a little color in her face. "I am no medical man."

"Precisely, that is what makes you acceptable."

"You are being utterly ridiculous." Richard rose and stood beside her, trying to summon up the look of a commanding officer. "Let us call for the surgeon."

"I will not see that saw-loving purveyor of tonic and potions." He slapped the seat cushion.

Richard snorted while trying to look serious.

"Colonel, would you fetch Mr. Darcy some brandy?" Miss Elizabeth pointed to the door with her chin.

Richard stared at her.

"Go man! That is the first sensible thing I have heard said." Darcy waved him off.

Richard dodged around Mrs. Reynolds and his valet who stood at the door.

"Fetch your master his banyan and some trousers. These breeches will not be comfortable—and some slippers, soft ones." She pointed at his valet.

"Yes, Miss." He scurried out.

Miss Elizabeth knelt beside the fainting couch, hand barely touching—or was it not touching—his shoulder. "I know Mr. Langley is quick to amputate in cases like this."

Darcy closed his eyes and swallowed hard. He would not die like his father had.

"That is certainly a drastic measure, but if necessary, to save your life, it should be done."

"It is not."

"I will look at your injury on two conditions." She looked directly into his eyes. Few ever did. "First, you and Colonel Fitzwilliam keep it in your confidence that I have done so, and second, you must trust my assessment. There is no point in putting myself out if you will not listen. I do not wish you to suffer any unnecessary procedure, but neither do I wish you to suffer for the lack of what may be necessary."

Her eyes were very fine indeed, filled with warmth and concern.

"Very well," he muttered.

The valet returned, required items in hand.

"Please remove Mr. Darcy's stocking so I might examine his injury. Mrs. Reynolds—"

"Do not worry, Miss. You care for the master, and I will see you are cared for."

She sat on a stool near his feet. "With your permission, I must touch your ankle to ascertain the degree of the injury."

He gritted his teeth and nodded, steeling himself for anther searing wave. But her cool fingers were gentle, soothing across the swelling, purple blotch.

"This will hurt." She pressed firmly along his ankle bone.

She was right, but the assault was short-lived.

Richard arrived, decanter, and glasses in hand.

"Your pronouncement, Miss Elizabeth?" Darcy whispered, dry-mouthed and hoarse.

"If Colonel Fitzwilliam agrees, I believe you may safely defer a call to Mr. Langley. In so far as I can tell, it is severely bruised, but not broken."

"What makes you certain?" Richard stood very close and peered over her shoulder.

"Let me show you."

He set the brandy aside and joined Miss Elizabeth in further poking and prodding of his colorful limb. Richard's touch was not nearly as gentle as hers.

"I am willing to accept her pronouncement, Darce. You are bloody lucky, you know."

Miss Elizabeth sucked in a sharp breath.

"Forgive me, madam. I usually remember myself in polite company." Richard lowered his face, chastened.

"But this is far from polite." She smiled her forgiveness. "With your permission, I shall brew some willow bark tea for your discomfort."

"You will check on the patient later?" Richard headed toward the brandy.

"If he desires it."

"Pray do."

"Then I shall." She disappeared and comfort left the room.

Richard poured brandy for them both. "She is certainly a steady girl. We are fortunate she was among us today. Your poor sister is at sixes and sevens."

He threw his head back. "I must—"

"Miss Bennet and Miss Garland are comforting her. She is in good hands. I did not know you had an aversion to surgeons. Should I find you a proper doctor?"

"Miss Elizabeth said it is only bruised. I am content to rest on her expertise. Kympton Parish has been well tended under the Bennets. I see no reason to suppose her care toward me would be any less diligent."

"It would be better for the estate to have a mistress, you know, not leave the vicar's family filling that role." Richard handed him a glass of brandy.

"You would choose to remind me of this now?"

"This may be an excellent test of Miss Garland's suitability. Surely, you would desire a wife who can be sympathetic and even useful to you when you are unwell. Much better to know her disposition toward the indisposed now, is it not?" Richard tossed back a large gulp.

"You mean I should accept her company in this state? Unable to even rise to greet her properly?"

"Precisely. If she recoils, then you will, at the very least, know what to expect of her. If she does not, then you might find more than her beauty and her dowry in her favor."

"I do not like it."

Richard pulled the stool Darcy's mother had embroidered close and sat near enough for private conversation. "You would rather remain ignorant of your potential partner's flaws? That does not sound like you, who investigates your business partners so assiduously."

"I do not like company when I am unwell."

"All the more reason to determine if you can tolerate her under those circumstances."

Meddlesome, intrusive—

"Darce, I do not mean to be cruel. But how long did your father spend on his sick bed before he died? Years, as I recall. It was only after he fell and the surgeon amputated his arm that the end came. While it was a mercy, I know it was traumatic for all of you. God forbid you follow in the lingering illness of your father. But if you should, would you not wish for a wife who would not abandon you at such a time, one who would not shy away from the unpleasantness of the sick room as Anne or Miss Bingley surely would?"

He groaned. Did Richard's reasoning have to be so sound? "Very well. After dinner, the house party may withdraw here rather than to the drawing room."

What were the chances that this did not prove to be a very bad idea indeed?

## ⚜Chapter 8

Darcy leaned his head back and stifled a groan. Changing garments in the parlor—what a mortifying and painful experience. But Miss Elizabeth had been right as usual: tight knee breeches, a stiff stock and cravat, and a form-fitted coat would have only added to his misery. A second glass of brandy along with the willow bark tea she brought helped him endure her further ministrations: anointing his ankle with pungent ointment and wrapping it to restrict movement.

He slept most of the afternoon, his brandy-induced dreams hard to recall but disturbing nonetheless. Now, near dinnertime, he lay back, staring at the plaster ceiling work, the dark gold curtains dimming the sunlight enough to create an odd twilight effect far too early in the day for such darkness.

Odd. He had never really paid attention to the molding between the ceiling and wall, nor the ceiling roses that had hung overhead all his life. Someone must have paid attention to them though—not a cobweb or tuft of dust to be seen on any of it.

The heavy drapes swayed in a slight breeze that brought soft green scents into the room. Another annoying reminder of why he was here.

Father had liked Mother's influences in this parlor, before he had been bed-ridden. The azure walls, especially, often calling them his favorite color. Often, when Darcy had been home on school holiday, Father had invited him into the parlor to read to him from one book or another. Those were rare moments that Father's drive for perfection could be satisfied. Even when he stumbled or said a word different to what the text contained, Father would just ignore the error and continue listening with pleasure.

Perhaps that was why he wanted Georgiana to read aloud well.

He shifted on the firm, royal blue upholstery of the fainting couch. It had never been a particularly comfortable piece of furniture for him, though the ladies seemed to like it well enough. No part of the seat fitted his frame, magnifying his discomfort. Ugh! Just how long would it take until he could make it upstairs to his room and to his bed and proper pillows?

Richard had offered to have the footmen carry him upstairs in a chair. His desperation would have to be far greater to agree to submit to the indignity his father had suffered. His ankle throbbed in time with his heart beat, his stomach growling a counterpoint. Just how long would this continue?

Behind him, the door swung open. Carefully, he turned to look over his shoulder. His valet trundled in with a dinner tray, Miss Elizabeth on his heels.

Her deep rose dinner dress complimented her fine complexion and light, pleasing figure. Utterly unlike Miss Garland, but pretty—definitely pretty. She looked at him as if he were properly garbed and polite. But he was not. He pulled at the lapels of his banyan. How appalling to be so informally attired in company.

If she noticed his discomfiture, she gave no sign of it. If she could pretend everything was right and proper, perhaps he could—and it might make it all easier.

The valet brought a small table near Darcy's seat and arranged the tray.

"I brought you more willow bark tea. I hope it will make you more comfortable for company this evening." She handed him the cup from the tray.

He sipped—much less bitter this time, but still unpleasant. She must have added the ginger and sugar after he complained of the bitterness. He downed the cup in two large gulps and handed it to her. "Thank you."

She curtsied and turned away.

"May I ask another favor of you? I know it is much to ask, but would you consider … no, never mind." He sighed and braced his forehead in his hand. He was being foolish.

"You would like company whilst you eat?"

He glanced up into her penetrating, perceptive gaze. How did she do that?

"It is no trouble for me to keep you company. Dinner is hardly a meal that should be eaten alone."

"It is hardly a meal that one should eat wearing banyan and trousers."

She smiled as though she understood how uncomfortable irregularity made him.

The valet moved an ivory wingchair with pale blue and yellow flowers slightly nearer the fainting couch.

"Bring a tray for Miss Elizabeth."

The valet bowed and disappeared.

"You have never been a great lover of company, even at mealtimes. You must need to be distracted away from your discomfort."

Damn it, she was right. How dare she be so prying, and why was it so comfortable?

"Your father did the same thing often enough." She removed the covers from his plates and arranged them in easy reach, whiffs of her light lavender scent punctuating each movement.

The valet arrived with a second tray.

"Now you may eat, Mr. Darcy." Her lips wrinkled in a funny little smirk. "Politeness no longer requires you wait for me." "

She busied herself with her tray.

Odd, she did not watch him. Anne and Miss Bingley always watched him to the point he felt like an exotic creature on display.

"You look as though you wish for conversation." She glanced up at him.

"I believe it is an accepted practice to have some conversation over a meal."

She sipped her soup—a creamy vegetable sort of concoction—for a moment. "I notice you have a copy of Shakespeare's histories on the table. Is it there for the beauty of its binding or for the pleasure of reading?"

"My sister would insist on the former—she has no taste for reading. I find it quite …."

"You must not say it is enjoyable. Your conscience will plague you if you do. You know it is improper to lie to one who so recently has done you a favor." One eyebrow arched in an oh-so-knowing lift.

He snorted softly. "I confess. I do not find Shakespeare's histories entirely suited to my tastes."

"What then do you prefer? His comedies or his tragedies?"

"His sonnets." Why had he said that? Anne would abuse him abominably if she knew.

"I can see why. A man who does not care to perform to strangers might well prefer works that do not demand performance in the way a play does."

Where was the teasing wit, the hint of reprimand that should have been in her voice? No, he had not missed it. Her voice and her eyes were soft, so soft and so very fine. Incomparable. He licked his lips and sipped his wine—why had his throat gone so dry?

"So … so what think you of Sir Alexander's work?" She blinked and returned to her soup.

"I have seen none of his other works on stage. But his offering for this house party is," he shrugged, "not objectionable."

"That is faint praise." There was that eyebrow again. Must she demand truth from him?

"I can see why his works have gained the level of notoriety they have. The themes are … appealing … to certain groups. He is able to turn a phrase quite cleverly. His use of humor to disarm those who would oppose his views is … astute. There now, is that more to your liking?"

"It is a more worthy assessment from a man of

your caliber." She dabbed her lips with her napkin. "I do not think you would choose to see his plays performed, though."

"You are correct. I would not. But that is a matter of taste. I heard you mention theater critics the other evening. What think you of their assessments?"

"I have it on great authority that gentlemen do not approve of ladies who suppose their information rivals his. It is, I am told, a very unattractive and undesirable trait, so forgive me if I defer to your opinion." She bit her lip and avoided his gaze.

"I would also very much like to deny what you assert, but I cannot. I have seen that sort of nonsense bandied about by individuals—of both sexes, to be sure—who are in possession of very little sense themselves. But it is my belief that men of sense do not want silly wives."

"I am not sure all who are at Pemberley now would agree with you."

"Consider Miss Garland. What say you of her?"

"She is certainly not silly." Her voice tensed.

"Would you consider her well-informed?"

"On matters that interest her, she is very well-informed. However, a great deal of wealth, a connection to title, and staggering beauty goes a long way in making a lady acceptable in many circles, no matter what her level of information."

Darcy raised his wineglass toward her. "I suppose you have a point."

"She has so many great virtues it is difficult to imagine any gentleman bothering to dwell upon a small vice like intelligence. Those of us not so well-favored do not have that luxury."

Unfortunately, she was correct. "What is your opinion of Miss Garland?"

Miss Elizabeth peered at him, an odd, almost sad glint in her eyes. "I cannot fully make her out. Though she is outspoken, she is not unkind, and she has taken to Miss Darcy very well. She seems at home in the country, though London pleases her as well."

"You speak in facts, not opinions." He leaned toward her. Pray she would be honest.

"She is certainly praiseworthy. I would like to know her character better, though."

Noise—this house party approaching—filtered in from the corridor. She rose and took the trays to the chest near the doorway.

And now he would never hear her opinion.

Georgiana rushed to his side. "Oh, Brother, I have been worried about you!" She grabbed his hand and clutched it to her shoulder.

"As you see, I am well. I shall be fine."

She sniffled. "I am so sorry."

Pray do not cry! "Stop, do not take the blame on yourself. It was an accident."

"Indeed, it was, Darcy." Garland came up behind Georgiana. "Frightfully sorry for it, too, you must know."

"I did not know you had it in you," Richard clapped Garland's shoulder, "to muster such force with your mallet."

"I dare say it was my dear sister who drove me to it. She declared me incapable, and I had to prove her wrong." Garland looked over his shoulder.

"And look what your bravado brought you!" Miss Garland shouldered her way past him. "Have you no thought as to how very tragic this might have been?"

She sat in the chair Miss Elizabeth had occupied minutes before, her face a portrait of concern.

"You really should consider the stage, for you have a decided flare for the dramatic." Garland harrumphed.

"I am afraid she is quite correct." Richard chewed his lower lip. "Men die of broken bones. You would not want that upon your conscience."

Georgiana blanched and swayed against the fainting couch.

Darcy slid back lest she fall upon his injured limb. Dear God, that hurt. "I am fine. There is naught but inconvenience here."

"Why do you not invite the Bennet sisters to play and sing?" Richard's voice dropped to a whisper. "Before Miss Bingley begins another concerto."

Georgiana giggled. Garland offered his arm and escorted her away, Richard on their heels and Miss Elizabeth lost in the rest of the company.

"You look reasonably spry for one who has suffered such an injury." Miss Garland smiled just a mite too much. "One might even wonder if it is merely an excuse to show off your fine banyan and your neck without a cravat." Her gaze lingered over him until he twitched. How could she be so impertinent and so intriguingly delightful all at once?

"Had this been intentional, madam, I would have found a way that did not relegate me to a fainting couch," he grumbled under his breath.

"I suppose you are correct." She turned her ear toward the little pianoforte in the far corner of the room and cocked her head. Such graceful lines from her neck to her shoulder. "Miss Bennet plays nicely, and her sister has a sweet voice."

"They are pleasant to listen to." When had Miss Elizabeth begun to sing?

"They are nothing to your sister, I assure you. Miss Darcy has a rare talent."

"Truly?" His gaze landed on Georgiana who stood near the musicians, brows furrowed in concentration, fingers moving as though she were playing with them. "I have never considered it so. She has such a difficult time learning anything. I worry about her."

"Surely not. She is one of the cleverest girls I have had the pleasure of knowing."

"Do not seek to flatter me or my family. Whilst I am pleased you do not think my sister a simpleton, I do not take kindly to your efforts to exaggerate her accomplishments."

She sat up very straight, blue eyes chill as ice. "And I do not appreciate your insinuation that I am prone to idle flattery. Not of anyone or in any situation. Whilst she may be no scholar, Miss Darcy is an exceptionally quick learner. I read her lines to her today—Alexander's hand is dreadful and often I am the only one who can decipher it—and she had the entire scene committed to memory the second time through. On the pianoforte, she plays pieces perfectly after hearing them only once. I would call that remarkable. It is a shame that you do not agree."

Were they talking about the same girl? "I am astonished, truly astonished. All her school masters have held quite a different opinion. They have deemed her everything from dull to lazy to quite willful, but never clever."

"That explains her mean opinion of herself. It is a shame, for she is far more accomplished than she or you believe her to be. At least Miss Elizabeth has proven an ally in my efforts to convince her of her own merit. That will be crucial before she has her come-out in London. A girl without self-confidence is often thrown to the wolves among the *ton*."

The crest of Darcy's ears burned. "It is good of you to take such an interest in her."

"She is a delightful young woman. I am pleased to consider her a friend." She turned toward Georgiana.

The firelight did marvelous things for Miss Garland's profile. Smooth, creamy skin formed into perfectly composed features, sloping into generous soft curves. The lace at her neckline only emphasized the plunging décolletage. A silk-stockinged ankle peeked from her hems, encouraging him to wonder at all that lay beyond.

She cast a sidelong glance at him and raised an eyebrow.

Botheration! He had been staring, and she had noticed. Where had his manners gone? How could he be such a brute?

Her eyelid twitched. Had she just winked? The turn of her lips surely suggested so. Great heavens!

"Do not be alarmed, sir, I do not take offense. I am quite accustomed to being stared at." The barest hint of a dimple creased her cheek.

"I was …"

"Of course, you were. Do not bother with prevarications. They only insult my intelligence. I am entirely aware of my propensity to gather stares and what they mean." Her voice, her bearing were so composed, with no hint of umbrage.

"I am intrigued. You must explain." He leaned back slightly and permitted himself to look directly into her sparkling eyes.

"People like to gawk at oddities. They gape at anyone unusual or extreme."

"You do not suggest I find you an oddity?"

"No, perhaps not. The notion is too extreme, but you definitely find me a curiosity." She matched his posture. "Not unlike a performer in a traveling circus."

He gasped. "Among the giants and the deformed?"

"Am I not the tallest woman you have ever encountered?"

"I will grant you that."

"How very good of you. As to deformity—is it all not some sort of continuum really, with the most hideous occupying one end," she extended her open left hand, "and the most beautiful the other?" She opened her right hand

"I had never considered it so." Nor had most philosophers he had read.

"Are they not polar opposites? One extreme does not exist in the presence of the other. So then, I am as curious as the horrid little creature displaying himself for the delight of ticket bearers." She extended her legs slightly and crossed her ankles. "In a way, I am at a disadvantage, for at least they are able to profit from the uniqueness of their appearance. At least in that manner, it seems they have all the advantage."

"How can you say such a thing?"

"Do you find me beautiful? More so than, let us say, your cousin Anne?"

He resettled himself in his seat, mumbling, "I do."

"Of course, that was an easy question. Your poor cousin carries the look of illness about her. But Miss

Bingley is certainly an elegant female. Do I surpass her?"

"Yes, you do." Impertinent. Brash. Disconcerting ...

"She is elegant in the way of many, so she is also ordinary. I agree. What of the remaining ladies? The Bennet sisters? Miss Bennet is regarded as very attractive."

"This is a most unseemly topic."

"I see now I have competition." She touched her cheek. "I think her a more ethereal beauty whereas I am more classic, timeless, if you will."

"I do not know how to answer."

"Of course not. Such a conversation with a woman you must consider quite improper. But if I am not uncomfortable, why should you be?" She studied him, challenging him with her gaze. "Are you offended if I declare you less tall than my brother?"

"No. It is a matter of fact."

"So, too, is a woman's beauty."

"Is there not a certain matter of taste to be considered as well? Height is a measurable trait, yet attractiveness is subjective."

"After a fashion, I suppose, but it hardly signifies unless one knows a lady well enough to consider her character as part of her beauty."

He rubbed his temples with thumb and forefinger. "I have no idea what you mean."

"I noticed you did not make any mention of Miss Elizabeth when we discussed the Bennet sisters." She pointed with her chin at the little group laughing around the pianoforte.

Miss Elizabeth was saying something—what, he could not make out—but it made the rest smile and nod. "She hardly rates a comparison to her sister."

"In some ways, that may be correct. But Alexander declares her the most attractive woman in the room."

He huffed. What was Garland doing looking at Miss Elizabeth? She was hardly of his station—not a woman he should be noticing. "I can hardly consider that a serious statement."

"I disagree. Were we in a London drawing room, I would consider her quite my stiffest competition for any gentleman's attentions."

"I cannot fathom why."

"She may not have my face or figure, but her wit is as sharp as mine and her understanding as quick. Moreover, she is blessed with what I lack, a warm and nurturing temperament, ready to take care of those around her, even at her own expense. Those are very attractive qualities." Why was she staring at him again? "It is to my good fortune she has neither wealth nor connections to solidify her position, or I would have to truly despise her. In such an environment, I could even see you—"

"You jest." He brushed the idea aside. Would that she would stop looking at him that way. "No. I should like to consider I have more to offer—"

"Than a woman with no fortune or connections might expect?"

"Are you jealous, Miss Garland?"

"Not anymore." Her cheek dimpled.

Georgiana and Garland took to the pianoforte. Darcy leaned back and closed his eyes, Joints stiff from enforced quietude protested every command to relax. Was there a single comfortable position on this blasted fainting couch?

"Are you well?" He opened his eyes into Miss Elizabeth's face, hovering just above him. "Might I see to anything for your relief?"

"You are a dear girl." Miss Garland rose and patted Miss Elizabeth's hand. "But I have the matter quite in hand. Do not fear."

"Of course. Forgive my intrusion." She curtsied and hurried away.

"I know just what you need, Mr. Darcy. I will return in a moment." Miss Garland dipped in the barest curtsey and disappeared from the room.

"Miss Bingley," Garland rose from the pianoforte. "Come play us something lively so that we may have a dance."

"That is a fine notion." Bingley moved closer to Miss Bennet.

"If you insist." Miss Bingley took her place at the keyboard.

Richard and Garland moved furniture out of the way.

Three couples assembled and made their bows and curtsies at Miss Bingley's opening notes: Miss Bennet and Bingley, Richard and Anne, Georgiana and Garland.

Miss Elizabeth stood in the shadows near the doorway, not entirely successful at hiding her crestfallen expression. Such was the uncomfortable reality of unequal parties of ladies and gentlemen.

She watched the dancers, the sparkle gone from her fine eyes. Her smile was entirely for show, nothing genuine about it. But she squared her shoulders and lifted her chin and watched on.

Miss Bingley finished her set and Miss Bennet was persuaded to play for the next, but none sought to dance with Miss Elizabeth. A few bars into her sister's first chorus, Miss Elizabeth slipped out.

## Chapter 9

Elizabeth dashed through the corridor and headed for the gallery. Enough, enough! There was absolutely no need to relive that nightmare again. It had haunted her dreams often enough. Foolish and childish thought it may be, she would never forget a cut like that. Forgive, yes, she must, but forget? Never.

If she went to her chambers, Jane would find her and insist they talk. Now was not the time for talk. Peace and silence—and perhaps air—were all she required.

Moonlight streaming through two still-open windows lit the long room. Forgetful maids—Mrs. Reynolds would surely reprimand them. The sunlight would fade the treasured paintings.

But for now, she would enjoy the silver tendrils streaming past the velvet curtains, turning everything to shades of soft grey, and then close the drapes when she left.

Had she not already been familiar with the room's marble and oil occupants, the moonlit effect might have been haunting. But these were not ghosts, rather old friends she met with each time she came to read to bedridden old Mr. Darcy. The old man could not speak much then, but his eyes were kind—like his son's. How sad the current Mr. Darcy never had the opportunity to see his father that way and the two never came to terms with one another.

She paced the length of the gallery twice, rubbing her hands briskly along her arms, her slippers whispering along the polished marble. Ridiculous! That is what old Mr. Darcy would have called her could he see her now. It was not as though this were the first time she had been without a dance partner. Most girls took their turns sitting out at Lambton's public assemblies. Was it really such a trial now?

Perhaps if Mr. Garland—Sir Alexander it was now—had not looked at her that way, it would have been different. Did he still take such glee in not dancing with her? Then to make such a show of asking Jane to dance with him.

How horrid and petty to be jealous of Jane. At least Jane never tried to make her feel inferior—no, that was better left to fine ladies like Miss Bingley and Miss de Bourgh. Raw and ill-used, that was how they left her.

Ironic how the gentlemen seemed to enjoy Elizabeth's company … at least until it was time to dance. Then beauty and fortune won over wit and clever conversation.

It always would.

She sank into a soft chair in a shadowed niche and slid into an ungraceful slump. What did unladylike posture matter when there was no one to notice? What did any of it matter when she lacked the traits that mattered to society?

The moon rose high above the horizon as she watched the moonbeams and shadows dance along the marble floor. She counted the floor tiles, first by horizontal rows, then vertical, and now diagonal. No one ought to be so expert in the dimensions of a marble floor. But it was soothing.

A tall figure entered the far side of the gallery, silk skirts swishing as she staggered and tottered.

What was wrong with Miss Garland? Leaden steps and a crumpled posture replaced her usual poise and grace. She crashed to her knees beside a window bench flanked by velvet curtains.

"Are you hurt?" Elizabeth dashed to her side.

"Miss ... Miss Elizabeth?" She turned her face toward Elizabeth, glassy-eyed, her features slack, head drooped and bobbing. "Elizabeth, dearest Elizabeth, my friend."

No scent of wine or brandy on her breath. She was not in her cups, but she certainly acted that way.

"I am ... am so glad to see you here." She pulled her head up and fluttered her eyes at Elizabeth.

"You seem in want of some assistance."

"You must call me Blanche, now for you are my very dear friend. Not like those jealous old tabbies around the ... the ..." she giggled into her hand.

"The parlor?" Elizabeth crouched beside Miss Garland.

"Yes, that is the room... the parlor. You are clever and quick and ... and ... not jealous. No, no, why would you be? We do not walk in the same circles, have the same aspirations. We ... we do not ... compete for the same attentions."

"You need to retire to your chambers ... Blanche.... You are not well. Let me help you stand." Elizabeth tried to pull Miss Garland's arm over her shoulders.

She yanked her arm away and sat down hard on the tiles. "No, no. I do not wish to go. It is nice here ... here with my friend."

Elizabeth sat on the window bench.

Miss Garland leaned her head in Elizabeth's lap. "Much better ... They hate me, you know. Miss de Bourgh, and Miss Bingley."

"Hate is a very strong term."

"Hate, definitely hate. I am far wealthier, prettier and have ... have ... my father ... he had a title, you know."

"I was aware."

"Your sister is scared of me! Can you imagine? Miss Darcy, though, she ... she likes me."

"She is a dear girl." How was she to get Miss Garland back to her chambers?

"I like you Eliza ... abeth. A pity ... such a pity."

"What is?"

"Mr. Darcy. He would like you very well if you were higher than you are."

Enough of this conversation! Elizabeth looked toward the door—surely there must be someone nearby to interrupt this trial.

"But you are not ... and he cannot ... and he must settle for me."

"You are very much mistaken."

"No, no, no, no. I am not. Not a little bit, my dear

friend." Miss Garland wagged an unsteady finger in front of her face. "No, I am not. Men stare at me all the time ... all ... all ... all the time. Fitzwilliam and Bingley, they stare when they do not think I see. They like my bubbies, you see."

"This is not proper...."

"No, it is not ... but they stare. But one can hardly miss something of this size, can one?" She looked down into her décolletage as she pushed it up to near-ly overflow her bodice. "But you ... you have naught but little ones ...."

Could this become more humiliating?

"But Mr. Darcy ... and Alexander, they ... both ... stare at you."

"They certainly do not."

"Yes ... oh, yes they do." She squinted up into Elizabeth's face. "I know ... I see them." She began to laugh and nearly fell sideways, catching herself on Elizabeth's legs. "But you have no fortune ... not a penny! You have got nothing. So, they cannot have you. And Mr. Darcy must settle for me."

"This is not a subject—"

"I said it because it is true. He made himself stare ... at me tonight. I must be sure ... to show him my ...." Miss Garland rearranged her bosom. "He likes them ... I think he does. He should ...." Tears pooled in her eyes and leaked down her cheeks. "I should not like you very well, you know."

How could she escape the gallery before this turned even worse, as it surely would?

"He likes you ... likes you very well ... but he will offer for me. I am jealous. I am not used to being jealous. Everyone envies me. Imagine, that I might envy someone like ... like you." Peals of laughter turned hysterical, mixing with sobs. "I want him to like me the way he likes you—not because he thinks he should, but because he does!" Her voice rose with each word and ended with a shriek.

She fell into Elizabeth's lap, wracked with sobs, clutching Elizabeth's waist. She held her breath and fought the urge to push Miss Garland away and run.

Mr. Darcy's valet strode up. "Excuse me, Miss. I heard—"

Merciful heavens, at last! "Miss Garland is quite unwell. Fetch her maid, and see her to her chambers."

He returned a few moments later with Miss Garland's lady's maid who seemed unsurprised by her mistress' condition. Lovely, just lovely.

Together they removed Miss Garland.

Elizabeth stood frozen. Her sanctuary violated; she smelt of Miss Garland's perfume. A bath would have been welcome, but it was far too late to make such a demand on the staff. Best find her way back to her chambers and be done with this awful day. Her foot slipped on something small and hard. She barely caught herself against the window frame. Good heavens! What was that?

Crouching, she retrieved a small, dark bottle. The moonlight played off the label. *A Lady's Soothing Tincture ~ a universal household medicine.*

Soothing, indeed. She shook the bottle. Empty but for a few drops. She poured one out on her fingertip and tasted it. Vile, bitter … and full of laudanum.

That explained Miss Garland's state. Why would a woman so well-blessed, so strong and confident, require a soothing tincture?

She left the gallery. Her stomach grumbled—she had missed supper after all. Below stairs seemed quiet. Perhaps she could sneak into the kitchen for a bite.

She crept downstairs along the dark stairway. Perhaps she would have to find a candle to assist her upstairs. At the foot of the stairs, she paused, a low moan filtered from the darkness. It must be from the parlor. Mr. Darcy?

She should not go to him, not like this, with everyone retired for the night. Bother, the valet was likely still upstairs assisting the maid with Miss Garland.

Another moan.

No one here had anything to gain by spreading gossip. Pemberley's staff was notoriously tight-lipped. She headed for the parlor. It was safe to err on the side of compassion here.

She cracked the door open.

Mr. Darcy thrashed on the fainting couch, moonlight painting wan shadows along his sweaty face. How had he become feverish? Could she have been mistaken? Had he actually broken a bone and it began turning septic?

She dashed to his side and laid her hand on his forehead. The skin was cool, not burning with fever.

He grabbed her wrist. "Must get up. I will die if I stay in bed."

"You must not risk further damage to your ankle." She pressed him back.

His grip tightened. "Do not leave me. I do not wish to die alone."

"You are not dying." She could just reach a footstool with her toes and pulled it close enough to sit beside the fainting couch. "Most likely, you have had too much brandy."

He blinked and shook his head. "Not so much. Only … only two glasses."

"That does not seem possible."

"One Fitz brought me … and Bingley gave me one whilst we read his lines from that ruddy foolish play. You … you were not here to help Georgiana. Why did you leave? Should have been here for her. She needs your help … and for me. My leg hurts."

"Let me help you get more comfortable." She eased his grip on her hand and helped him settle back, arranging the pillows beneath his injured foot and behind his shoulders. "There now, you should find that more comfortable." She wiped the sweat from his face with a napkin left from tea and biscuits and resumed her place on the stool.

"Wanted your willow bark."

"Shall I go and make you some?"

"The Valkyrie gave me wine instead. Tasted strange … so strange … so sleepy."

So, that was why Miss Garland had the bottle of soothing syrup.

He clutched her hand with one hand and swung at an unseen assailant with the other. "Away! Away!"

She ducked his failing arm. "There is nothing there."

"Cannot you see the Hound of Hell? It comes for me. I must … If I do not get off this bed, it will take me!" He sat upright and swung his feet to the floor.

She grabbed both his hands. Even now he was so strong. "Calm, yourself. There is nothing here. I promise. You are quite safe."

"I will not lay down again."

"Then prop your foot on this stool and sit quietly."

His bandaged foot landed heavily in her lap. She caught her surprised squeal before it escaped. His head lolled back over the back of the fainting couch.

"Read to me—as you did to my father. He said it kept the hound at bay."

"I cannot read in the dark."

"Then sing to me with your pretty voice."

"Very well." Given his state, he would hardly recall her performance in the morning. Even if he did, he could hardly find fault with it, given the circumstances. If it might calm him, it was worth it.

What did one sing under such conditions? A simple country tune with many verses and choruses. After three such songs, her throat grew raspy and her voice hoarse.

"She would not sing for me."

"Who?"

"The Valkyrie."

"I assure you, there are neither hell hounds nor Valkyries in the house."

"She was here, in the parlor! She played pianoforte and read lines with Georgiana and wore blue silk." He waved into the darkness.

Miss Garland? She was his Valkyrie?

"She is very lovely, the Valkyrie. I like her. Richard likes her … a great deal, you know. Would even … offer … if he had more. She does not like second sons, you know."

"No, I did not." Not that she wanted to know, either.

"Calls them … pred … predator … wolves. Wolves! Do you think Richard is a wolf? I … I am not a wolf."

"Of course not."

"Do you think she likes me?"

"It is not for me to say." Elizabeth swallowed back the bitter taste in her mouth.

"Or perhaps ... my fortune, my house. Do you like my house?"

"It is a very fine property. But is not a man more than the sum of his property?"

He attempted to cock his head, but his chin fell to his chest. "A nice thought, truly ... truly." He laughed bitingly. "But that is not the way of things ... no ... no ... no .... I am naught but a fortune and estate ... a name and connections ... no one sees more ... cares more than that."

"That is a very sad philosophy. There is a great deal more to a man than positions and possessions."

"You are very good, Miss Elizabeth, very good. No one else sees that, you know. Just you. Only you. My wife will not see it that way."

"How can you be certain?" She looked toward the door—surely someone had to come in soon. Then again, that might only make this even worse.

"Richard wants the Valkyrie for my wife." He laughed drunkenly. "Do you think it a good idea?"

"I ... I ..."

"You are a good friend. A great, good friend. I hope she will be like ... like ... you." A moment later, he snored.

She tried to shift his foot off her lap, but he moaned and cried out. By all rights, she should leave, should flee this situation. Alone, in a dark room, with a gentleman? Had she been mercenary, she could use the situation to her advantage, to great advantage.

She peered at his sweaty face, bathed in the moonlight. He groaned again. She smoothed her hand along his forehead, just barely in her reach. He sighed and some of the tension eased.

No, she could not treat him that way. His intentions toward her had always been clear and proper. It was right and fitting that he be interested in Miss Garland. Even if he thought of her as a Valkyrie, she would be a fitting mistress for Pemberley.

And since she considered Elizabeth her friend, perhaps Elizabeth could remain a friend to Mr. Darcy as well.

Early morning sun peeked through the window, teasing Elizabeth's eyes open. She pushed her shoulders up from the fainting couch where she had finally collapsed beside Mr. Darcy, its bright blue upholstery made slightly violet in the rosy morning light. His foot still lay in her lap, heavy and still swollen. She stretched, though it was difficult to manage without disturbing him. Stiff aching joints confirmed she had indeed been there the full night.

Footsteps shuffled at the door. She jumped enough to make Mr. Darcy stir.

His valet hurried to her side. "Let me help you, Miss." He shifted his master's leg, and she slipped off the stool.

Her legs and feet tingled; her knees barely straightened.

The valet caught her arm and helped her to her feet. "Can you walk?"

"I believe so." She limped to the corridor, but the stairs to her chambers, where she might finally get some proper sleep, were far too intimidating. Little chance that her spirits would settle enough for rest, though.

A walk, yes—a marvelous idea! Still hobbling, she trudged to the garden doors. Lovely, inviting rays of sunrise urged her to forget the emptiness that plagued her. Why did her heart ache as much as her back?

Dewy morning air carried the faint, sweet scent of flowers, beckoning her down the garden path. Glittering dewdrops glistened on bluebells that waved at her from beyond the garden walls. Bluebells were always worth visiting. Something about the way they carpeted the woods in humble grandeur—who could resist?

A certain woman had worn a gown that shared a hue with the modest blossoms. What would she do now with what she had learnt about Miss Garland? One should keep a secret, but what harm might be done in keeping that confidence?

More important, what was to be done about the night just spent in Mr. Darcy's company? Breathe, she must breathe! It would not ruin her. Nothing had taken place. And no one knew.

"Ho there!"

She cringed and squeezed her eyes shut. No, not him! What rummy timing. She looked over her shoulder.

Sir Alexander, jacket and cravat rumpled, trotted into the woods toward her, crushing bluebells with every step. "How delightful to find you here, Miss Bennet." He doffed his beaver hat and bowed.

If only she shared the sentiment. "You are about quite early this morning."

"I keep unique hours. Last night's company proved so stimulating, I spent the rest of the evening at work on a new manuscript. My muse is positively enchanted with the atmosphere here!" He sucked in a deep breath of bluebell-perfumed air and settled his tall hat back into place.

"I have heard a muse can be a very fickle thing, indeed."

"You have no idea. No idea at all! One moment, I must chase her as a huntsman pursues his prey, over hill and field, running all the way. The next, she is a slave driver lording over me with her whip, demanding I complete whatever task she desires. Then there are those times as last night, that she is a lover who has perfumed the sheets and invited me to her bed." His gaze raked her from eyes to bosom.

Face burning, she inched back.

"But my fickle lover was not pleased with me last night." He stepped closer, and his voice dropped heavy with suggestion. "Do you know why?"

"I have no idea." Nor did she care to have one.

"It was entirely your fault." His pointing finger nearly touched her collarbone.

"I do not understand."

"Why have you told no one that we have met before?"

Her belly tightened in a knot more intricate than his cravat. "I do not see how that intelligence might be of use to anyone."

"But you remember." His face reformed itself into a wholly new expression, something vulnerable and even sincere. "I was unforgivably rude and unfeeling toward you."

"It is of no matter. It is long past." At least that should have been true.

"I might have believed you, save I saw your expression last night." He slipped closer, uncomfortably close. "When the dancing started and you were without a partner. I saw your face as you left."

She turned aside. Perhaps if she ran, he might not follow. "I was fatigued. My head hurt."

"Perhaps, that is true. I believe there was more than that. I have seen that expression before."

"It is of no matter." She sidestepped around him and strode off down the path, away from the blue-bells and into the woods. What a time for her knees to still hurt.

"It is a very great matter. When a man, a gentle-man insults a lady, it is a grave mark against his honor." Blast! His long legs made it far too easy for him to advance on her.

"It is of no matter. Pray, let it rest."

He laughed, a full-throated, full-bellied laugh, but devoid of mirth. "You say that, but I have known too many ladies to believe for a moment that it has been laid to rest. You probably remember every foolish word that fell from my mouth like the foaming slaver of a mad dog."

Her feet rooted in place. His expression, the way he tied his cravat, even the scent he wore as he spoke those words—yes, it was all as fresh as the night it had happened. She balled her fists.

"At a party given by Sir Alfred and some of the other theater patrons. Your aunt and uncle brought you. Your first soiree in London, I was told."

"Also, my last. I care not to discuss it."

"I imagine the fault for that is largely mine."

"Do not take credit you do not deserve." She forced herself to glare at him. Perhaps that would put an end to this conversation.

"No woman willingly gives up the pleasures of a London Season... unless they have heard a gentleman declare her pert opinions were not offset by her fine eyes … that she was not handsome enough to tempt him … and that he had no need to give consequence to young ladies slighted by other men."

How little he understood. "There is no need to recount it. The past is past, and I am quite done with it."

"You were a perfect lady that night, and I a perfect boor." He stood so close, his shoulder brushing hers.

If she fled now, he would only catch her arm. She would surely shatter if he touched her.

"I could tell you I was deep in my cups that night and beg you to excuse what I said." His breath had traces of coffee, not brandy.

"One must never take to heart the words or acts of one suffering from too much wine."

"Brave words from a woman wounded to her core."

How dare he talk of her feelings as though he understood them, as though they mattered to him. "It is of no matter. I pray you, forget it."

"No, I cannot. In the scene I wrote last night, I saw—I finally understood my transgressions. My conscience has tormented me since. Pray forgive me, I spoke unconscionable things to you and wounded your womanly spirit. Forgive me."

"It is forgotten. Think no more of it."

"You never spoke a word against me, despite the distasteful way I used you to indulge my ill-humor that night. You are far too kind and thoughtful and good for any of us."

"You mistake me for my sister Jane."

"I have heard you intimate such a thing before. It is not pleasing. I think it a rather ill-guided attempt at modesty that neither suits nor does either one of you justice."

"Exactly how do you see that?" Bother! How had he baited her into this conversation?

"You have grown so accustomed to hearing your sister's beauty and temperament praised, you ascribe all good things to her in a vain attempt to prove to all that you are not jealous."

"You understand me so well." She sneered, unladylike gesture though it was.

"You are so busy proving yourself not jealous that you show yourself quite green with envy."

"If that is true, it is a wonder that any can stand to be around me."

"You really can be quite unpleasant. Anyone who dares compliment you is soundly slapped for his impertinence. How dare we pay attention to you when there are women like your sister or Blanche in the world. They are worthy of attention, but not a lowly Elizabeth Bennet, of little beauty and no wit."

"Thank you for enlightening me. Pray excuse me." She forced past him and marched away, dry leaves and underbrush crunching under her half boots with each footfall.

"You really must harden yourself to the fact that you are worth looking at."

"What a fickle creature you are. I am both not handsome enough to tempt you, yet really worth looking at. Next you will be telling me I am the wisest fool you have ever met." She slapped a low hanging branch out of her way.

"You took the very words from my lips. I have rarely heard as excellent sense as I hear from you, yet, on this one point, you are utterly intractable."

"Intractable because men such as yourself have assured me of my accuracy. Now if you are finished impugning my beauty and intellect, I will leave, unless you have designs upon my character as well."

He chuckled, warm and condescending at the same time. "You are quite adorable when you are piqued. I must say I never thought to see a woman who could rival the appeal of my sister in high dudgeon. But you will do quite nicely."

"I will do? For what?" She whirled on him.

"I should very much like to take you under my protection." All elements of façade shattered as he faced her with naked, raw emotion.

She backed away, nearly tripping over a tree root.

"You fascinate me, inspire me, body, soul, and muse. Ever since those stupid words tumbled out of my mouth, your fleeing image appears to torment me, to chase away my inspiration and remind me of how undeserving I am." He licked his lips. "Now I have been fortunate enough to find you again, I do not wish to lose you. I can offer you your own establishment, an allowance. I will even have a solicitor write up an agreement so you can be certain of my intentions."

"As your mistress." She could barely force the words out.

"As my inspiration, my muse, my heart, and soul."

"Your mistress."

"I cannot marry you. Surely you understand that."

"I understand that very well."

"Then you will consent?" His hazel eyes lit.

"You do not know me at all if you believe I would agree to such an arrangement."

"Of course! Your father—I should have thought. I

am certain I can work on him. Darcy will help me, I am sure of it, especially if Blanche applies to him. Blanche will approve, you know. She will be happy for such a sweet, steadying influence upon her Bohemian cousin. You will be the making of me, Elizabeth, dear, the making of me."

"No, I will not, for that would be the ruin of me."

"How can you say that? I promise—"

"To use me for a price. What will become of me when you have gotten what you want from me and your muse has found another inspiration?"

"Do not think such unhappy thoughts. I cannot see such a day coming. You need not fear." He tried to take her hand, but she snatched it away.

"While you may have no concern for tomorrow, a woman must. All I have is my reputation and my few accomplishments. Should my father pass from this world, I might make my way as a companion or governess. But if I trade away my reputation for an uncertain life with you, where am I to go? What is to become of me?"

"You could be courtesan to a nobleman, even a king! Do not underestimate how far you could go. You could travel with me. I will introduce you—"

"To other men to whom I might sell my company?"

"You sound as if you are being sent to a brothel."

"Is not the only difference the price at which I would sell myself?" Why did he seem so shocked? "I suppose I should acknowledge the compliment you attempt to offer, but I must decline."

"To hold out for an offer of marriage?" He sneered. "From Darcy? After last night?"

"What happened?" She gulped. What did he know?

"I did not see Darcy drink enough to be in his cups, but I suppose some men cannot hold their brandy. He and my sister seemed to enjoy one another's company—greatly—last night. They were both—unguarded—shall we say. I expect he will make her an offer soon, and he will not keep another woman."

"What have his intentions to do with this conversation? Why should I be concerned with someone so wholly unconnected to me?" She pushed past him and ran for the manor.

## Chapter 10

Over the next two days, Darcy's ankle remained inflamed and grew more painful by the hour. The housekeeper and his valet flitted in and out of the parlor with cool compresses, wrappings, and willow bark tea. Miss Garland offered more soothing syrup, but, given the headache and the disquieting dreams he suffered having taken it once, he declined. A glass of brandy addled his mind and spirit much less.

He leaned back into the fainting couch, his head throbbing—the consequences of sleeping too much. With the parlor drapes drawn so tight, the sunrise stood no chance of rousing him at a proper hour. Oh, for a proper bit of activity. How many hours had he spent staring at the ceiling roses now? Long enough to know each one by name as well as the spider that had taken up residence in the corner nearest the fireplace.

Naming spiders surely was not a good sign. Perhaps that soothing syrup still had lingering effects.

Were those memories or dreams of a conversation with Miss Elizabeth? Had she spent the night in the parlor with his foot propped in her lap, reclining awkwardly next to him? The things he might have said to her. Snippets, mortifying snippets teased him, but more substantial memories remained tantalizingly out of reach.

Just as did the lady herself.

He stretched against the fainting couch's too-firm cushions. When he recovered, he would surely have the piece refitted to be more comfortable. Or perhaps simply burnt.

He grumbled. Was there no comfortable attitude on this blasted chair? Why had Miss Elizabeth not been to see him?

Everyone else in the house, including Miss Garland, had been to the parlor to keep company with him. She had been very amusing, whilst she stayed. But her visits had been brief. Miss Elizabeth would have stayed as long as he had wished for her to. She was good company when one was laid up.

A knock—too loud to be Miss Elizabeth's, sounded at the door frame. He jumped and craned his neck.

"How are you feeling this morning, Darcy?" Bingley sauntered in. How dare he sound so pleased with life.

"Beastly."

"I though you would have enjoyed a solid excuse to remain away from your noisy party these past two days." He pulled a chair near and sat, one arm draped casually over the back.

Had Bingley never learned proper posture?

"I am glad you consider my hospitality so pleasing." Darcy crossed his arms over his chest.

"You do not mean to tell me you have suddenly developed a taste for large parties and loud companions?"

Darcy grumbled under his breath. "Pray open the curtains whilst you are here."

"That is more like you. You must be feeling better. When do you think you will be up and about again?" Bingley laughed and threw open the drapes. Cool morning sun poured into the room. The walls matched the morning sky.

"I have no idea. Mrs. Reynolds thinks a fortnight before I am fit to even use walking sticks." Darcy struggled into a sitting position, balancing his ankle on a nearby stool.

"That is a spot of bad luck."

"Never fear. Richard can accompany you and Garland hunting and fishing if you like."

"You think me so shallow? That I think of nothing but sport whilst you are injured?"

"I expect you three are in need of respite from constant female companionship."

"You are too severe on members of the opposite sex. Far too severe." Bingley snorted.

"You do seem to be enjoying the company here. Some company in particular."

Bingley clucked his tongue and nodded. "I suppose I have always been a bit obvious in my regard. Say, are you are displeased—"

"That you and Georgiana have not—no, not at all. She is far too young and not even out. The whole point of this house party was to give her an opportunity to practice being in company before she comes out, not for matchmaking. She needs to meet more of society before she considers anyone."

"Garland seems to pay her a lot of attention." Something about the way Bingley wrinkled his lips suggested he did not approve.

"He enjoys flattering, I think, and she likes being flattered. Miss Garland says such harmless flirtations are a regular practice. Perhaps it is good for Georgiana to discern between polite and genuine attentions from a man."

Bingley shrugged.

"You are much in Miss Bennet's company." The lovely, sweet, and rather insipid Miss Bennet.

"She is a delight, is she not?"

"What I think is of little consequence."

"Actually not. I had hoped to seek your opinion." Bingley tugged at his collar. "Yes."

"In what capacity do you seek her company?"

Bingley paced along the length of the room, raking his hair. The bright sun only highlighted the color that rose from his throat to his cheeks. "That is the problem, I suppose. Caroline thinks her a pleasant girl."

"And that is a bad thing?"

"Not bad, but she—Miss Bennet, that is—has little in the way of a dowry, and her connections are in trade. Caroline does not think her a fitting wife. But she said she would … understand if I desired to set up an establishment for Miss Bennet."

"How generous of her." Darcy dragged his fist across his mouth.

"Indeed … indeed. I cannot believe the gall of her, attempting to direct me in such a way."

"I do not know why you allow her to discompose you so, or even live with you for that matter." Darcy craned his neck—if only Bingley would stop his bloody pacing.

"You do not know Caroline."

"Nor do I care to."

"Much to her disappointment."

Darcy shuddered. "Regarding Miss Bennet?"

"Yes, yes—what do you think?"

"About what? I do not expect her father would be pleased to see her under your protection."

"No, no! As a wife!" Bingley stopped directly in front of him, hands thrown in the air.

"Your acquaintance has only been of a few weeks. You wish to marry her?"

"Marry who?" Richard peeked in, then sauntered across the room to sit in the chair Bingley recently vacated. "Who wishes to marry whom?"

"Bingley." Darcy jerked his head toward him.

"Who?" Richard rubbed his hands together briskly. "Miss Bennet? Can you afford her without a fortune?"

"Yes, that is manageable." Bingley bobbed his head.

"Does she like you?"

"I believe so."

"Do you like her?" Richard laced his fingers before him.

"Very much."

"Then go to it man. Why do you stand about?" Richard gestured toward the door.

"Oh, yes, very well then. Thank you, Darcy. I knew I could count on your advice." Bingley straightened his coat and strolled out.

"That was simple enough." Richard leaned back, extended his legs and crossed his ankles.

"You make it all sound very simple." Darcy pinched his temples. Richard always magnified his headaches.

"It is for him. He needs only a gentlewoman to increase his standing without the encumbrances you or I face. His choice may be an easy one. Frankly, I envy him for it. No need for you to go and muddy it up." Richard leaned forward, his tone losing some of its light-hearted edge. "Speaking of women and marriage—you and Miss Garland seemed to enjoy each other's company very greatly the night of your injury."

"She is witty and charming."

"And well-endowed in many ways. Do you not remember …."

Darcy winced and raised his hand. "I do not remember much of that evening."

"Well, I do. I have never seen you so unable to hold your liquor."

"I think she gave me some tonic with the last glass of wine."

"You ought to avoid any more of it lest you find yourself trapped."

"Trapped?" The word echoed in his skull.

"You do not remember? My friend, in any other company, Miss Garland could call you out for compromising her and insist you marry her. I am surprised neither she nor Garland have spoken of it to you. Luckily Georgiana had retired—but Darce—"

"I thought it a dream." Darcy fell back against the fainting couch, squeezing his eyes shut. If only he could recall.

"It was no dream. Anne was utterly scandalized. You could not keep your hands—"

"Were we alone at any time?"

"No, she was in her cups as well. We sent her upstairs as soon as we could separate you."

"Oh, bloody hell. What am I to do?" Darcy scrubbed his face with his hands.

"There is one obvious option. You could marry her. She is rich, beautiful, intelligent, and connected. You could do far worse. And she seems to like Georgiana very well, too. If you are so upset, make her an offer of marriage, and the matter of honor will be settled. If it helps, you could remember that is why I invited them to join us."

"I will think on it." Darcy groaned as he shifted his leg.

"Shall I send Miss Elizabeth to see if she has any more tricks to alleviate your suffering?"

"Yes, do that."

Richard left.

Darcy clutched his head. He had always been so careful, so moderate, so temperate, never to permit improper behavior on his part to darken the family image. Now, in his own home, to be found so wanting—

"Mr. Darcy?" Miss Elizabeth peeked in. She entered without any of her usual lightness of step.

"Are you well?" Clearly, she was not. Her hem was dusty, muddy in places, with dry leaves and grass clinging to it. Her hair was something less than disheveled, but with the light sheen of perspiration on her face and throat, it seemed she had just been running. Twice he had encountered her in a similar state when her mother was very ill. Miss Elizabeth was apt to engage in very strenuous walks when distressed. "Is there anything I can—"

"How are you feeling today? Are you in a great deal of pain? May I look?"

He grunted, and she sat in the nearest chair. She had deflected his questions when he asked during her mother's illness, too.

Her cool gentle fingers soothed his bruised and swollen flesh. "I do believe we were correct, there is no break in the bone."

"I am relieved to hear that. But what of you, you seem—"

"Do you wish for more willow bark tea, or perhaps something stronger?"

"No, nothing stronger. I do not think stronger potions agree with me."

She nodded, but there was something odd in her countenance. Had she too—those other images of his dreams, of lying beside him! "Oh, bloody hell." He clutched his temples and pitched forward.

"Excuse me?"

"Forgive me, please I forget myself." He pressed his eyes and grimaced. "I am not a master at word craft, so I shall just come out with it. I fear I may have behaved quite improperly, ungentlemanly, the evening I was injured. Have I been offensive to you in any way?"

Why would she not meet his gaze? "You were not yourself that night."

"So, I have heard. I am afraid I have very little clear recollection of anything that evening."

"Perhaps that is for the best." She clasped her hands in her lap and stared at them.

"How badly did I behave? Was I wretched to you?"

"No, only most uncomfortable, and you did not wish to be alone." She wandered to the window.

"How long did you stay?"

"If you do not remember, then there is nothing to discuss."

So, she had spent the entire night. He dragged his hand down his face. "I do not know what to say."

"You need say nothing. You were addled by a tonic and by no means in a right state of mind."

"You forgive me?"

She turned and looked directly into his eyes. "Nothing more need ever be said."

"Is there anything I might do for you to make up—"

"Avoid such tonics in the future. I will ask no more from you."

She could ask far, far more and rightfully so. "I can see there is still something bothering you. Pray tell me; let me help."

"It is not a matter for your concern."

"I wish to know."

"Truly, you do not. I shall prepare your willow bark tea." She rushed out before he could respond.

Elizabeth dashed into the corridor, nearly running over a young maid heading toward the parlor. This would not do. She had to gather her wits. She forced herself to perch on a hall chair. Slow, deep breaths, that is what Papa always recommended at such a time.

Papa also said that it was a burden to know too much. As she did right now. What was she to do with those truths?

"Miss Elizabeth." Miss Garland strode toward her. What beastly luck.

Elizabeth stood and dipped a shallow curtsey. "Pray excuse me. I am on my way to prepare some willow bark tea."

"For Mr. Darcy? Oh, do show me how. It seems to be such a useful little brew. It quite eased the headache I had yesterday when my maid brought it to me."

"It is quite simple. I showed your maid—"

"No, no. Better you show me as well." She looped her arm in Elizabeth's and pulled her to the kitchen.

The warm room, centered around a large stone fireplace, hummed with activity, echoing with the noises of cooking and cleaning. The fragrance of baking tarts and stewing puddings filled the air with comfort. Was it odd that the kitchen had always been one of her favorite places? The cook nodded at Elizabeth but raised her brow in a dark scowl to Miss Garland.

"How charming that the staff here seems so comfortable with you." Miss Garland's smile was as thin as her voice. "You are quite a fixture here, I suppose."

Actually, she had a very good idea of what was meant, but pursuing that was even more distasteful than the current conversation. "I have spent a great deal of time here."

"You must know Mr. Darcy well." Her voice dropped to just above a whisper. "You see, I have a bit of a difficult situation, and I am in quite the quandary."

"I do not know why you would ask my advice. Would not Miss Bingley or Miss de Bourgh be in much better positions to offer you direction?"

"I hardly think so. More likely they would begin a chain of very ugly gossip. Your discretion I can rely upon."

"I am not fond of secrets." Swallowing did not relieve the bitterness in the back of her throat.

"That is the problem. None of this is a secret, and I do not know what to do. If, let us suppose, a gentleman of a good name and good fortune behaves improperly toward a lady whilst drunk ... that is to say, he does not recall matters—" Miss Garland pressed a hand to her heart. She was not attractive when she pretended innocence. "But her sensibilities are nonetheless offended, what should be done?"

Offended? Opportunistic was much more likely. Horrid creature! "Then if she is a true lady, she should forgive the matter entirely and never give mention to it again. The finest sensibilities must acknowledge charity as the highest motivation."

Elizabeth took a boiling kettle off the hob and led the way to a work table near the window.

"Would that it were that simple." Miss Garland sighed as Elizabeth poured boiling water into a bowl of willow bark. "If only the woman were able to make a room of witnesses forget."

"That does make a difference." Elizabeth's hands shook.

"I thought you might see it that way. So, what then?"

"Then it behooves the gentleman to protect the reputation of the woman he has compromised."

"And she is not out of place to request such protection?"

"All this talk of his comportment does make one wonder. What was the nature of her behavior? Was she entirely proper herself? Or perhaps might she have been similarly influenced by wine or perhaps something even more *soothing*, that might have caused her behavior to be regrettable as well?"

"What are you suggesting?" Miss Garland gasped, ice coating her voice.

"Only that it is wise for one to treat another in the fashion that they would most wish to be treated—especially when one is most vulnerable."

"You imply I … a woman might be taking advantage of such a situation? What is impure about the desire of a lady to protect herself and her reputation?"

"Nothing at all. I would just wonder whether it is best to do that before or after *soothing* oneself." Elizabeth poured off the willow bark tea into a large cup and added ginger and sugar.

"You judge me because my nerves are of a delicate constitution?"

"I do not imagine you to be very delicate." Perhaps that was not the wisest thing to say, but what sensible person could possibly resist?

"You question my character? Do not judge me. You are but a vicar's daughter. Despite your fine eyes and ready opinions, you know very little of the world."

"I do not claim to know of the world or much of anything beyond the simple virtues taught by my parents." Elizabeth stirred the ruddy tea as whiffs of steam rose from the brew.

"Simple and quaint, but of little use to those of us with more sophisticated concerns."

Elizabeth strode to a nearby shelf and retrieved a small tray. "Perhaps that is true, but remember, it was you who came to me seeking my opinion. I did not seek you out to offer it."

"Too true. I thank you for pointing out my error. I shall refrain from making it again." Miss Garland flounced from the kitchen, little puddles of bitterness left in her wake.

Elizabeth pulled a stool close and sat upon it. If only she could warn Mr. Darcy—poor, poor man. Had he any idea of her true nature?

# ⁂Chapter 11

Darcy resettled on the fainting couch yet again. He would definitely burn the foul piece of furniture when he recovered. Moreover, he was beginning to hate the upholstery's particular shade of blue.

To be able to pace around the room, or better still, to move freely about his own home. Never again would he take for granted the simple ability to walk. Yes, he should be grateful that he would walk again and that the surgeon was not on his way with his saw. It hardly mattered when every fiber of his being ached to pursue Miss Elizabeth and discover—no, more like demand to know—why she sent the willow bark tea, carefully seasoned with sugar and ginger, with Mrs. Reynolds. Why did she not bring it herself?

Had he been so offensive that evening that she could not bear to see him? In spite of her pretty words about forgiveness, she seemed so troubled.

Why would she not simply tell him? She had never before hesitated in telling him when he had stepped on her finer sensibilities. Why should she avoid him over it now?

She said it was not him, but something else. But what else could it be? What other reason? Had Anne and Miss Bingley finally nettled her too much? Surely neither Richard nor Bingley would have been anything but charming. And Garland paid her little notice—he did treat her rather officiously in all matters concerning that damned theatrical. But that hardly seemed the thing to discompose her so.

He grumbled under his breath and flexed his hands. Why had she not come?

"You are appearing most animated this morning, Mr. Darcy." Miss Garland whisked into the parlor and stopped in a sunbeam, the door closing softly behind her.

The sun sparkled off her golden hair and caressed her creamy skin, glowing along her cheek and neck, down to her generous bosom. Concern lined her lovely face, so lovely. What kind of boor had he been?

"Are you in pain?" She pulled a chair very close and sat, peering deep into his eyes. "May I procure something for your comfort? I see you have already had some willow bark tea. Brandy, perhaps?"

"No, no, I am well."

"Your expression says otherwise."

"Do not trifle with me, Miss Garland." He propped himself up into something resembling a proper posture.

"Excuse me?"

"My cousin has addressed my behavior of the other night with me and informed me of how wanting it was."

She turned aside, cheeks coloring, hands clasped in her lap. "That is a rather a delicate issue."

"Pray, do not play games with me. I have neither skill nor patience for them." Darcy clutched his forehead.

"You were influenced by too much wine, I am sure."

"And perhaps the tonic you gave me."

Her eyes flashed, wide with a hint of something— anger perhaps? "Forgive me, but you did not receive it by subterfuge. You took it from my hand, knowing exactly what it was. Do not blame me for your behavior."

"I did not mean to suggest you were to blame, only to offer a more complete explanation for my untoward conduct—an assurance, if you will, that it was entirely out of character and unlikely to occur again. I accept full responsibility for my actions."

"The question, though, is: what does that mean, to take responsibility?"

"It is to admit my failings, seek forgiveness, and make reparations where I can."

"Reparations? You are a man of integrity. I am impressed."

Was that a compliment or insult? "You have not answered the question at hand. Was my behavior toward you that night unacceptable?"

She rose and moved to the same window where Miss Elizabeth had stood not long before. Stunning, simply stunning. "Yes, your behavior was unacceptable and uncouth. I have never been subjected to such ill-mannered, boorish treatment in a private home. Any lady of quality would have been offended."

The hair on the back of Darcy's neck prickled.

Miss Elizabeth had not been. But she and her family were longtime friends and not movers in society. Perhaps that made the degree of offense less.

She ran her graceful fingers along the mullions. "My larger concern is my reputation."

"Your reputation? I do not follow."

"Whilst I trust Alexander and Colonel Fitzwilliam to keep the sordid details to themselves." She looked at him over her shoulder. "I do not know Mr. Bingley's propensity to spread tales. As for Miss de Bourgh and Miss Bingley, I am quite certain they will be both quick and happy to spread scandal about one who is—well, forgive me for dwelling upon the point—above them. Women are always pleased to drag down someone who is higher than themselves."

"What would make things right?"

"It is not for me to say. Is not the man the active principal and a woman to have only the power of refusal?"

Darcy pinched the bridge of his nose. "You seem to enjoy making this difficult for me."

"As much as you enjoyed my person that evening?"

His gut knotted so tightly he could hardly draw breath. The one situation he swore he would never be placed in! But was it so bad, really? He had been considering making her an offer. Why should he feel so differently now? It should not matter; by all rights, it should not. And even if it did, there was honor to be upheld, and he must do his duty by that. His father would have expected as much.

He cleared his throat. "Miss Garland, would you consider an offer of marriage?"

"I suppose that is the only thing for it. Is it not?" She returned to the chair near him, but did not look at him.

"Is my offer so very abhorrent?"

"No, not at all. You are a very eligible, desirable match." She frowned a little and peeked up at him. "You must allow this to be a most business-like proposal."

"I am what I am, and am unlikely to change. If you need the drama and romance offered by someone like your brother or even Richard—"

She brushed the idea away with a flick of her delicate fingers. "I have no need for wastrels and second sons. I do not need to lower myself to an unworthy alliance."

Which of them did she consider a wastrel? "I could instead offer to buy Miss Bingley's and Anne's silence."

"They would both demand you marry them to ensure their silence, and since we cannot make a bigamist of you, I suppose I shall have to marry you myself." She smiled, finally.

He would have to hire a painter to capture that expression.

"I thank you for the honor of your hand." This was not what he expected from the moment of his betrothal. "I will send word to my solicitor to draw up the settlement papers as soon as I am able."

She took his hand and laid it against her cheek. "I have every confidence in your ability to accomplish the necessary tasks."

"I shall not disappoint you."

"I have no doubt." She slid his hand down her face and neck to rest upon her swelling décolletage.

His heart raced, and his mouth grew dry. What glorious softness.

"I am content to wait as necessary for the settlement to be worked out." Her chest heaved beneath his hand. "In the meantime, though, I have a small concern regarding Miss Elizabeth."

He tried to pull his hand back, but she held it fast. "What of her?"

"My dear Mr. Darcy." She laughed, the sound of liquid light. "Have you not noticed? The poor girl worships you. She is quite in love with you. I fear she may react badly when our happy news is announced."

"That is preposterous. She has no feelings but friendship toward me and my family."

"I will defer to your greater knowledge then. But should she begin acting oddly or disagreeably, be gentle with her, for her hopes have been cruelly dashed."

"I am certain it is utterly unnecessary."

"As you say. Perhaps we should turn our thoughts to more pleasant ideas." She pressed his hand down along her well-filled bodice. "I have some very pleasant ones which we may consider when you are more recovered."

He swallowed hard.

She lifted his hand to her lips, kissed each finger, and released it, a wistful look in her eyes. "Shall we make the happy announcement tonight, after dinner?"

"As you wish—"

"Blanche. I should like you to call me by my Christian name now."

"Blanche." The name played on his lips, sensuous and tempting.

"I like the way you say that. I anticipate the pleasant time we may share when you have better recovered." Her eyes raked him with a glint he had never seen in a woman's eyes before.

Blood roared in his ears, and his cheeks heated to flame. Surely, she did not—

She licked her lips and lifted her brow.

She did.

"You will forgive me. I should go. I am all a flutter and need to recover from this very happy turn of events." She flashed her brows once more and left.

He stared after her, blood racing, groin aching. Had she just offered him a carnal invitation? His body thrilled—oh dear God, how it thrilled—at the prospect.

But the ease with which she offered it—those were not the reactions of a chaste woman. Or were they? Perhaps she expected that such an offer would please him. How was he to know?

Miss Elizabeth would certainly be able to explain—but no, this was hardly the kind of matter upon which he could consult her.

A chill crept along his cheeks. What had Blanche said? Miss Elizabeth in love with him? No, that could hardly be. She was far too sensible for such nonsense.

Still, it might be considered unseemly to continue to seek her advice now that he was betrothed. But whom would he consult now? He pressed his hand to his cold, aching belly. He had relied on her for so long. What would Pemberley be like without her?

Elizabeth sat in the morning parlor near the window, wrestling with a bit of fancy work that was determined to vex her. With all vestiges of breakfast cleared away, only the polished mahogany furniture and large bowl of lilies kept her company. Usually her stitches behaved like good little school children, sitting in their pretty rows. Not today. How unsurprising.

Might as well set it aside for the day. The sun had just passed its zenith, and shadows crept in, turning the pale blue-green walls the color of the sky before a storm. The light would be better tomorrow.

Miss Darcy rushed in, skirting around the table to reach Elizabeth. She clapped and bounced on her toes. "I have had a splendid idea, Miss Elizbeth. Tonight, dinner should be brought to the parlor so Fitzwilliam might dine with us. It will be such fun."

It was certainly a novel notion, but not necessarily a good one. "Have you mentioned it to your brother? He does not always like new things, and surprises make him uneasy."

"Miss Garland very much likes the idea and assures me he will be delighted."

"And her brief acquaintance with him makes her an expert on his likes and dislikes?"

"You are jealous to think anyone else might know him at all." Miss Darcy had never spoken to her that way before.

"I am sorry you could think it of me." Elizabeth tossed her sewing aside and strode from the room.

Soft girlish steps pelted after her. "Wait, please, wait."

Perhaps she should.

Miss Darcy caught up halfway down the corridor,

near the grand stairs. "I should not have said that. Please forgive me."

"How could you think such a thing?" Elizabeth climbed the stairs.

"What else am I to think?" Georgiana stomped behind her.

"A great many things, actually."

Rapid footfalls rang along the staircase. "Stop it. Do not run off whilst I am talking to you."

Elizabeth reached the top of the stairs and tried to turn down the corridor toward her chambers.

Miss Darcy blocked her way. "You are angry with me."

"Yes, I am."

"You never get angry with me, no matter how stupid I have been."

"You are not stupid. You know very well that is my steadfast belief. Do not play that game with me. What you said to me has nothing to do with being smart or stupid. It has to do with kindness which is a very different thing altogether."

"You think I was unkind?"

"Do you think otherwise?"

"I had not really considered it." Georgiana scuffed her pink slipper along the carpet. "I am sorry."

"It is very much unlike you. Who has influenced you to behave this way—or to believe such things about me?"

"No one."

Elizabeth rolled her eyes.

"You can hardly be surprised that neither Anne nor Miss Bingley like you very much. You are smarter, nicer, and prettier than either of them."

"And they are far richer and better connected than

I will ever be which counts for far more in the eyes of society. I understand my place in society; it is as it is, and there is nothing more to be said."

Miss Darcy's voice softened. "Are you ever jealous of any of them? Like your sister or Miss Garland?"

"They are both lovely ladies. I do sometimes feel wanting in their presence."

Miss Darcy laughed a little sadly. "I feel that way often."

"I know you do. But you have so many advantages, you need not compare yourself to anyone."

"Sir Alexander told me the same thing."

"He did?" And he was probably the one convincing Georgiana that Elizabeth was jealous of every other lady in their party. Lovely man.

"Yes. We talk often, and he encourages me in the same things you do. He speaks highly of you."

"I am surprised he speaks of me at all." What did he hope to gain by talking of her to Miss Darcy?

"You do not like him?"

"It sounds as though you do."

"Pray, do not tell anyone." Miss Darcy bit her lower lip and lowered her face.

"He pays you a great deal of attention?"

"Mostly when we are rehearsing his play. But I so enjoy the time with him."

"He is very well able to please when he desires it."

"What do you mean?"

"Only that you should guard your heart. You have not even made your come out in society yet. You have a sparkling Season waiting for you in Town next year. You should not set your heart on anyone now, when there is so much yet to be explored."

"You do not like him. Are you—"

"Stop there, I will not hear any more of your accusations." Elizabeth raised an open hand. "Sir Alexander is much older than you and conversant in the ways of the world—ways which you are completely unacquainted with. Your brother and Colonel Fitzwilliam would not approve either. A playwright is not entirely respectable regardless of his fortune."

"I see him talking to you a great deal."

"You mean am I interested in him and trying to dissuade you from him so as to avoid the competition?" She drew in two deep breaths—hands trembling at her sides. If only she could tell the truth, but that would make matters worse. "I will set your mind at ease. I have absolutely no interest in him whatsoever. Even if he were to pursue me, my father would not permit it. He would not want any of his daughters so close to the theater."

"But you could elope."

Elizabeth tucked one hand behind her back and tightened it into a fist. "Only in the pages of a Gothic novel or perhaps one of Sir Alexander's plays. You do realize that without a settlement, one could be left penniless, alone, and with no recourse. Ask Miss de Bourgh or Miss Bingley or even Miss Garland. I assure you none of them would consider marriage without a clear settlement and a generous one at that. No, elopement is not in my future nor in any sensible woman's future. Sir Alexander is completely outside my notice. Any advice I have for you regarding him is motivated only by friendship. Just as everything I have ever told you has been."

"I am sorry to have been so silly. I should not doubt you."

"No, you should not." Would that she could walk away and end the conversation now. It would be entirely satisfying, if a little harsh. "I understand it is difficult to be on the verge of coming out and to begin considering the possibilities of young men and marriage. While the opportunities can be wonderful, there are those who will hurt you and take advantage of you. It is wise to guard yourself."

"I suppose you are right, but it makes it all seem so dull and dreary."

"Good sense is often quite dull and unappealing." And trying. It could be very, very trying.

"But what about dinner tonight? Must we give up those plans?"

"I never said you had to give them up, just ask your brother if they are agreeable to him. Honor his sensibilities, and I expect he is likely to agree to your request."

"But what if he does not?"

"Then honor his wishes. I know it might be disappointing, but it will be for the best."

"You are not very much fun. Come with me and help me ask him?"

"No, you must learn to speak to him on your own." Elizabeth curtsied and brushed past Georgiana to her room.

No wonder Mr. Darcy was often at his wits end with her.

Mrs. Reynolds herself came to Elizabeth's room to announce that dinner would soon be served in the parlor. She did not hide her displeasure well.

Elizabeth tucked a final pin in her hair and smoothed her gown—a crisp pink muslin trimmed with embroidered roses and yellow ribbons, all gifts from Uncle and Aunt Gardiner. It was one of her nicest and very fitting for her station in society, but nothing in comparison to the other fine ladies of the party. She lifted her chin and left for the blue parlor.

Merry voices and soft music in the background made it easy to slip in unnoticed, the last of the house party to arrive. Jane sat at the spinet with Mr. Bingley, playing a simple duet. He beamed with a smile that matched hers. They were a lovely couple. No doubt, something would be announced soon. They would surely be very happy together.

Miss Darcy, in a white lawn gown, sat on the long settee near the windows between Colonel Fitzwilliam and Sir Alexander, with a look that suggested she was rehearsing her part again. With her lines memorized, she pursued perfecting the dramatic elements with an almost frightening zeal. How single-minded she could be when interested in something.

Miss Garland sat close to Mr. Darcy who still kept to the fainting couch, looking rather ill-at-ease. Still though, they looked well together. Very well together. Society would approve of the handsome couple they made. That would be good for them both. She swallowed hard.

"Excuse me." A footman bearing a laden tray scooted past her. Faint aromas of soup and roast pork wafted up from the tray.

Had she been standing in the doorway gawking all this time? Where had her manners gone? She hurried to an open chair beside a small table in an unoccupied corner. The painted screen beside her—illustrated by

Mrs. Darcy years ago—concealed her from the observation of the rest of the party while allowing her a clear view of the room.

Two footmen and a maid circulated through the parlor, offering the diners delicacies from their trays. After everyone was served, the dishes were arranged on a sideboard, and the servants left.

Mr. Bingley lifted his crystal wine glass. "To Miss Darcy and her inspired idea to sup together tonight."

Colonel Fitzwilliam raised his glass. "And her stodgy brother who permitted such irregularity on his watch."

The ladies tittered politely while Sir Alexander roared. Elizabeth winced. Mr. Darcy did not like to be teased. Perhaps she should—no, she should not. It was not her place to interfere. Miss Garland was beside him. She would look after his wounded feelings.

Elizabeth took the barest sip of her wine. If it was to be an evening of toasts, she could not risk drinking too much.

Conversation filled the room, conversations which did not include her. She forced herself to eat, but everything tasted dull and flat. How odd that a single chair sat in isolation, ensuring someone could not participate in the company. Mrs. Reynolds would not have arranged the room this way.

"My dear Miss Elizabeth." Miss Garland, resplendent in an ivory gown and blue jewels of some sort, stood before her.

When had she approached?

"It is not right that you should be all alone. Alexander, help me move Miss Elizabeth's table to the rest of ours."

Sir Alexander rose. "Always happy to be of service to you."

Miss Garland took her glass, and Sir Alexander the table and brought them close to Miss Garland and Mr. Darcy's places.

How lovely. She wanted to sit near neither of them, but protest would be unseemly at best. Where was a powerful headache when one needed it?

"Thank you for the willow bark you sent earlier. It was much appreciated." Mr. Darcy said with a note in his voice that declared something was bothering him.

"I am pleased you found it helpful. I have written a receipt for Mrs. Reynolds including the ginger and sugar so she may prepare it for you whenever you have need."

"That is very good of you." Miss Garland patted Mr. Darcy's hand. Why was she touching him in such a familiar way? "How thoughtful of you to make sure he would have it even in your absence."

"Absence? The parsonage is but a mile away. Miss Elizabeth is hardly ever absent from Pemberley." The words seemed to tumble from his lips unexpectedly, leaving him with a sheepish look when he finished.

Miss Garland's eyes flashed with something very much like anger.

"When one is in need of willow bark, a walk of a mile can be very inconvenient," Elizabeth whispered.

Miss Garland nudged Mr. Darcy with her elbow. He cleared his throat and lifted his glass. "I should like to propose a toast." The room fell silent. "To my betrothed, Miss Garland. May she enjoy a wonderful London Season as the new Mrs. Darcy."

Elizabeth raised her glass and drank, not feeling, not tasting, barely hearing the happy voices that ranged around her. "May you both be very happy." On shaky knees, she rose, managed a curtsey and quit the room.

She trudged up the stairs as an unfamiliar heaviness settled over her. It was good for them to have matters settled between them. It was good.

Tears began flowing as soon as she shut the door. They must be tears of joy. He had what he wanted, what he should have, and that must be a very good thing.

The revelry had extended late into the night, with toasts and song and even a bit of dancing, which Miss Garland enjoyed on Richard's arm rather than Darcy's. Now the room was dark, quiet, and empty, with only slivers of moonlight slipping in around the edges of the heavy gold drapes. On such a night, should he feel the same—dark, quiet, and empty?

Perhaps he was simply too rational to be passionate.

He stirred against the fainting couch and grumbled. Tomorrow he would ask Miss Elizabeth to bind his ankle. Then, he would try the walking sticks Richard had procured for him. With any luck, he would see the outside of the parlor soon. Very soon. Even just making it to the morning parlor or the dining room would be a welcome release.

But would she come?

A dull ache crept across his limbs, settling into his chest. She had not yet brought him tea, and she had left dinner early. Was she avoiding him now?

Blast and botheration! He slapped the arm of the

fainting couch. Thoughtless, inconsiderate girl! Of all the times when he needed her, why did she prove so flighty now?

He had just taken the biggest step of his life. Richard and Georgiana's reassurances were pleasing to be sure, and Bingley's effusions agreeable, but the affection and encouragement he most desired were distressingly absent. He raked his hair and struggled to find a comfortable position on the too-hard, and now lumpy, cushions.

Why should her opinion matter so much? It was not as though she was in any way connected to him. Yet, she was such a part of Pemberley. A part he must now learn how to do without. Miss Garland— Blanche—would now take that role.

He pressed his forearms hard into his stomach. Who would have thought Blanche would cost him his friend?

## ❦ Chapter 12

Elizabeth slept fitfully and rose just before the first rays of dawn touched her windowsill. The fine bed linens itched and stung as though she had been scoured by nettles. Even her soft nightgown chafed.

Enough. She pulled on a simple morning dress and pinned her hair into a plain bun. If she left quickly, no one would see her, and she could return before Miss Bingley or Miss de Bourgh arose to cast their judgment upon the simplicity of her toilette.

She crept downstairs and waited by the garden doors for first light. Mrs. Reynolds tried to offer comforts—tea, coffee, warm bread with cheese. Elizabeth declined the hospitality with a mumbled excuse that made no sense even to her and rushed outside. Cool, damp air wrapped her like a shawl. She ran for the path into the woods, the one through the bluebells.

Gentle perfume and sheltering tree limbs embraced her. Here she was safe, safe from Pemberley.

How could she return to face the jealous Valkyrie hovering around Mr. Darcy? How could she avoid him when he demanded her ministrations and advice? How many would judge her as petulant and ungrateful for her reluctance, validating Miss Darcy's accusations? How had it gone all out of kilter? She increased her pace.

Rounding a shadowy bend in the path, she collided with a huge dark form.

"Oh, my knee!" she screamed and fell.

Sir Alexander staggered back and clutched a nearby tree. "Who goes—Oh! Miss Elizabeth?"

She rolled to her side, amidst the dirt and deadfall, and pushed up on her hands. Sharp dried twigs and underbrush bit at her palms and against her hip; the cool, green scent of loam filled her lungs.

He appeared beside her on his knees, peering into her face. "Forgive me. I had no idea that was you. Pray, allow me to help you."

She waved him off.

Strong hands under her arms pulled her to her feet. "You are injured."

Merciful heavens, that hurt! "It is nothing."

She gasped as he released his grasp on her elbow. "The way you stand conveys a very different story."

"Do not be so concerned. Pray excuse me." She turned on her uninjured leg and limped several steps.

"You are a terrible actress. Perhaps it is well you are not participating in our theatrical." Miserable sot, first pushing her and causing her to fall, now laughing at her.

"I am so pleased to know." She dragged herself several more steps.

"You are hurt."

"And when have I been a fitting concern for you?"

"Since I first saw you in London." Heavy, crunching footfalls approached.

"I do not want your concern."

"You know he is engaged to my sister now."

"What has that to do with me? Pray, leave me alone." She leaned on a nearby tree, panting. Exertion and pain were not a pretty combination.

"You told Georgiana that you had no interest in me, and your father would not approve of me besides." He blocked her way, arms crossed loosely over his chest.

"That was a private conversation, not meant for your ears."

"Much like the one you overheard in London those years ago."

She drew herself up straight. Heavens, that was a bad idea! "No. What Miss Darcy told you, I have already said to you directly. Moreover, I did not insult you. Had I said you were the last man in the world I would ever marry—"

"So, you have considered marrying me." He wagged a finger at her, chuckling.

"I have not."

"You are lying again. It is good you do not play cards. You have little signs that always give you away."

"You did not offer marriage, so why would I have considered it?" She hobbled around him and several steps farther to lean on a tall, ragged tree stump—a large oak tree struck by lightning. Anything to take the pressure off her twisted knee.

He turned to face her and leaned back on the tree. "Too true, too true. Do you know I have regretted that conversation?"

"It was mortifying. I would rather never have heard any such comments directed at my person."

"I thought you might have reconsidered."

Ghastly brute. She dragged herself several steps, stopping at a cluster of saplings. Foolish things offered little support.

"You should know, I have reconsidered."

"Reconsidered what? I gave you my answer. There was nothing unclear about it."

"Not your answer, my offer to you." Several long strides brought him her side. "I should never have offered you my protection."

"I forgive you. Pray excuse me now."

"I should have offered you marriage."

"What?"

"I have your attention now? That is gratifying." He took her hand. "I was a boor and a cad, offering as I did to make you my mistress. You were right to refuse me. So very right. I have been forced to consider my ways and realize that I have been selfish and short-sighted, wanting the pleasures of today at the cost of a far better future."

"You sound like one of your characters making a speech." A light breeze raised prickles along the back of her neck.

"I suppose I do. But only because I am as a man walking in a dream, suddenly seeing a path before him, no longer obscured by a veil. I too easily dismissed the possibility of being married to you, my dear Elizabeth."

"Do not speak in such familiarities and endearments. I do not welcome them."

"Of course, you would say such a thing. You will always be the voice of my conscience."

"I have not agreed to be anything to you." She pulled her hand away.

"Of course not, for I have not asked. I have become so accustomed to the unstable life of an artist that I had momentarily forgotten. I am a baronet and able to enjoy the rights and privileges of that rank."

"That seems unlikely."

"Perhaps, but it is true." He slowly circled the saplings, shoving aside the ones that dared block his way. "And what is more, I have no need for a rich or connected wife. I have all that I need with my estate and inheritance."

"I hardly think you are prepared to give up the theater in order to manage your assets."

"Is that the price of your hand? It is one I think I could gladly pay."

She shifted more weight off her knee. "You are not more suited to a sedentary life than Miss Darcy is to the schoolroom."

"That is a cruel cut."

"You willfully misunderstand me. She is ill-suited as a student, you are ill-suited—"

"To be a gentleman?" He sneered, towering over her.

"For a conventional life. Surely you must see, we are not at all suited for one another. We are complete opposites."

"Precisely why I need you so much. You are my balance, my anchor."

"Who will become a millstone around your neck." As he strangled the life from her.

"You are so fast to your principles; you inspire me. I must be near my inspiration."

"My father would never agree."

"Let us seek him now then." He swept her up into his arms.

She shrieked. "No! You are hurting me again! Put me down!"

"Coming to your aid will only endear me to your father. Besides, you clearly cannot walk the half mile to the parsonage. You would have deserted me by now if you could."

Unfortunately, he was right. Fighting him would be useless and would only leave her further disheveled with all the implications that might come out of that.

Half a mile had never hurt so much.

Papa met them on the gravel walk up to the parsonage. "Great heavens! What happened?"

She reached her hand toward him. "I am fine Papa, merely my knee."

"She could hardly walk, sir." Sir Alexander headed resolutely for the vicarage door.

Papa let them in and directed Sir Alexander to the cluttered parlor where he laid Elizabeth down on the faded floral couch.

"Her sisters—where are they? They should tend her."

"Perhaps you have forgotten, but this is my house, not a stage under your direction." Papa tapped the floor sharply with his cane.

"I am fine, Papa. Pray, do not disturb my sisters. I

thank you for your assistance, Sir Alexander." She cleared her throat. "Although, I could have managed on my own."

"I think that very unlikely. You could hardly stand." The lift of Sir Alexander's eyebrow suggested more amusement than ire.

"You embellish the tale for your own purposes. Even so, I am quite safe and well in my father's care. You need trouble yourself no longer."

Papa regarded her carefully. "Thank you for the service you have rendered my daughter. I am bewildered how it is you came upon her in such a state. One might even wonder if you had something to do with it."

"Are you accusing me of deliberately injuring her?" Sir Alexander puffed out his chest and pulled his shoulders back.

"A guilty conscience is one that hears accusations where none exist."

"He did not hurt me. It seems we both favor early morning walks and chose, unbeknownst to one another, to walk the same path. In the dim light, we ran into one another and not surprisingly, I bore the brunt of the mishap."

Papa's lips wrinkled up in that thoughtful expression he wore when searching for the truth. One might never lie to him. He always knew.

"My intentions are entirely noble, sir." Sir Alexander bowed dramatically. "I am at your and her service. Though, perhaps, I might request a favor of you."

Elizabeth snuffed a sharp breath. Papa raised an eyebrow, and she bit her lower lip.

Papa laid his hand on her shoulder. "While I am pleased to be of service to my fellow man, I do feel it incumbent upon me to see to my daughter's needs first. Now is not the time for a favor."

"But now is the ideal time. If you will only hear me out."

"As I said, now is not a good time. I must insist you allow me to attend to Elizabeth."

"Allow me to summon the apothecary or the surgeon."

"When I have ascertained what is necessary, you can be certain I will procure the help she needs."

"I insist you permit me just a few moments." Sir Alexander drew himself up, tall and formidable.

"And I insist you treat me with the courtesy due your elders." Papa poked him in the chest with his walking stick. "Need I remind you, young man, you wish to approach me for a favor? This is not a good way to receive a positive response."

Sir Alexander stepped back. "Of course, sir, please forgive me. You are correct. Please attribute my incivility to my deepest concern for Miss Elizabeth's welfare."

"Very well, very well. Then you will bring word to Pemberley of her injury and her safe establishment here. I do not wish Jane or the Darcys to experience undue concern."

"A service I shall be pleased to render." Mr. Alexander bowed and removed himself from the parlor.

They stared at each other until the front door opened and closed again. Elizabeth sagged against the back of the couch, grimacing as she shifted. Papa called for the housekeeper who examined her knee and pronounced it sound enough, but twisted something fierce. She trundled off to fix a poultice and a soothing tea.

Papa closed the parlor door and pulled a lyre-back chair up beside the couch.

Quiet and safe, nothing could harm her here in their humble little parlor with him at her side.

He set aside his walking stick and took her hand. "I imagine there is a great deal you wish to tell me, and I am not averse to hearing."

She giggled. Papa was quite the best listener in the county, perhaps in all of England. "I do not know where to begin."

"Ordinarily I would say at the beginning, but perhaps in this case, you should tell me more about Sir Alexander. It seems there is a great deal of story to be told." He lifted his brows and tucked his chin, his special warning that he wanted the entire truth immediately and would not brook disappointment well.

"It is complicated, Papa."

"I am a clever man. I dare say I shall be able to follow your tale."

"I do not think you shall be very pleased with me." She squeezed her eyes shut and dropped her chin to her chest. Though he was never unkind, few things were worse than Papa's disappointment.

His calloused finger tipped her chin up. She peeked into his rich, warm, worried eyes.

"Lizzy, you know you can tell me anything, and it will be well. Has he imposed himself upon you?"

"Yes ... no ... after a fashion ... I do not know." She pressed the heels of her hands into her eyes. "Do you remember the Season I spent in London four years ago?"

"How could I forget? I have never seen you so utterly despondent."

"That was because I met him there."

"What happened? Why did you not tell me?"

She peeked at him through her fingers. "We were introduced at a ball. His friend wanted him to dance with me. He was only Mr. Garland then, and hardly amenable."

"Is that all? Even at sixteen you were made of sterner stuff than that."

"He did not simply ignore me. He declared to the entire room that my fine eyes were hardly sufficient to offset my pert opinions, which were more fitting to a courtesan than a lady. Moreover, he had no need to give consequence to young ladies slighted by other men. Whispers began about my reputation …"

"No doubt your aunt and uncle put an effective stop to those. Their connections—"

"They did, I am sure. But whenever I went out, there were whispers—at least I was certain that there were. I could not …" She covered her face with her hands.

Papa crossed his arms and drummed his fingers along his upper arms. "That is why your aunt said you declined all invitations, keeping yourself at home with your young cousins?"

It would have been nice to give him a fully formed answer, but all she could manage was a sad little squeak and a nod.

"Dare I ask, or do I already know? He has continued his boorish behavior here?"

"Yes and no. I encountered him walking once, and he declared his wish to kiss me."

Papa growled deep in his throat. Had he ever made such a sound before?

"Be sure, he did not. He used the opportunity to apologize for his cruelty in London." She studied her fingernails.

"What else?"

Of course, he knew there was more—and he would persist until she told him. "He made me an offer."

"Of what?" The words were tight and clipped.

"First he …." She huddled into the couch and whispered, "He offered to bring me under his protection."

Papa sprang to his feet and stalked across the room, waving his walking stick. "The ruddy blackguard." He continued muttering for some time, using language he had never before used.

"But then … this morning … he made me an offer of marriage." She looked him directly in the eyes. "I told him no—that you would never approve."

"And you? Do you …."

"Heavens, no! He is not at all the kind of man I wish to find myself associated with. His principles are too … vague. He is far too changeable for my liking."

He harrumphed and returned to her side.

"I fear he desires to make you believe that I have been compromised somehow so that you might compel me to marry him."

"I would not have you marry such a man under any circumstances." He gripped her hand hard, reassuring and constant. "But you must be honest with me now. Have you been compromised?"

"I … I do not know." Her hand trembled in his.

He gripped her fingers harder. "What do you mean? What did he do?"

"Not him."

"Someone else? What has been going on at Pemberley? I trusted Mr. Darcy to look after you and Jane." His eyes narrowed as he studied her face. "Darcy? I cannot believe that of him."

"No, not like that. He was injured, and I helped care for him." The entire story of his injuries, the night in the parlor, and his betrothal to Miss Garland tumbled out in a breathless rush. "I cannot go back, Papa, not ever. How can I show my face there again?"

"You have done nothing wrong, my dear." He slipped his arm around her shoulder. "Except for falling in love with Mr. Darcy."

She flinched as if struck in the face. She loved Mr. Darcy? How could he suggest such a thing?

Because it was true.

She contained the first wave of sobs, but the next overpowered her and drove her into Papa's strong shoulder.

He held her tight and stroked her back. "There, there, child. I should not have permitted you to stay there, feeling as you do."

"But … but …."

"I know, you did not even recognize it. But your mother did, long ago. That's why we have always taught you the importance of keeping to the social sphere to which you were born. We thought that would be enough to protect you."

"I am so sorry. I did not mean to. Truly—"

"I do not blame you. The heart makes its own choices—not always the wisest ones. Why do you think all the conduct writers advise against marrying for love?"

"I know it is foolish, I am—"

"You are no fool, Lizzy. You would make a fine

mistress of Pemberley. But the differences between you are too great. I had hoped the house party might be pleasant and put you in the way of meeting other agreeable gentlemen—perhaps even encourage you to try another Season in London with the Gardiners."

"What am I to do now? I cannot face Pemberley's society now—perhaps not ever." She wrapped her arms around her waist lest another freshet of sobs escape.

"Of course not. I would not ask you to. I hate for you to leave me, but perhaps a visit to your Aunt and Uncle Gardiner might be in order. The Season will begin soon. She just wrote to invite you and Jane to go."

"But Jane is much pleased at Pemberley with Mr. Bingley."

"So, I have gathered. I shall not insist she go. But I think it time for you to have another taste of society. The circles the Gardiners mix in are much more appropriate for you to keep company with. How soon can you be ready?"

"Are you in such a hurry to be rid of me?"

"Of course not." He sighed and swallowed hard. "I am a selfish creature who would far rather keep you to myself. But Mrs. Green and her daughter will be traveling to London in just a few days and inquired whether one of you girls should be available to join them. I think Mrs. Green believes her daughter would enjoy the journey more with someone of her own age to travel with. I do not think your sisters are ready for such a journey, but you?"

So soon? How could she leave her home? "I can be ready to leave with them. I do not really see any other choice."

"I will write to her directly. When you are ready, we will call Mary and Kitty to help you upstairs. They can help you pack." His shoulders slumped as he made his way to the door.

London. She worked her tongue against the bitter taste at the back of her mouth. How could it be that things here had gotten to the place where London seemed better than Lambton? How utterly arsey-varsey. Would things ever be right again?

## Chapter 13

The day of Miss Elizabeth's accident, Richard had presented Darcy with a pair of walking sticks, permitting him to leave the parlor for the first time in—how long had it been? If only those walking sticks had permitted him to make it all the way to the parsonage to find out firsthand how Miss Elizabeth fared.

Three days later, Darcy sat at his desk in his study. The orderly shelves and tidy surfaces offered evidence that not quite everything in his life was turning upside down. Why had she not come back to Pemberley? That would have been the sensible thing. The staff was much better able to care for her here than her frail father and feather-pated sisters. It made no sense that Garland should have taken her there. That man became more insufferable by the day.

And now this! He reread the neatly penned message. According to her father, Miss Elizabeth's knee was healing well, but she was now much needed by her aunt in London and would not be returning to Pemberley's house party. Mr. Darcy's invitations were very kind indeed, but family responsibilities must come before parties of pleasure.

He crumpled the paper and threw it aside. It rolled drunkenly along the regular lines of the carpet's geometric pattern, landing in the shadow of his favorite wingchair. How dare she? She had refused all offers of the apothecary and surgeon, and now she turned her back on his invitation. He was her family's patron, showing them every favor, every blessing in his power. How could she treat him thus?

And how was he to tell Georgiana?

He grabbed his crutches and struggled to his feet. Pacing with these monstrosities was not nearly as satisfying as stamping about freely, but it was better than being trapped on that blasted fainting couch. Today he would conquer the staircase and make it back to his own chambers, no matter what.

He clomped into the corridor, the walking sticks announcing to all that Fitzwilliam Darcy, invalid, was on the move again. Several servants paused to stare at him, ostensibly to ensure the master did not require their assistance. But it seemed to be more gawking than anything else.

Damn ankle throbbed with every step—searing but bearable. Blanche would surely be there to offer her encouragements, if she knew of his plight. But in some things, an exposed décolletage was not as useful as a friend's steady shoulder and words of wisdom and encouragement.

Once he made it to his chambers, though, there were other inducements to look forward to. Blanche made sure to remind him of it. Regularly. He licked his lips, heat prickling his neck.

Still though, with so many in the house, the notion left him equal parts delighted and uneasy. At least Miss Elizabeth would never know.

Why did that even matter?

"Fitzwilliam! You are so much steadier on those walking sticks than yesterday!" Georgiana rushed down the grand stairs to his side.

Darcy leaned hard on the walking sticks and lifted his injured foot so only his toes rested on the floor. "I have just received some news from the parsonage."

"Elizabeth has not suffered something awful, has she?" She clasped her hands with a pleading look.

"No, she is healing well, but now is needed by her aunt in London. She will be going there directly."

"She will not return to us and be here to watch our play?"

"I am afraid not. Are you very upset?" Pray no tears, not today.

"If her aunt needs her, then it would be selfish of me to wish her here. Oh, but I am disappointed. I had counted on her to help with some new lines Sir Alexander has written. And I have worked so hard on the rest. I wanted her to see how well I have done." She traced the edge of a marble tile with the tip of her pink slipper.

"Perhaps Miss Garland—Blanche—can help you. She will be your sister soon. It might be good for you to become accustomed to her help."

"I suppose so."

"You like Blanche, do you not?"

"Yes ... yes, of course I do. She is very kind. I enjoy playing pianoforte with her ever so much. But—

and I know it sounds foolish—she is not Elizabeth. When do you think Elizabeth will return?"

No, Blanche was not Elizabeth. "I do not know. But even when Miss Elizabeth does return, I think you should expect her less at Pemberley than you have been accustomed to."

"Why? She is my friend."

"I expect she will be concerned that her long-time familiarity with Pemberley might make Blanche uneasy as she steps into her role as mistress."

"But I may still call upon the parsonage? That should not trouble Miss Garland, should it?"

"I do not know, but perhaps it might be time for you to cultivate other relationships, ones more in keeping with our own sphere. You will have your come-out soon. Blanche will be able to guide you and introduce you to a far wider acquaintance than you have ever had."

Georgiana pouted. "I still do not see why I must give up my friend."

"Do not fight with me about this. Things will be as they need to be. We do not always get to have our choice." No, indeed one did not.

"But ... could you ... would you find out where she has gone, so I might write to her, and maybe ask when she will return?" She turned pleading eyes on him.

"You wish to write a letter?"

"I will ask Mrs. Reynolds to help me ... to ensure it is a good letter. I will not embarrass you. Please?"

She would ask for the one thing he could not refuse. "I shall enquire after directions to her uncle's house. Perhaps later today, while you and the house party are out riding."

"Thank you, you are very good to me." She squeezed her eyes shut. "Might Anne use the phaeton whilst we ride? She and Miss Bingley have declared themselves unable to ride and will stay here and keep company with you otherwise."

"Then, by all means, the phaeton will be at their disposal." Being trapped in the house with Anne and Miss Bingley—the back of his neck twitched.

"You will join us for breakfast now?"

Fresh clothes and a bath would have to wait. Darcy followed her to the morning parlor.

The mahogany table was set with a crisp white cloth and the marble-topped sideboards laden with an array of fragrant dishes. The Bath buns smelled particularly good.

Garland studied a sheaf of handwritten pages, probably his blasted script, beside Richard who sipped his coffee. Anne tried to interest him in some bit of conversation, but Richard gave her the same empty nod and stare he offered his sisters when they chattered. Miss Bingley lectured Miss Bennet on the shape of fashionable sleeves this season.

Bingley, his attention fixed on Miss Bennet, declared it a marvelous day for a ride and the rest of the company concurred. The rest, except for Miss Elizabeth. And Blanche who was also noticeable by her absence.

Mrs. Reynolds appeared at his shoulder, a folded note on her silver tray. He opened it. The elegant flowing script could only belong to one person.

*Please give my regrets to your dear sister as I shall not be able to join the riding party. I have a ghastly headache which renders me most indisposed.*

Beneath that in much smaller letters, she added:

*I have availed myself of a remedy which generally sets me to rights in just a few hours. Perhaps you would consider coming to me and seeing to my comfort once the party has departed.*

His mouth went dry and blood rushed to his face and loins. He shifted in his chair.

"Are you well, Darcy?" Richard asked.

"Miss Garland expresses her regrets at being unable to join you for your riding this morning as she is quite indisposed with a headache."

Richard cocked his head and his eyebrow rose.

Darcy looked away. Were his responses really that easy to read?

"That is most unfortunate. Mornings like this should not be wasted." Garland folded his napkin and laid it on the table. "She is prone to missing out on many things due to those headaches of hers."

Georgiana looked crestfallen, but Anne brightened noticeably.

"We will certainly miss her company, but I believe we may still be a merry party nonetheless," Miss Bennet said with a smile meant for Bingley.

"Shall I see the horses readied?" Richard rose, glanced at Darcy and snickered. "I imagine the beasts are fairly jumping at the chance to have a fair romp this morning."

Garland coughed. Or was that a chuckle?

Heat crept up Darcy's neck and over his jaw.

"I look forward to our *ride*." Garland nodded at Georgiana. "It is a shame, sir, you cannot join us in the *exercise.*"

Richard snorted. "Shall I arrange the phaeton for you, Anne—or do you prefer to have a carriage and driver?"

"I should prefer to drive myself. You may accompany me, Darcy, if you would like. I should be happy to drive you."

Richard and Garland looked at each other and sniggered.

"I do not believe our cousin is—up—for that this morning." Richard barely choked out the words.

"Best he stay at the house and … rest." Garland kept a perfectly straight face.

"Of course, you should, Brother. You must get well as soon as may be possible. After all you can hardly perform—"

Richard and Garland broke out in a bout of coughs. Georgiana eyed them with some alarm.

Words, many words he would have with them later.

"Then, ladies, I expect you shall wish to dress for the occasion. And we gentleman shall supervise the horses." Richard ushered them out of the breakfast room with a final backward glance and wink at Darcy.

Richard had spent entirely too much time in low and coarse company.

He struggled up from the table and rang for Mrs. Reynolds to call for the butler and his valet.

Who would ever have thought a simple trip upstairs would require the assistance of two grown men and leave him winded, and with his heart racing? Reaching his chambers had never been so welcome.

To celebrate, he called for a bath. Warm water and his favorite scented soap floated away layers of curmudgeon. How pleasing to be clean and properly dressed, a gentleman once again.

Now he might engage in more pleasurable pursuits. The crutches tarnished the picture, but only a little. He clomped for the door.

*Remember your place, Son, your duty to your family. Do not offer your attentions unworthily. They shall always find you out.* His father's sharp, judgmental voice rang in his ears.

But she was his betrothed, and the settlement in process of being drawn up. Why should he hesitate to accept what she so freely offered? It was a done thing.

He paused and leaned against the tall mahogany bedpost. Her offer was quite free. So free as to be unmaidenly. The very air she carried herself with was one of confidence and knowledge.

Carnal knowledge.

He sank into onto his mattresses. Breathe. He must breathe. Just how much knowledge had she?

He dragged his hand along his freshly shaven cheek. Was it wrong to expect his wife to come to him a maiden, chaste and untouched? He had maintained himself under good regulation, at least since his grand tour. His future wife should have as well.

But Blanche's reputation was beyond reproach. If no one considered her compromised, no one held any transgressions against her, did it matter what she may or may not have done?

He chewed his knuckle. How was he to know her past? He needed to know—perhaps it was unreasonable, but he had to.

Richard and Bingley would be of no help. And his surest source of wisdom was most certainly not to be consulted now, even if she were at Pemberley, which she was not. He raked his fingers through his hair.

The only person with whom to discuss the matter with was Blanche herself. Not a conversation he relished, but it must come before any other diversions.

He struggled to his feet and hobbled to her door. The hard wood stung his knuckles, like the sting of a schoolmaster's ruler.

A soft sound filtered through the door, indecipherable, but enough to give him leave to enter.

The rich guest chamber had been appointed by his mother specifically for the pleasure of female guests, with everything soft and dainty and delicate. Georgiana begged to have her chambers made up like it when she had turned thirteen.

Sunlight filtered through the sheer pink silk drapes with a complexion-flattering glow. Floral paper hangings and a pale green counterpane with matching pillows lent the room the air of a spring garden.

Blanche lay across the bed clad only in the sheerest silk nightdress, teasing him with all that was barely hidden. It draped every womanly curve to greatest advantage, lighting his every nerve on fire.

"Blanche." Where had his voice gone, suddenly lost to a dry, scratchy throat?

She murmured and shifted, her gown falling open over an exquisite breast.

He worked his tongue over the roof of his mouth. "Blanche, I have come."

Her face turned toward him, and her eyes peeked open. She blinked and squinted at him.

Did she not recognize him? He limped closer. Damn the walking sticks.

"Da … arcy?" She slurred as though her tongue was too thick for her mouth.

"Are you unwell?"

"Had a headache … told you that." She rolled to her side and fumbled around the bed for something. "Took my tonic." She held an empty bottle out to him. "Better now."

A splash of cold as sharp as spring water struck his face and trickled down, cooling every kindled fire.

She glanced down at her gown and loosed another tie. A small tug and her other breast tumbled free of its covering. "Do … do they … please you?" She smiled up crookedly.

Her form was as beautiful and flawless as a marble sculpture and the passions sparked anew. Her sloppy drunken laugh quenched them.

"You are unwell. I shall call your maid."

"I do not need a maid. I need a man. I need you." She reached both graceful arms toward him.

"No. I shall leave you now."

"But you … you have not had … what you …what you came for." She pushed up to sit, unsteady and teetering.

"I have had all I care for. Good day." He bowed from his shoulders and clomped out as quickly as he could.

He would not, could not avail himself of what she offered, not like this—a shiver snaked down his spine. Though she invited him now, would she remember she had done so when her tonic wore off? No, this was too much like taking advantage of her and that he could not do.

His valet met him in the hall. "Have my coach readied. I will go to the parsonage."

"Need you some willow bark tea before you leave, sir?"

He grumbled under his breath. Damn. Miss Elizabeth would have already prepared that for him had she been here. "Yes."

The valet bowed and hurried off.

A carriage—he required a carriage for the mere mile journey to the parsonage. Humiliating. But things would soon be better.

Soon, he would know when Miss Elizabeth would return. Then he and Georgiana might be comfortable again.

The driver helped him down in front of the vicarage all covered in white climbing roses, just beginning to bloom. Gah! To be handed out like a lady! He would never, never play pall-mall again, nor even set foot on a mall for the rest of his life.

He rapped at the dark oak door that gleamed in the sunbeam and smelt vaguely of polish. How long could it take to answer a knock?

The housekeeper showed him into Bennet's study. Cluttered and filled with books and journals and papers, it was nothing like Darcy's own, but somehow it managed to be warm and inviting just the same. Little paintings and samplers, surely done by his daughters, decorated the two longest walls. A squat bowl of cut garden flowers stood slightly off center on a side table near the fireplace on the wall opposite the desk.

Bennet rose, silhouetted by the window behind his desk. "Mr. Darcy. What may I do for you, sir? Shall I call for some tea? It is excellent to see you up and about once again."

"Thank you, but I do not prefer tea. I am, though, enjoying the freedom of movement once again."

"I think it a far underrated privilege, indeed. Please, sit and take your ease, or stand if that is more satisfying to you right now."

"Yes, well, it is actually rather more pleasing at the moment." Darcy stood near a threadbare brown wingchair near the desk, cushions lumpy, with faded stains.

"What brings you to call? With a full house party in residence, I hardly imagine it is company you seek." Bennet came around the front of his desk and perched against it.

"My sister requested that I inquire after Miss Elizabeth."

"I see." His voice cooled. "And what would you inquire about?"

"Georgiana would like to know where she might direct a letter for Miss Elisabeth. You must understand, Georgiana has never wanted to write letters and that she would wish to now is both notable and pleasing. I would prefer to get her the direction before the whim departs."

"I believe Elizabeth would enjoy a letter from your sister." Bennet searched the jumbled desktop for a pencil and a scrap of paper.

"She also asked if there was a date upon which we might anticipate Miss Elizabeth's return."

Bennet scratched out the direction and handed him the irregular scrap. "As to her return," He tossed the pencil on the desk. "You may tell your sister ... oh, bother ... I do favor honesty ... tell her I do not expect Lizzy to be returning at all."

Darcy collapsed onto the wing chair. "Have I heard you correctly? She is not returning?"

"Going forward, she will reside with her Aunt and Uncle Gardiner in London."

"Whatever for?"

Bennet wandered away from his desk and stopped in the window. "Lizzy is nearly one and twenty."

"What has that to do with anything?" Darcy clutched the arms of the wingchair, the worn fabric giving way under his fingers.

"At such an age, a young woman's thoughts naturally turn to her future. Lambton's society is quite limited."

"But she has lived all her life here, in the shadow of Pemberley. Why should she leave? Georgiana needs her friendship and her guidance."

"We need her here at the vicarage as well, but some things cannot be helped."

"But why? Why should she wish to leave … here?" Darcy gulped back a lump in his throat.

"I suppose she finally understood she could no longer stay."

"Has someone been untoward to her? Unfeeling? Inconsiderate? What has suddenly made … Pemberley's society intolerable to her?"

"Nothing untoward, I assure you. Just the normal course of things opened her eyes to the true nature of life." Bennet turned to him.

"You speak in riddles."

"My daughter is a tender-hearted young woman whose feelings I will not expose to inspection by those who cannot properly have concern for them."

"Her feelings? What feelings?"

Bennet peered down his nose and scowled. "None

you need be aware of or concerned with."

"But Georgiana misses her company dreadfully." So did he.

"For that I am heartily sorry. But I cannot ask Lizzy to sacrifice her future for the comfort of your sister who is well able to find new friends. Her aunt and uncle are well-connected in London. It is time for her to be introduced in society and to eligible suitors. She needs a home and a family of her own—and…." He met Darcy's eyes with a pointed gaze. "It is quite clear she cannot find them here."

"Why so suddenly? Are you, or your family, in need?"

"Mr. Darcy, you must forgive me, but I will say no more to you on the matter. Your sister may write to Lizzy if she wishes. But pray, ask Miss Darcy not to entreat Lizzy to return. This is what is best for my daughter. I ask you to honor that."

"Yes, yes, of course." He folded the direction and tucked it in his pocket. "I should leave you then. Good day." He bowed, grabbed his walking sticks, and shambled out.

Darcy grumbled as the driver handed him into the carriage. "Take the road that circles the lake."

He threw the walking sticks to the opposite side of the coach and fell back against the squabs. How could she abandon him and Georgiana when they most needed her? Who else could, who else would, advise him on his household, on Georgiana, on Blanche and her tonics? He needed her right now. What business had she being anywhere else but Pemberley?

What had Bennet been blithering about her future? What more could she want for? She had a home and a parish that depended upon her. How could she just walk away from her duties to seek ... marriage to some nameless gentleman?

A sick, cold knot tied itself between his shoulder blades. Bloody walking sticks seemed to do as much harm as good.

Whom would he talk to now? Who would advise him on these baffling matters?

She had not even said goodbye.

He returned to Pemberley near sunset, ankle and head throbbing a counterpoint to one another. Best confine himself to his room lest he materially damage one of the ladies' refined sensibilities.

Richard caught him at the staircase. At least, he had no refinement to offend. "Do you need assistance? You look like the very devil himself."

"Kind of you to notice." Darcy trudged up the first step.

Fitzwilliam maneuvered to his injured side and grabbed his elbow. "You had a memorable morning?"

Darcy snarled as his injured foot made contact with the steps.

"That was not the response I expected."

"What do you expect whilst invading my privacy?"

"Privacy? A beautiful woman sends you what I assume was a carnal invitation and you believe there is any privacy left to be had? You are a wonder."

"A wonder who does not require gawkers." Darcy would have pulled his elbow away had he not needed the support so much. "What leads you to believe there was any invitation?"

Oh, the look Richard gave him! "You do take

yourself far too seriously, you know. Any man would dream of the favor you were granted."

"My father would not."

"He is dead and before that too disabled—"

"Stop. I will not discuss this."

"Fine, fine. Go on then thinking of your father as some sort of departed saint. It might do you well to realize he may not have been the man you thought he was."

"This is not about him."

"I beg to differ." They reached the top of the stairs, and Richard released him to his walking sticks. "It is, as is everything you do. He is dead all these years, and yet you still seek to please him as much now as when he lived. With about as much success, I might add."

"What is that supposed to mean?" Half way down the corridor, almost to his chambers, and he would be free of this conversation.

"For all that you admired him, he was a taciturn fault-finder to the core. No one could ever do enough to satisfy the old curmudgeon. You, me, my father, the king himself! No one would ever satisfy him. Even your saintly mother bore his constant dissatisfaction. When are you going to stop trying to please him and start living?" Richard shoved open the white paneled door to Darcy's chambers. "I had hoped today might be that day."

Darcy paused, panting. Was it the conversation or the exertion that rendered him so breathless? "Come to my dressing room. Things are complicated and I … I need advice."

Richard's eyes widened, and he shut his mouth hard.

The dressing room caught the rays of sunset against the warm, dark oak paneling, leaving the room comforting, somehow appropriate for a conversation he did not want to have. Darcy laid aside his walking sticks, tumbled into his favorite leather chair near the fireplace, and put his foot up on a nearby footstool. They would need candles soon.

"Let me help you off with your boots lest your foot swells, and you need to cut them off." Richard grabbed the heel of Darcy's boot. "Hold on. This will not be pleasant."

Richard was a master of understatement.

"Nothing like a wee bit of torture to loosen the tongue, you know." Richard headed to the brandy decanter in the corner cabinet. Richard always knew where to find brandy. He poured two glasses. "So, tell me of this complication."

Perhaps this was a bad idea, and he should keep his own counsel. Richard dropped onto a nearby chair, his gaze never leaving Darcy's face. Gone were the traces of levity in his eyes, replaced by a furrowed brow and tight lips.

"As you suspect, I tried to call upon Blanche— Miss Garland—this morning."

"Clearly it did not go as you expected. Were you … unable …."

Darcy ran a finger around the edge of his collar and sipped his brandy.

"You would not be the only man to whom it has happened—especially with a woman as extraordinary as she."

"My performance was not the issue. It was hers."

"Hers? What has she to do but lie there—"

"She was unconscious."

"Excuse me?" Richard set his glass hard on the table between them.

"Or all but in any case. She invited me, but in her condition—" Darcy lifted open hands.

"Her condition? I do not understand."

"There was an empty tonic bottle in the bed beside her. She was all but insensible. Call it what you will, but I could not, not with her in such a state. Go on, mock me. Tell me I am a fool for not partaking of such easy fruit."

Richard sipped his brandy, swirled it and sipped again. "I cannot mock you, and I cannot laugh. You have a very real problem. I have seen too many caught in the grips of laudanum to think light of it in any way."

"What am I to do?"

"You must confront her, forbid her from the stuff lest she offer it to Georgiana."

"Georgiana?" Darcy fell back against his chair. "I had not even considered that."

"Well, you must. The poor girl is only now coming out of her shell. You know how tumultuous a Season in London can be. Think of what could happen if she were to offer Georgiana something to calm her nerves. I mean no offense to your sister—"

"But you can clearly see her falling victim to its soothing properties."

"Indeed, I can. This is very bad. Do not waste a moment. Take charge of your betrothed, and put a stop to this before it goes any further."

"But how?" Darcy raked his hair with both hands.

"How? Just go in and speak your mind. I have never known you to have a problem with that. Finish your brandy and go to it, man. Do not delay." Richard rose and rummaged in the large wardrobe. He handed Darcy a pair of slippers, ones embroidered by the Bennets—a gift from several Christmases ago. Darcy gulped down his brandy and slipped them on. Perhaps they might carry a little of Miss Elizabeth's wisdom with them.

Blanche's lady's maid informed him that she was sleeping and had left orders that she was not to be disturbed. He penned a note—a summons for Blanche to attend him in his study and gave it to the lady's maid.

The woman turned positively white. That could not be a good sign. She warned him that her mistress sometimes took considerable time in recovering from such a headache. So much for dealing with the matter without delay.

## ❦ Chapter 14

The next morning, Darcy shut himself inside his study and paced the floor—without the walking sticks, relying only on the support of his riding boots for his injured ankle. Richard peeked in and interrogated him on his choice to forgo the walking sticks. Yes, riding boots in the house were highly improper and yes, his ankle still hurt; no, he probably should not be doing it. But if there was a time he did not need to feel like an invalid, it was now, so damn the advice; he would do as he pleased. Richard beat a hasty retreat.

Darcy stalked straight down the center of the impeccably neat room, along the line made on the geometric-patterned carpet as the morning light streamed in through freshly-washed windows. Every chair was in its place; each book sat on the proper shelf, arranged by category and title, all bound in the same custom Pemberley black leather binding with gold print; the curtains hung straight as they should; and the folios on his desk were lined up perfectly with one another. In short, the room was exactly as it should be.

Yet, nothing was right.

His valet had brought him a note with his breakfast tray that Blanche would see him in his study after breakfast.

Apparently, he had failed to account for the difference in their habits. For her, breakfast was far later than for him. He had been in his study failing to accomplish anything useful—except to increase the ache in his injured ankle—for nearly an hour and a half now.

A soft knock at the door stopped his heart. What was he going to say? For all Richard's insistence that Darcy was quick to speak his mind, that only held true when Darcy knew what he was going to say.

"You look so serious this morning." Blanche glided into his study. The Valkyrie had returned, clad in white silk flowing over her curves like a spring flowed over pebbles, caressing and bringing them to sparkling life.

"I trust you are feeling better today." He shut the door behind her and pulled his shoulders back. She must not distract him from his purpose.

"I am rather put out, you know." She stood very close, her shoulder brushing his, angling herself just so as to offer him the best possible view.

Darcy stepped back. "Excuse me?"

She ran her finger along his shoulder and down his chest. "I seriously considered ignoring your summons. After all, you ignored mine." She turned her face up toward him and blinked slowly.

He stepped out of her arms' reach. "I beg your pardon."

She dropped her hands to her hips. Her tone turned cold and sharp. "Oh, do not be so prudish, Darcy. I gave you an invitation that any man in England would have answered in a trice and not only did you keep me waiting, but you walked out on me. You have humiliated me, and I expect a very pretty apology."

She wore indignation well—very well. Had she tried to tempt other men this way? How many?

"Do not look as though you do not know what I mean. What more invitation do you need? The door was unlocked for you."

"Being conscious would have been attractive."

"I was hardly unconscious. I remember your visit quite well."

"You were insensible."

"Who are you to judge?"

He strode behind his desk and braced his hands on the solid mahogany top. "Have you forgotten that I am your betrothed?"

"Not at all. Would I have invited you otherwise?"

"I am not certain. To whom have you offered this sort of invitation before and how often?"

She whirled away from him and stalked toward the windows. Did she intentionally arrange her shoulders so the light emphasized the graceful curve of her neck? "How dare you! I do not like the implication of your question."

"I do not like the state in which I found you."

"You have no right to question my behavior. My reputation is impeccable."

"As your betrothed, I have every right—"

"To ask for what I offered you, and you refused! Do not think I will forget that easily. You have insulted—"

Darcy slammed his fist on his desk. "I did not refuse you, and I have not insulted you."

"I remember quite clearly. You turned your back on me—"

"On an insensible drunk who could hardly form a coherent thought. Lying with you would have been insupportable!"

She pressed her hand to her bosom. "You call this insupportable? I am … my person is insupportable? No man has ever—"

"And just how many men have had the opportunity to."

She spun and stamped toward him, eyes flashing with fire. He caught her upraised hand before she could strike him. "Release me!"

He held her wrist for three more breaths then released it. "You will not raise your hand to me or to anyone in my household ever again."

"Or what?"

"Is my command not enough? I need to follow it up with a threat?"

"You seem the sort of man who would do such a thing."

"Clearly you do not understand my character."

"You have impugned mine liberally enough."

"Enough!" Bloody hell, he sounded like his father. He drew a deep breath and moderated his tone. "Enough. I have said nothing of your character, only of your behavior. You will eschew any further use of your tonics whilst you are under my roof."

Her eyes grew wide, and her jaw dropped. "You have no right."

"I have every right. I am master of Pemberley, and as such, I will decide what is acceptable within its borders. I do not abide by my household raising hands against another either, and I will not tolerate any more soothing tonics in my home."

"You do not know what I suffer. I am in great need—"

"Then I will employ a surgeon or a physician, if you like, to alleviate your discomfort."

"I already have what I need."

"But I do not." His face prickled; he had not realized it until the words came out, but it was true—and it was not her.

"You had the chance—remember you turned your back on me." She tossed her head with an elegant little sneer.

"I need a wife with whom I can entrust Pemberley."

"Are you saying you cannot trust me?"

"How can you manage anything if you are insensible?"

"I have managed my life very effectively, thank you, or do you find fault with that as well?' She threw her hand in the air, an elegant practiced motion. "I am finished with this conversation. I will not stand here and be insulted at every turn by the man who is supposed to—"

"Do not change the focus of this discussion. I will not be baited into that game."

"Enough. I am finished!" She balled her fists and

stormed out the door, slamming it behind her.

He clutched the desk and sank down into the chair behind it.

What had just happened?

And what was he to do now?

A full week now, Elizabeth had been in London. A week of rain and fog and strangeness that would have to become as familiar to her as the wilds of Derbyshire had been. The city air smelled odd, heavy with smoke. The sheer number of people one encountered simply walking past on the streets—would that ever feel less smothering?

She sat in the lyre-back wooden chair near the dainty oak writing desk and pressed her cheek to the window's cool glass. Aunt had given her the second-best bedroom near their own despite there being an available guest room on the floor above near the nursery. It was Aunt's way of making her feel wanted and welcome. Pale green paper hangings with tiny vines of climbing roses covered the walls, and matching fabric dressed the windows and the bedcurtains, reminding her of the rose-covered vicarage.

Just a week away from there—she missed everyone so, especially those she had no right to miss. Papa was right. She could not go back. What was the point in clinging to the possibility? She would never get on with her life if she had hope of seeing him again.

It should become easier, should it not? But her hands trembled, and her mouth went dry at the prospect of reading Jane's letter that mocked her from the writing desk.

Enough of such silliness. She snatched up the letter and broke the seal. The red wax cracked and fell away, several fragments bouncing on the desktop. There, the worst was over, and she could read it comfortably now.

More or less.

She slid her chair into a bright sunbeam. Jane's hand was so delicate and thin. The perfect penmanship was sometimes difficult to read without sufficient light.

*My dearest Lizzy,*

*Is it selfish of me to tell you how much you are missed? I am sure that it is. I know you must be such a comfort to Aunt Gardiner that it is wrong of me to wish you were here with us.*

*And yet I do.*

What had Papa told Jane and the rest of her sisters about her new residence in London? Certainly not the truth. That was something that would never again be spoken of, not even between Papa and herself. He had probably intimated that Aunt was increasing again and could not manage by herself any longer. At least half of that was true. It was difficult to imagine any one so capable as Aunt Gardiner.

*It will come as no surprise that Lydia and Kitty are jealous that you are in London and they are not. They come occasionally to Pemberley on Miss Darcy's invitation, to help in the painting of scenes for the theatrical. I am surprised by Kitty in particular. She is a far better artist than any of us knew. Mary has made herself useful sewing costumes. All three of them have been very well-behaved, I am pleased to say. I suppose Papa's preventing them from acting has had its desired effect.*

Good, he did not need her sisters to be difficult to

manage on top of her absence. She leaned back against the chair and turned her face into the warm sunlight, but the warmth did not penetrate. She reached behind her to the dresser and retrieved a shawl. It was good that they did not need her—surely, it was.

*Miss Darcy misses you tremendously. Although any of us who are available work with her to learn yet more new lines— yes, Sir Alexander continues his endless revisions—I think Miss Darcy would rather have your help. The way she looks at me, sometimes, I think she wants a sister to confide in and is wondering if I will do.*

*So far, she has always decided that I will not and keeps her own counsel. I think that is for the best as I do not have your capacity for insight and wisdom. But with Miss Garland available, I have no doubt she will soon find the guidance she needs.*

*I cannot say too much right now, but Mr. Bingley has gone this afternoon to talk to Papa. I can only hope that you might guess what they are to talk about. I can hardly breathe, hardly think, waiting to hear the results of their talk. You told me before you left of what you expected and how you anticipated Papa would react. I do so hope you are correct. But then, I should not worry so, for you are very often—almost always, really—correct. So instead of being all aflutter, I should rejoice. I should, and yet I still will not breathe again until he has returned, and I know that you might wish us joy.*

Elizabeth, closed her eyes, sighed, and let her chin fall to her chest. Good news at last.

As distracted as Mr. Bingley could be, it was difficult not to wonder if he would forget that he had not made an offer to Jane and leave without ever saying a word about it. Who had reminded him? Colonel Fitzwilliam? Sir Alexander? Mr. Darcy himself?

That hardly seemed likely. He did not like to interfere in the affairs of others.

*The only thing that mars my hope is my observation of Mr. Darcy and Miss Garland. Since they announced their own happy news, neither one has been well. Miss Garland hardly ever joins us in the drawing room after dinner and only rarely appears when Mr. Darcy might be present. As for the man himself, we only see him at dinner and when Sir Alexander insists that we all rehearse the theatrical together. Mr. Darcy performs his part with perfect memory but with no emotion and excuses himself as soon as might be arranged.*

*Miss de Bourgh has whispered that now he is betrothed, he has no further reason to keep up the thin veneer of sociability he wore. But I think that a very cold estimate of him. Still, though, I wonder what might have changed.*

*Papa is very well these days ….*

Elizabeth laid aside the letter and pressed her hands to her cheeks.

Mr. Darcy rarely became taciturn without some clear reason. Not all would necessarily consider it a good reason, to be sure, but there was always a reason. She chewed her knuckle.

Something had happened with Miss Garland. He was too sensitive to how it would look if he avoided her company to do so easily. Perhaps she had learned of Georgiana's difficulties and spoken ill of her. That would certainly upset Mr. Darcy. Or perhaps he had—

A knock, Aunt Gardiner's, sounded on the door.

"Pray come in." She placed the letter, face down, on the writing desk.

Aunt Gardiner opened the door, peeked in, then finally entered with soft, purposeful steps. "Is everything well with your family?" She glanced at the letter.

"Everyone is well, thank you. My younger sisters are even making themselves useful, which, to be honest, is quite the news. One might wonder if my absence has done them good."

Aunt Gardner sat on the bed near Elizabeth. Sunbeams shone off blonde curls that escaped her mobcap. Despite four children and a decade of marriage, her complexion remained the same peaches-and-cream it had been when she had married, and her figure was straight and trim. Her sweet temperament helped allay some, but not all, of the inevitable jealousy in her circles that surrounded her good fortune. She smoothed her dark pink muslin skirts over her lap as though collecting her thoughts to speak. "Have you thought about what we talked about when you arrived?"

Elizabeth looked through the window; the children played in the mews garden below, their nursery maid watching over them. Laughter filtered through the open window on the same breeze that fluttered the edges of the rose-printed curtains. "I have."

"And have you come to any conclusions?"

"I have."

"Pray do not play this game with me. If you do not wish to talk, I will not pry. You know that. Simply say so, and I will leave the topic be." Women were rarely so direct as Aunt Gardiner—a trait which had lost her more than one friendship—but at times like this, it was refreshing, if challenging.

"I am not unwilling, just, it is difficult. I had never thought about leaving Papa or Lambton until I actually did so. Finding myself here is an abrupt change, and as much as I love you and Uncle, it does require getting accustomed to it."

"Is there anything else we can do to help?"

"No, I cannot imagine anything you could do to make me feel more at home. I suppose it is upon me to take the next step. I will do as you advise. Pray help me to engage in London society. I know better what I am facing now, and I think I can manage it with far greater equanimity than before."

"I cannot pretend not to be glad to hear that. I have not stopped feeling guilty for—" Aunt Gardiner squeezed her hand softly.

"Would it help you to know that he was one of the guests at Pemberley just before I left? He made a point of seeking me out and apologizing for his boorish behavior." Aunt definitely did not need to know the full story.

"I am all astonishment. I would not have expected such a man to realize, much less repent of his errors."

"As far as I am concerned, the matter is finished. And nothing remains for you to feel guilty for."

"Your uncle and I have some introductions in mind to make for you, if you are amenable. We know a young barrister who has told your uncle many times that he has yet to find a woman who can talk enough sense to hold his interest for more than five minutes. I think he would find you a very refreshing change of pace." Aunt Gardiner lifted an eyebrow and the corner of her mouth.

"You think I would like him?"

"His manners are excellent. He is known for his kindness toward his old mother who lives with him, and he is a very good dancer."

"All equally excellent qualities I am sure, though

perhaps his dancing is the most important among them." Elizabeth chuckled, and it was not entirely forced.

"It is a joy to hear your sense of humor has finally returned. We have been invited to a card party on Thursday night to which I believe he has also been invited. Will you join us?"

"I will."

"Good, good. You will permit me one more indulgence? Come to my sitting room. I have several gowns that have not fitted me well since little Thomas was born. But I think with just a few alterations, they will do very nicely for you. I have a lovely box of trims that your uncle has brought home from his warehouse. With a little clever needlework, I think we can craft some lovely new things for you. There is nothing like a new dress to set one in the right frame of mind for an outing."

"May I finish my letter from Jane first? I have just a bit more to read."

"Of course. I will see you in a few minutes." Aunt Gardiner left.

Elizabeth stood and leaned against the window frame. The children still played in the garden below.

No, this wasn't Pemberley, or even the countryside. But if those things were closed to her now, she would make the best she could of the opportunities she had. Maybe there was a barrister who would find a clever woman more agreeable than a stupid one.

# ꙮChapter 15

Darcy stood beside the window of his chambers, peering down on the lawn below. The breeze from the open window teased the heavy blue curtains into a fickle dance against his cheek and shoulder. Behind him, the room was neat and tidy, the heavy dark oak furnishings dusted and polished until they shone. Every shelf, every drawer, even the closet was in order—he could have laid hands on anything he wanted with his eyes closed.

If only the rest of his life might be so easily ordered.

On the lawn below, Blanche instructed the ladies of the house in archery, whilst the men looked on, appreciating the pleasing show of their figures in the late morning light. Georgiana was much improved and even Miss Bennet now attempted the activity. Since Miss Elizabeth's departure, Blanche had rallied the ladies to engage in the sport several times. No doubt she was aware of how well the activity made her appear, especially in comparison to the other ladies.

Thirteen days. It had been thirteen long, difficult days since his world upended itself and began its descent into chaos. Blanche had mentioned it during the few minutes she spent in the drawing room last night.

"It has been close to a fortnight." She stood behind him, leaning her back and shoulder into his. "I should wonder that you are not quite put out and tired of it all."

"Who is to say that I am not?" He shifted his weight to his injured foot, away from her.

"So, you do have a limit after all."

"Everyone has their limits."

"I was beginning to wonder." She pressed into him a little harder.

He stepped away, and she nearly stumbled. "What is that supposed to mean?"

"It is all in your hands you know. I am quite willing to end this stalemate."

"Then you agree—"

"Once you have provided me with a properly pretty apology, we can end this ridiculous state of affairs."

"An apology? You expect an apology?" He clenched his fist.

"That is the conventional mode when one has been wrong."

"I am quite willing to apologize on those occasions when I have been wrong. But this is not one of them."

"You treated me horribly."

"Requiring that you behave in a manner befitting the mistress of Pemberley is not treating you horribly."

"You have no right—"

"I have every right."

"Not when you are wrong." She stormed out of the drawing room and slammed the door behind her. Everyone in the room stared at him as though he might have an explanation.

He turned his back and perused the shelves for a book. A few minutes later, he quit the room entirely.

How was he to bring her to understand? Richard's tales of opium-addled soldiers would hardly affect her. Neither would Garland be of any help. Clearly, he knew of his sister's tonics and made no effort to address the matter.

Her laughter wafted up through the open window. Georgiana had hit an inner ring of her target—her best performance yet. It was good to see her succeed—she needed successes in her life. Miss Garland could certainly help her find them—if she did not ruin Georgiana with her tonics.

He would not marry Blanche without her capitulation and safeguards in place to ensure she did as she promised. Yet she seemed equally determined to have her way. That might have worked with other men, but not here.

It was possible to break off the engagement. No announcements had yet been sent to the papers. Miss Bingley and Anne might still talk, though, in such a way to damage Blanche's reputation. That would not do.

If only he had been more prudent, more careful

before he had offered for her. He had been far too impulsive. He should have talked to … to Miss Elizabeth before making any decision.

Oh, dear God. The room spun.

He grabbed the window frame for balance, dizzy and ready to cast up his accounts. No, that was not enough. A chair! He must have a chair. His hand landed on a small wooden chair. Skidding back, it groaned as it caught his weight.

Oh, dear God.

He knew exactly what Miss Elizabeth would say. She had already told him when she had been quite as compromised by his tonic-addled behavior as Blanche. Even more so, as she had spent the entire night in the parlor with him. With his foot propped in her lap no less! How much more improper could it have been? Bennet would have had every right to demand he make his daughter an offer of marriage if he had found out.

But he did not. No one had.

Because she had wanted it so.

He laced his fingers behind his neck and braced his elbows on his knees. Even when he had asked her what he might do to make things right, she asked nothing for herself. She forgave him the entire incident and promised that she would think of it no more.

It was what a friend would do, she said.

What did that make Blanche? How could he marry a woman who was neither his friend nor someone he loved?

And what would he do without the friend whom he loved?

Stomach still churning, Darcy presided over that evening's dinner that included the entire Bennet family, save, of course, the one Bennet he longed to see. The room glittered with the reflected light of many candles, bouncing from mirrors, to crystal, to polished silver. The rich aroma of roasted veal rose up from the platter before him. Abundant dishes demanded mirth and good will from the company.

Everyone but him seemed to oblige.

Once he had carved the joint, Darcy pushed food around his plate and avoided being part of the conversation.

After the wine was poured and the dessert course served, Bingley stood, wearing an entirely self-satisfied expression.

"Are you planning on leading the ladies out?" Richard lifted his glass toward Bingley.

"We civilized folk permit the hostess to do that, you know." Garland added with a smirk toward his sister.

Darcy worked his tongue against the roof of his mouth.

"Mock me all you will. You shall not stay me from my happy announcement." Bingley looked down on Miss Bennet and offered her his hand.

She stood beside him, blushing, hand in his, even more lovely than usual in the flickering candlelight.

"Miss Bennet has made me the happiest of men, accepting my offer of marriage and consenting to become my wife."

"Jane!" Miss Mary squealed, clapping her hands to her mouth.

Suddenly, all the Bennet sisters crowded around Miss Bennet, chattering and chittering.

"Charles? You never mentioned such a thing," Miss Bingley said through a forced smile.

"A brother hardly needs a sister's approval of his plans, now does he?" Garland winked at Blanche. "On the other hand—"

"No, no, no." Blanche waved a finger at Garland but looked directly at Darcy. "Do not try to perpetuate the myth that you are in any way in charge of me."

Garland lifted hands in surrender. "Far be it from me to suggest such a thing. Besides, it is no longer my problem now, is it, Darcy?"

Darcy cleared his throat and lifted his wine glass. "I believe a toast is in order …."

Thankfully, others followed suit, offering many toasts to the happy couple.

Half an hour later, Georgiana invited the ladies to the drawing room. Blanche took Miss Bennet's arm near the door and followed Georgiana out. Hopefully she would not have too much sage advice for the newly-betrothed lady. Bingley did not need that sort of cunning in his life.

Bennet made Bingley the center of conversation while the gentlemen enjoyed their port and cigars. Neither sat well with Darcy this evening, so he sat back and observed as the rest partook. Little by little, the gentlemen trickled out to the drawing room, until he was the only one left.

Damn it all, every last bit of it.

He should be happy for Bingley—happy that his friend had found what he wanted and that all around supported the notion.

He should be.

Father had warned him to assiduously avoid jealousy—it only led to misery, he said. Obviously, he was right.

Was it so wrong to want to be as pleased in his own betrothal as Bingley was? It seemed a small enough thing to ask.

But no, dwelling on that would not make it any easier to get through the rest of the evening. Best make his entrance into the drawing room before someone came to find him and required an invented explanation for his tardiness.

Few candles lit the long corridor from the dining room to the drawing room. Disapproving eyes glared down at him from the portraits along either side. The darkness, heavy and oppressive tonight, muffled his thoughts and the sounds from the other part of the house.

Wait, were those voices, in the morning parlor? Yes, they were coming from there.

He quietly made his way to the half-closed door of the morning room, stopping just beside the doorway. Closing his eyes and holding his breath, he focused on the soft sounds.

"Was that right? Did I deliver that line properly this time?" Georgiana sounded hopeful.

"Almost." Garland's breathy whisper was far too intimate. "I rewrote that line two days ago."

"I had not realized."

"I specifically remember giving you the pages. Did you not read them?"

"I am sorry. I know I should have. But Miss Bennet has been so busy with Mr. Bingley…."

"What has she to do with any of this?"

"She helps me … sometimes my eyes are so tired—"

"That reading is difficult for you?"

Georgiana sniffled.

"Why should that make you cry?" The rustle of cloth must be a handkerchief being produced from Garland's pocket.

"I do not think others have such difficulties."

"Everyone has difficulties, my dear, Miss Darcy. You have no idea what my sister suffers, for she never utters a word of it. She is a brave soul, much like you."

"Do not call me that. I know it is not true."

"Of course, it is. I can see it in you all the time. "

"You are merely flattering me."

"I only speak the truth. One does not flatter his muse. One treasures her, protects her—"

Darcy lunged through the door. Garland and Georgiana stood very close, silhouetted in a silver moonbeam near the window.

"Who—oh Darcy! What are you doing there?" Garland stepped back from Georgiana.

"Perhaps I should be asking that question of you." Darcy stalked around the table to stand between them.

"We were looking for a pair of chairs to dress a scene." Georgiana put her hands on her hips and lifted her chin. The moonlight painted her as more child than woman.

"Indeed, we were. And these should do very well. There is a particular speech in the third act that must be delivered whilst seated." Garland manhandled two chairs away from the morning table.

"And just how much longer do you think it shall be before this theatrical is performed?"

"What say you, Miss Darcy? Five days should see us ready?"

Georgiana avoided Darcy's gaze. "Yes, I think that will do."

"Perhaps you can press Miss Bennet for help with invitations and publicity, since it seems your good brother has frightened away Miss Elizabeth." Garland laughed, but there was something about his tone that did not sit well.

"I believe I have already made myself clear on the matter. I will not have my home turned into a public venue. You may invite the Bennets, but that is all."

"A gentleman's home is his space within which to interact with the rest of the world. Or have you forgotten that? Which means you must interact! Blanche can assist you. Is that not what the mistress of such a home does?"

"Pemberley is my home, and it will be my say who is to be here. Only the Bennets—do not cross me in this." He leaned a little closer to Garland.

"Must you be so inflexible?" Where had Georgiana acquired that high and snippy tone?

"Another whine like that, and I will cancel it all together."

Garland laughed in his face. "It is unbecoming to make idle threats."

"My words are never idle, sir. Do not test me. Now that you have found your set dressing, it would be appropriate for you to join the rest of the party in the drawing room and wish Bingley and Miss Bennet joy."

Georgiana huffed and flounced out of the room,

Garland sauntering behind her.

Darcy followed, shutting the door behind him. He leaned against the wall, squeezing his temples.

First Blanche, now this? What was he to do?

Aunt Gardiner's "several" gowns turned out to be three evening dresses, a ball gown, and two half-dress ensembles, one with a matching spencer, the other with a pelisse. An entirely new wardrobe, fitting for a young lady out in London society. Though she protested that Jane should have them as her wedding clothes, Aunt insisted Elizabeth ought to resign herself to the trial of having new and pretty things.

Aunt's doting attentions were lovely and yet bittersweet. While Mama had tried to conceal her favoritism, Jane, the prettiest, and Lydia, the liveliest, had been Mama's pets. One did not easily forget being not-the-favorite. But now was not the time to dwell upon such things, not when there was an evening's entertainment to be anticipated.

Elizabeth slipped on the blue velvet cape that matched the blue silk evening gown Aunt Gardiner had given her and turned this way and that in front of the long mirror in her room. The unique sound of swishing silk would take some time to get used to, but what a wondrous feeling the fabric had as it cascaded to the floor. With a feather and ribbon ornament in her hair and matching reticule and shoe roses, she looked more like a fashion plate than a country vicar's daughter. Who was that woman in the mirror and did she want to be her?

Uncle called up the stairs. The coach was ready

and such philosophical reflections would have to wait.

A brief ride carried them to Bow-Street and the Doric portico entrance of the Covent Garden Theater. Within, four tiers of boxes, painted white with gold and green borders that could seat twelve hundred, and another six hundred seats in the pit greeted her with a cool, impersonal welcome. How could one not feel lost and insignificant within?

The little music room theater at Pemberley was less than nothing compared to this. No wonder Sir Alexander was ever in some sort of pique over the staging of his production.

Despite the production being a comedy and utterly unlike Sir Alexander's play, the experience rang too much of disquieting afternoon rehearsals at Pemberley with Sir Alexander's character saying most inappropriate things to Miss Darcy's. Thankfully, the crisp night air embraced her as they waited at the edge of the street for the coach to come for them, dissolving away the ephemeral illusions of the theater, reminding her of the realities of London.

Much improved, and better still, the night had only just begun. A card and supper party awaited.

The coach stopped at a first-rate townhouse, not unlike the Gardiners', lit by a pair of tall street lamps on either side of the steps. Fresh white paint —very fresh, enough to still smell it—and crisp black ironwork greeted them as they approached the friendly red front door. Elizabeth hung back a little and swallowed hard.

How similar this scene was to that night years ago when she first met Sir Alexander. He had just been Mr. Garland then. Mr. Garland the playwright; Mr. Garland the heir presumptive; Mr. Garland the handsome-not-exactly-a-rake-but-do-be-careful-of-him bachelor.

No, those thoughts were for another time. Best focus on this evening and only this evening. He would not be here, and perhaps, more importantly, she was not a silly girl of sixteen who wore her heart on her sleeve and took overheard remarks to heart.

She followed Aunt Gardiner inside.

A maid stood waiting to take their wraps before they proceeded past the entry hall. The butler led them down the marble-floored passage lined with striped paper hangings, to a winding staircase that finally opened onto a landing and a large drawing room. The room extended the entire width of the house with the left-hand windows facing the street and the right overlooking the mews. The space could have accommodated six card tables, but only four, all matching and delicately painted white with gold scrollwork, were set up. A small pianoforte was tucked in the corner nearest the mews-facing windows. A sofa and several white and gold bergère chairs had been pushed into a tight cluster near the instrument. Two sets of shelves held garniture and objects of curiosity between the street-facing windows. Perhaps she could discreetly make her way to those shelves—what a family collected always revealed much about their character.

"Mrs. Gardiner, Miss Bennet." Mrs. Lovington, their hostess, a middle-aged mother of five who looked barely old enough to be married herself, hurried toward them. Her ginger hair was plaited and arranged into a deceptively simple style, fixed with pearl pins and ostrich feathers. Her ivory silk gown, elegant and simple, fitted her so perfectly that it was no wonder Aunt Gardiner was the only person with whom she had shared the name of her modiste, lest she be too busy to make Mrs. Lovington's gowns.

"Thank you so much for inviting us." Aunt Gardiner extended her hands and kissed Mrs. Lovington's cheek.

"There is no greater pleasure in the world than having my friends join me. I am so glad you are here, Miss Bennet. Now that my daughter is near coming out, your aunt and I will have so much more to share. I cannot tell you how grateful I am for that." She smiled broadly, her green eyes sparkling.

If Aunt had not warned her that Mrs. Lovington was entirely genuine, it would be easy to distrust her very open, artless manner.

"Your invitation was most gracious. I have been in London such a short time, I have hardly any acquaintance." Elizabeth curtsied.

"Indeed so. But tonight, we will remedy that. Come, allow me to introduce you to my friends." Mrs. Lovington took Elizabeth's arm and headed toward the nearest cluster of ladies.

A quarter of an hour later, Elizabeth could count a dozen new families added to her acquaintance, all of whom were gracious and enthusiastic about adding a new young lady to their circle.

Mr. Lovington burst into the drawing room, his warm baritone filling the room ahead of him. Tall, with a bit of a belly, his unruly dark hair sported narrow streaks of grey. A party of gentlemen, presumably from the billiards room followed, several of them young enough to be in want of a wife.

Elizabeth swallowed hard and forced what she hoped would be a pleasing expression on her face.

"You must be on your best behavior tonight. My wife has a new friend in our midst, and you would not want to miss your opportunity to dance with her." Mr. Lovington bowed. The two young men with him followed suit.

"Miss Bennet, may I present Mr. Boyle and Mr. Cluett?"

"I am pleased to make your acquaintance." Elizabeth curtseyed just deeply enough. They were all equals here tonight.

Mr. Boyle, on the left, was handsome, but not tall. He resembled Mr. Darcy a bit, except for his coloring, which was very fair. Mr. Cluett, on the right, was very tall, taller than Mr. Darcy, but not particularly hand-some. His hair was dark, but his eyes were a most arresting shade of grey.

"It is our pleasure." Mr. Cluett bowed deeply.

With a flash of his eyebrows suggesting he was not to be outdone, Mr. Boyle bowed more deeply. "We have been anticipating this moment all day."

Elizabeth cocked her head.

Mrs. Lovington blushed. "I hope you do not mind, but I might have implied that we were much antici-pating your company tonight."

"And you promised us dancing." Mr. Boyle elbowed Mr. Cluett. "I certainly mean to dance tonight. I would be most pleased if you would dance with me, Miss Bennet. The first dance, perhaps?"

"Then I insist upon the second, if I may." Mr. Cluett thumbed his lapels.

"I ... I ... thank you very much."

"Excellent. I shall find my sister who would be much gratified to be the first young lady to exhibit tonight—she plays a lively reel." Mr. Boyle hurried away.

"I think I might suggest to my cousin that she take her turn after that. Do you like a country dance?" Mr. Cluett scanned the room, doubtless for said cousin.

"I do."

"Excellent. Excuse me." He hurried off.

"Are they always so very enthusiastic?" Aunt Gardiner's gaze followed both men through the room.

"You know how young people can be." Mrs. Lovington laughed. "But truly, they are excellent young men. Mr. Boyle has just taken a living in Kent. A lovely parish with a very nice vicarage as I understand. The patron is a friend of his family who has been holding the living until he could take it. He is a very fortunate young man. Mr. Cluett is a new barrister who has some excellent connections, and a very promising career. But do not think me a matchmaker, heavens no. There is far too much mischief in that. I have only introduced you because it would be difficult to have you together in my home and unable to speak to each other. No, if anything comes of this, it is entirely of your own making. Pray excuse me to open the pianoforte."

"I believe she means it—she is not a matchmaker. I do not want you to feel pressured in any way. This is an evening of pleasure, nothing more," Aunt Gardiner whispered in her ear.

"I confess, it is strange to have so much attention directed toward me, but I shall find a way to endure it with great equanimity." And she would do just that.

A few minutes later, Elizabeth found herself claimed by Mr. Boyle, who was a very good dancer and an excellent conversationalist. He was most pleased to discover they shared a taste in novels. He had little taste for Shakespeare, but that was hardly a fatal flaw, even if Mr. Darcy harbored a great fondness for the Bard's sonnets.

In the next set, Mr. Cluett demonstrated an excellent sense of humor when he found himself turning right instead of left in the first round of the dance. The misstep did not seem to discompose him—his happy confidence saved his dignity—and her own good humor—from the gaffe. Mr. Darcy had always been so serious in everything he did; every mistake was a matter for concern. But considering his father, that was not surprising.

No, he was hardly Mr. Darcy, and this was hardly Pemberley. Still though, Mr. Cluett's easy humor and composure were most intriguing ... perhaps worth getting to know. Mr. Boyle might be as well. So, too, were several of the young ladies Mrs. Lovington introduced her to. Hardly the London she remembered from those years ago.

Perhaps she would be able to adjust to London after all.

# ✣ Chapter 16

Seven days later, Darcy paced the blue drawing room. The azure walls and furniture chosen by his mother were supposed to calm his rankled nerves. But his injured ankle still twinged despite the boots he wore—improperly—in the house. How galling being forced to dress inappropriately in order to accommodate a foolish injury inflicted by a thoughtless situation. No shade of blue was sufficient to overcome that indignity.

What a sevenday it had been. Blanche ignored him the whole of it. Her tenacity was as remarkable as her beauty. She seemed surprised that he remained steadfast as well. Apparently, she was accustomed to winning at this game.

What was the line between stubborn and willful? Surely, she was approaching it, if she had not already crossed it. What was he to do about it?

Neither the upending of his peaceful, orderly home nor the turning of the music room into a theater made the matter easier to sort out. Had any room in the house escaped having its appointments pillaged to satisfy the needs of the set? Was a green vase not adequate? Why did the blue one from the library need to be used instead?

He pressed his temples. When was the last time a headache had not been thundering in the background?

Garland had become more and more temperamental—according to Richard, "tyrannical" seemed a better description—particularly as the day of the performance approached. Garland went so far as to punish Darcy's stance on publicity and a large audience by writing him out of the play entirely. Did Garland realize it was more reward than rebuke?

At least it would all be over soon. In a few short hours, the dreadful home theatrical would be but a memory, and he could begin putting his home and his life back together.

Hopefully.

"The Bennets have arrived," Mrs. Reynolds announced from the parlor doorway. She stepped aside, and the vicar and his three younger daughters poured in.

"This is so exciting! I can hardly believe the time has arrived!" Miss Kitty clasped her hands before her and twirled.

Bennet lifted his eyebrows and shrugged.

"I still do not understand why we could not have a larger audience. The backboards I painted are so lovely. It is a shame that they will not be seen." Miss Lydia's face formed into a pout.

"Another word and you shall go home without seeing it at all." Bennet glowered at her.

Miss Lydia sniffed and slumped—capitulating but rebellious. So very much like Georgiana. She turned to her sisters, and they spoke softly among themselves.

Bennet approached. "I understand you are no longer acting."

"No, the playwright determined that the father's role was unnecessary."

"I recall making your participation a condition of my daughters' participation."

"It was a very recent change. Would you rather I had permitted publicity and a wider audience?"

Bennet grumbled. And glanced over his shoulder. His daughters whispered among themselves and giggled. "No, that would not have been an improvement. But you should have told me. You were to participate so as to be able to protect my daughters and your sister."

"Georgiana wrote to Miss Elizabeth, but she has not written back." Darcy clasped his hands behind his back and stared over Bennet's shoulder, through the open parlor door.

"I am sure she will soon. Lizzy is an attentive correspondent."

"Georgiana misses her friend very much. She says she has been waiting for Miss Elizabeth's advice on a matter."

"Lizzy's aunt has kept her schedule very full."

"Doing what?"

"Though it is none of your concern, her aunt and uncle have been introducing her to their rather broad circle of acquaintances. As I understand, Lizzy's company has been quite in demand. On their at-home days, there are callers constantly coming and going, and their evening engagements have been equally full."

He swallowed hard and clenched his teeth. "It would be disappointing to think that she would forget Pemberley."

"It is not like Lizzy to forget her friends. Mark my word, she will write to your sister soon."

"Mr. Darcy! Mr. Darcy!" Mrs. Reynolds ran in, red-faced and panting. "I cannot understand it. I do not understand."

Miss Mary took her arm and helped her to a chair.

"What is wrong?" Darcy's pulse hammered in his temples, throbbing behind his eyes, fuzzing the edges of his vision.

"Miss Darcy. It is Miss Darcy. I cannot find her. I have searched the house twice and I cannot find her."

"She is probably just nervous about the performance and is in the garden rehearsing." Miss Mary patted Mrs. Reynolds' hand.

"Lydia and I shall go and find her." Miss Kitty grabbed her younger sister's hand, and they skipped out.

"There you see, it will all be well in a few moments." Miss Mary knelt beside Mrs. Reynolds.

"No, no, you do not understand." She pulled a scrap of paper from her sleeve and passed it to Bennet and Darcy.

Bennet unfolded it, squinting and turning the sheet this way and that. "It is difficult to make out."

"Georgiana must have written it!" Darcy edged behind Bennet and peered over his shoulder.

"I have…" Bennet pointed at a smudged word.

"Decided?"

"Yes, I think it is: 'I have decided. I am going with him.'" Bennet looked over his shoulder at Darcy, brows knotted.

"Lord, no!" Darcy staggered backward, room spinning, breath knocked away as though he had fallen from his horse.

Mrs. Reynolds choked back a sob. "I cannot find her. Her dressing room is upturned, and there are gowns missing from her closet."

"I will find her maid. I am sure she can explain what is going on." Miss Mary dashed from the room as Mrs. Reynolds burst into tears.

"I found them, together in the morning parlor one night," Darcy whispered.

"I had no idea he would stoop to such a thing." Bennet trudged to the settee.

Darcy collapsed beside him. "What do you mean? Had you any idea he had designs on Georgiana?"

"I am as shocked as you are on that account. I was certain if she were away, then all would be safe." Bennet covered his face with his hands.

"What are you talking about? Did he impose on Miss Elizabeth?"

"If I had only known earlier, I would have required the girls to return home at once. But she did not tell me."

"I demand to know! What happened?"

"After Lizzy wrenched her knee, she told me that one morning whilst she was walking, he sought to kiss her. Apparently, you conveniently walked in and stopped that scheme, never knowing what had happened. Then he offered her his protection—"

"To be his mistress?" If he ever saw that wastrel's face again….

"After she refused him, he recanted and made her an offer of marriage, which she also refused."

Damn and bloody hell! "That is why she had to go to London? To be away from him? Why did you not tell me?"

"It is my business as her father. Not yours."

"It is my business as master of Pemberley, and as her friend. I should have known."

"No, it is not your concern." Bennet met Darcy's gaze. "She is not of your sphere. Your concern needs to be for your sister."

"You will write to Miss Elizabeth and ask her to come home? She is much needed here."

"No, I will not. Pemberley is your home, not hers. She is about the business of establishing her own home now, and nothing that happens here should take her from that. Miss Garland must be the one you turn to now." Bennet's voice was firm, but not unkind.

Damn it all, he was right—but everything about it felt wrong.

Miss Mary dashed in, dragging a young maid by the hand. "Tell them what you told me. No one will be angry with you. I promise you will not be sacked." She looked into Darcy's eyes with an expression reminiscent of Miss Elizabeth.

"What do you know, girl? Tell what you know." Mrs. Reynolds rushed to the maid.

"Tell me the truth, and you have nothing to fear," Darcy said.

"The young mistress, this morning, gave me clear instructions on the things she wanted packed up into her trunk and to have sent to be loaded on the baronet's coach."

"Do you know when they departed?" Bennet asked.

"Not for certain. But, I think, I think it might have been three hours ago." The girl wrung her dusty hands in her smudged apron.

Bennet leaned close and softly said, "And in what direction did they go?"

"I ... I ... did not see the carriage leave. I have no idea."

"Why did you not tell Mrs. Reynolds?" Darcy asked.

"The young mistress said I would be sacked if I said anything. Please, sir, my mum is ill. I need to pay the apothecary."

"Of course, girl. There would be no way for you to know that Miss Darcy could not follow through with such a threat." Bennet cleared his throat and stared at Darcy.

Hardly subtle, but appropriate. "Indeed. Mrs. Reynolds, see the apothecary bills brought to me."

"Thank you, sir." The girl sobbed into her hands.

"Come." Mrs. Reynolds helped her out.

"Mary, go and find Kitty and Lydia and take them home. It is best you tell your sisters that Miss Darcy has taken ill. Not a word of this is to be spoken to anyone under any condition. Do I make myself utterly clear?" That was a tone that not even Darcy would dare cross.

Miss Mary, pale and wide-eyed, scurried out.

Bennet rubbed his chin with his fist. "The question is: where would Sir Alexander go? Perhaps Colonel Fitzwilliam or Miss Garland might be able to offer some insight. I imagine they are better acquainted with him than you are."

"I will find them." Darcy strode out as briskly as he could manage.

Where would Blanche be? The music room, check that first.

He all but ran down the corridor, nearly stumbling as he flung himself into the music room.

"Darcy? Heavens, what has taken hold of you?" Blanche put down the flowers she had been arranging and moved toward him with languid, elegant strides.

"Your brother, where is he?"

"How should I know? Before a performance, he is usually hidden away somewhere brooding and does not come out until the last possible moment. This is entirely normal for him."

"Georgiana is missing."

She flicked his concern aside. "Stage fright, I am certain. The poor dear will do very well indeed, but she has been imagining disaster from the very beginning. The performance will do a world of good for her confidence."

"She left a note. She said she has gone with him." He grabbed her shoulders.

Blanche gasped and lost a bit of color in her face. "No, no, I am certain it is not possible. Georgiana's hand is so atrocious. I am certain it was misread."

"A maid said she had instructions to pack Georgiana's trunk and send it to be loaded on your brother's coach."

"No, no, no!" She pulled herself from Darcy's grasp and paced the width of the room. "Foolish, foolish boy. Both of them, utterly foolish!"

"Where might he have taken her?"

"How should I know? It is not as if he discussed this with me. Has he no compassion on any of us? Does he not know how this will affect our reputations, my reputation?"

"What are you talking about?"

"You and I—we are tainted with the very association with them!" Who knew that a Valkyrie could shriek?

"This is not the time for those concerns. I need to know where to find her." Darcy balled his fists until they trembled at his side.

"This is Bennet's fault. Miss Elizabeth should never have been sent away. If she had been here to distract Alexander, he would never have bothered your sister." She turned on him, icy fire in her blue eyes.

"He already offered her his protection."

"Foolish girl! She should have taken it. The ridiculous article should know she will never have a better offer than that. How dare she put my reputation at risk—"

"Hang your reputation! I do not care—" Another word on *her* reputation and he would surely shake her. "I must protect my sister."

"It seems a little late for that now."

"Where might he have taken her?" Darcy took her hand and pulled to her to face him. "Tell me where they might be."

She wrenched herself away. "Unhand me! I do not know. He writes for a private theater company in Derbyshire; they might go there. He also has connections to London theater as well: two private companies and a friend associated with Drury Lane. There may be one or two beyond that."

"Write their names and directions for me, now—all of them."

"Do not order me about like a servant."

"You are my betrothed, and I expect you to act like a helpmeet to me. I insist."

"I shall go upstairs and find the directions and send a maid with them directly. I have a devastating headache now and do not wish to be bothered for the rest of the evening. I am most truly and completely distressed." She swept out of the room, dodging Richard as he stormed in.

"I just heard—Bennet told me. What is to be done?" Richard fell into a chair that was supposed to have been for the theatrical's audience.

"I am still working that out." Darcy paced through the fully-dressed set, skirting the awkwardly placed chairs and the scenery boards left at awkward angles. "All I can say for certain right now is that I will have Mrs. Reynolds see to it that all the staff have sufficient incentive to keep quiet about what has happened."

"And the Bennets?"

"They would never betray me. Neither would Bingley, and he will see to his sister. Anne is connected to us and will support us. Since Georgiana is not out and not known in society, there is still a chance her reputation can be spared. We must find her before her identity is known."

"Will you force them to marry?" Richard steepled his hands and pressed the to his chin.

"Not if I have any alternative. The man is a bounder. I would not see her attached to such a creature if there is any other way." It was already too late for himself. "As soon as Blanche gives me the directions she promised, we must be off."

"The sun is nearly set, and there will only be a sliver of moon tonight. We cannot travel now."

"I insist—"

"No, we will do her no good if we are killed by highwaymen or thrown from our horses who cannot not see the road in front of us."

Darcy pounded his fist into his palm "At first light then."

"I will handle the horses. Come, we must pack."

Richard was right, of course. But first, Darcy would share his plans with Bennet—it was as close to Miss Elizabeth's advice as he could get.


Bennet's sympathy was genuine, not the uncomfortable kind that made him wish he had never mentioned his trouble. Moreover, Bennet offered useful direction on how he might approach Georgiana, if and when he found her; how to talk to her; how to encourage her to come back under Pemberley's protection—if that was even possible. And if it was not, Bennet had thoughts on how to learn to live with that potentiality without losing his sister entirely.

How did Bennet manage to be so entirely without judgment for both him and Georgiana? How had he overlooked the caring wisdom Bennet carried for so long? It should not have been surprising; they were the selfsame traits that Miss Elizabeth possessed.

Near midnight, Mrs. Reynolds knocked at his dressing room door. Face drawn and eyes red, she offered him a letter she found in Georgiana's dressing table. From Miss Elizabeth, it had arrived earlier that day. The wax seal remained intact. Georgiana must have set it aside in favor of all the activity of getting ready for the play. Perhaps he might find something useful in it.

His hands trembled, and he tried to swallow through the cotton wool that filled his mouth as he stumbled toward his wingchair near the fireplace. Only two candles flickered from the mantelpiece, casting their faint glow along the dark wood paneling. Dim light, but sufficient.

The letter was from her, the voice, the wisdom he longed for. The single person he desperately needed right now. No, it had not been written for his eyes, but what mattered that now? For a few moments her words would be there with him and perhaps something might begin to make sense.

Heart hammering his ribs hard enough to ache, he cracked the seal and unfolded the missive. A bit of the wax fell off into his lap. He picked up the irregular red lump and worried it between his fingers.

*My dear Miss Darcy,*

*I pray you, please, talk to your brother before you allow Sir Alexander to speak with you again. I implore you, do not allow his clever words to confuse you from what you know to be right. I understand how compelling he can be, but remember his craft is theater. He loves the dramatic far more than he could care about anyone, even you.*

*I know you cannot be happy to hear what I have to say, but you know I can only tell you the truth.*

*I also know you are angry with me for leaving you. I understand, I truly do. I wish there had been any alternative. I fear you will not believe me when I insist there was not. I expect you are tempted to ignore what I have told you simply because you are angry.*

*So, I offer you another source of counsel. Before she died, your mother left you and your brother letters, tucked into the Darcy family genealogy in the drawer of the chest beneath her portrait in the gallery. My mother helped her write those letters.*

*Your mother was like you—beautiful, brilliant, accomplished, and unable to read or write properly despite the best schools and tutors. She feared there would be a day you needed her and she would not be here for you, so she made sure my mother and I knew the location of those letters.*

*I considered telling you of them many times, but your mother insisted that it would be very clear when the right time was, and I am certain it is now.*

*Go and find your mother's letter and let her voice guide you to make the right and honorable choices. Then talk to your brother. He is a trustworthy man in whose support you can always be certain. He is the best of men. You will not regret confiding in him.*

The letter fell from his hand, half-sliding off his lap. Breathe, he must breathe. But how could he force air into a chest so tight?

Mother was just like Georgiana? He had never known? How was it possible? How much more did he not know?

Perhaps the letter for himself was still there.

He grabbed a candlestick and made his way through the dark house. Dark, judgmental portraits stared down from the gallery walls, disapproving of his late-night wandering. Sweat trickled down the side of his face as he set the candlestick on top of the bombé chest.

Cold, smooth drawer knobs so unfamiliar in his hands. Should he? He had to know. The drawer squealed and protested every inch he opened it. The Darcy genealogy—a black leather-bound tome with gold lettering—looked up at him, smelling of old leather and paper, much like the library and the study, his favorite sanctuaries. A pair of folded letters protruded from between the pages. He pulled them free. One bore Georgiana's name. He set it aside and opened the one addressed to him.

*Fitzwilliam*

The lovely, feminine loops and swirls that formed his name called to him in his mother's voice, even if they were in Mrs. Bennet's hand.

*My son,*

*I would rather say these things to you myself, and perhaps I will have the opportunity, but it is too important to chance that these words are left unsaid.*

*You are so very observant; you probably already know my secret.*

No, not until a moment ago ....

*I am sure you have noticed; Mrs. Reynolds reads my letters to me and writes my correspondence for me. She is an excellent woman, and I hope that you will find a way to allow her to retire on Pemberley with a portion when the time comes—I value both her service and her silence that much.*

*I hope you can forgive what I have done to your father. He did not know the truth about me until after we married. It was very difficult for him to trust me after that revelation.*

*It is my fault that he has been so very difficult, so very hard on you. When you were born, you looked so much like me, and he feared that you might also share my failing. But you did not. I think he believed that it was because he was severe with you and had high expectations. You will not be surprised to know I disagreed with his sentiment.*

*I know he was hard on you, and you have had moments*

*where you hated him for that. If only you could understand the deep concern for you that was forever on his mind. Ask Miss Elizabeth about it; she will be able to tell you.*

*I hope that she is still with you when you read this. I hope that you have not taken her friendship for granted or failed to appreciate all that she brings to the shades of Pemberley. I know she is not of our sphere. But that is not the only, or even most important quality in a wife.*

*Be patient with your sister for she is like me ....*

There was more—pages more, but his eyes blurred, and the words faded into one another. Mother was like Georgiana? Miss Elizabeth knew?

"I thought I would find you here." Blanche's slow steps whispered along the marble.

Darcy dropped the letter in the drawer and shut it so hard the candle sputtered. "What do you want?'

"I need to talk to you. I have the names and directions you wanted."

"Give them to me. I am in no mood to talk."

"I regret that, but I understand you are leaving first thing in the morning. There will be no opportunity to talk to you later."

"I do not wish to discuss anything right now." He stepped around her, but she cut him off. Flickering candlelight caressed her face. Even now, the image would make a stunning painting.

"Here." She pressed a folded paper into his hand. "I hope that it will help."

"I do not know how long we will be gone."

"I will not be here when you return. I am going to Sicily. My friend has taken a villa there. I would like to see it."

Cold suffused through his chest, into his limbs, rendering his tongue nearly too thick to speak. "Sicily."

"It is quite lovely, as I understand."

"How long will you be there? I thought you did not like to travel."

"Send word to your solicitor. There will be no need for—"

"You are jilting me." The word fell from his lips and clanked against the marble floor.

"Jilting? That is a strong word. I thought you did not like the dramatic. No announcement has been made in the paper. There has been no public presentation. I am certain you can keep your friends quiet and pay for your staff's silence. The whole affair was just a momentary impulse under the influence of too much wine. Nothing more need be said."

It had not been too much wine, but what matter whether it was wine or laudanum? The effect—and the emptiness it left—were all the same.

"I see. Good evening then, Miss Garland. Since I will not see you in the morning, safe travels. Sicily is lovely this time of year." He did not look at her as he strode past, his footfalls echoing through the long room.

Eight days after they left Pemberley, London rose on the horizon, encased in a heavy fog. Fitting, considering the final address suggested by Miss Garland proved no more useful than the others. There was no choice but to take refuge at Darcy House and sort out what to do next.

When they arrived, Darcy stalked to his study— the housekeeper had only just received word of their plans and their rooms were not yet ready—and shut the door behind him.

The room was just like he left it when they were last in London. Every book in its place, every piece of furniture unmoved, every surface dusted and polished. Everything exactly as it should be. The unmitigated gall of a room to be so perfect when everything else was so completely out of order.

He fell into the wingchair that matched the one in his study at Pemberley, near the fireplace, head in his hands. The more time that passed, the greater the likelihood that Georgiana's identity would be discovered, and he would be reading of their elopement in the papers.

What point in hoping now? She was lost to him, utterly, completely lost. Father had made him promise to care for her, to keep her safe until delivered to a suitable husband and home of her own. She would have none of that now.

He had failed everyone who depended upon him: his sister, his guests, Miss Elizabeth.

His entire family would consider him inept. They might speak words that would say otherwise as they condemned Georgiana for her foolishness, but underneath all that, they would think him a failure.

It was difficult not to blame Richard for bringing the Garlands into his midst. But there were too many instances where his own choices had led to where they were now—teetering on the brink of disaster—so that he could not lay all the blame at someone else's feet.

Richard cursed Miss Garland under his breath—he was not one to suffer disloyalty lightly, and Miss Garland's defection was of the worst sort, second only to Garland's. Such language! Some of it Darcy had never heard before, which was saying a great deal.

The only person who might possibly understand, who might be able to offer him solace in this storm, was lost to him because of his own failures, too. Insensitivity, failure to protect her as he had promised her father ... and failure to recognize her value, how very essential she was to Pemberley. To him.

That morning he came across her and Garland on the footpath, he should have been more aware; he should have noticed. She had not been herself; upset and distracted, her color was high. Garland responded like a schoolboy caught where he did not belong. It was all there right in front of him, but he ignored it. He was too occupied with his own concerns to take the time to recognize what he should have.

Would she ever forgive him for that? Would he ever have the opportunity to apologize?

How could he face Pemberley without Elizabeth by his side, at his shoulder knowing what he needed, understanding him in his strength and his weakness? No, it was simply not possible. He could not do it.

And yet, what choice was there?

The chair beneath him creaked as he rocked, face in hands, barely able to breathe.

# ❧ Chapter 17

Elizabeth sat at the dressing table—again—pretending to adjust the ornaments in her hair. Three and a half weeks she had been in London now, nearly a month complete. This new routine, days filled with her nieces and nephews, social calls and evening entertainments, should be feeling more comfortable now, more normal, more natural. Perhaps it was, but some days it was difficult to tell. All the new places, new people, new experiences while pleasing, sometimes made one wish for home.

No, that was not a right thought. London was home now; she just needed a little more time, and it would all feel right and natural. Like Derbyshire had.

The sun danced on the edge of the horizon—just another quarter of an hour and they would be off to the theater again. Her reflection taunted her. When Jane had pinned up her hair, it was always simple—

pretty, but simple. Aunt Gardiner's maid crafted fancy French styles that matched Elizabeth's lovely new gowns. Yet—she adjusted a floral pin—was it really herself she saw in the mirror anymore?

Who was she in this place?

Enough of staring at her own reflection. Elizabeth moved to the writing desk, pale apricot silk swished against her knees and lacy ruffles fluttered with each step. She slipped Jane's most recent letter out of the drawer and perched on the edge of the cool, green-covered bed.

Jane had not sounded like herself in her letter. Not that she had said anything was amiss—in fact, the missive contained little information at all, except to describe the pleasure that her engagement to Mr. Bingley brought to one and all. While Jane tended to dwell upon the positive, this seemed extreme, even for her. It was almost as if there was something she had been specifically told not to mention, so she was going out of her way to avoid discussing anything that might be at all displeasing. It was a Jane sort of thing to do.

But what could be so distressing—

"Lizzy? Are you ready?" Aunt Gardiner called from the other side of the door.

"I am coming." Elizabeth slipped the letter back into the drawer. Whatever was—or was not—troubling Jane would have to wait until after the private theatrical at the Lyceum and the supper party to follow.

The curtain closed and the principal actor came out to recite the play's epilogue, but Elizabeth could hardly breathe, hardly think, much less hear, what was going on. The audience murmuring in the pit and the more polite company in the boxes around her faded into a noisy gray haze. This could not be possible. None of it could be possible. Not even in a novel of fairy-land could this be possible.

She pressed her temples and sucked in slow deep breaths. *The Appearance of Goodness*—how could they have performed Sir Alexander's play? Granted, there were a few differences; some of the changes he had made immediately before she left Pemberley were notable by their absence, but in all essentials, it was the same.

Uncle Gardiner tapped her shoulder and helped her to her feet. Concern lined his face, but if he had asked after her, his question was lost in the noise of the withdrawing crowd. He took her arm and led her outside.

"What did you think of the play?" Aunt Gardiner smoothed her skirts and settled back into the soft squabs of their coach.

Elizabeth settled in beside her, barely able to feel the smooth leather beneath her.

"As I understand, it is a very recent—some say yet unfinished—work. I am told the playwright does not wish his name revealed because of it," Uncle Gardiner said. "What was your opinion?"

"It had its good points, to be sure." Aunt Gardiner's tone did not quite match her words. "The heroine seemed too naïve, even for a young girl, and the suitors lacked subtlety. It was far too easy to predict their true natures."

"Then you may have some very interesting conversation tonight. I think, and it is only a supposition, that we might have the opportunity to meet the playwright himself at the party. He provided the tickets our hostess gave us for the evening. Perhaps he will give us some additional insight into the drama." Uncle Gardiner thumbed his lapels.

"That would be very ... interesting," Elizabeth said. Interesting hardly captured the potential, but what other word might be polite to offer in the circumstance? Distressing, disturbing, and gut-wrenching were definitely not considered polite.

How could Sir Alexander be here when he was supposed to be at a house party in Derbyshire? And what was she to do if she saw him here?

A stuffy, silent butler took their wraps and showed them into an equally stuffy, but less silent, drawing room. The floor was filled with fashionable furnishing and the walls covered, nearly floor to ceiling, with a dizzying array of paintings: portraits, landscapes, still-lifes, flowers, and even what appeared to be a map.

Clusters of people, many recent acquaintances, milled around half a dozen card tables, talking and sneaking surreptitious peeks at the covered dishes perched on three sideboards that lined the longest wall of the room. A young lady played softly on the pianoforte tucked into the corner farthest from the sideboards, a lovely, lively tune while a pair of sisters—they must be sisters, the way they favored each other so—sang passably on either side of the instrument.

Mr. Cluett waved from across the room and sauntered to her side. His coat and breeches were exquisitely tailored—it was true, a man of middling looks could be made far more handsome by an excellent tailor. "Were you at the Lyceum as well? I thought I saw you in a box on the right-hand side, but I was on the left."

"You were in the third box on the second tier?"

"Yes, that was the one. I am flattered that you would have noticed." Mr. Cluett seemed very pleased. He was a pleasant enough fellow. Had she met him prior to knowing Mr. Darcy, her opinion of him would likely have been higher.

Unfortunately, most men paled in comparison to Mr. Darcy.

"You must tell me what you thought of the play." Mr. Cluett's eyes sparkled as though in anticipation.

"I have not yet had time to think it over and form an opinion." Hopefully she could put the entire thing out of her mind and avoid thinking on it at all.

"How remarkable. Most women I know have a very ready opinion on such things. It is singular that you would have to take time to dwell upon it."

"Do you consider it a bad thing that I should not have already formed a judgment?"

The corner of his mouth crept up, crinkling the corner of his eye. "It is rather pleasing, I think. It certainly suggests an opinion well worth listening to."

Her cheeks flushed.

"There's a thought." He rubbed his chin as he glanced over her shoulder and scanned the room. "I have an idea to give you further insight into the play we just saw. Come." He beckoned her to follow him through a milling crowd.

They broke through the throng to stand very near a very large man wearing an exceptionally well-tailored blue coat, who turned to face them as they approached.

"Lester! I do say! Come, meet my friend." Mr.

Cluett pushed nearer. "Miss Bennet, may I present my friend, Mr. Samuel Lester."

Sir Alexander stared down at her, smiling, though the expression did not extend to his eyes.

"I am pleased to meet you … Mr. Lester." She nearly stumbled over the name. What was he playing at?

"The look on your face suggests you have some acquaintance with my sister, Miss Davis." Sir Alexander edged closer to a young woman beside him who did not look up.

Elizabeth blinked several times. "Indeed, I do. It has been sometime since we last met in the country-side. Are you well, Miss … Davis?"

Miss Darcy, dressed as a young lady out in society, peeked up at Elizabeth, color high. She nodded fractionally and made a tiny curtsey.

"Well, who would have guessed you might already be acquainted? What a happy coincidence." Mr. Cluett rocked on his toes as though very pleased with himself. "I shall get us some punch directly, and we may sit down and discuss that play of yours, Lester, what say you?"

"Capital notion." Sir Alexander's eyes fixed on Elizabeth.

Mr. Cluett disappeared into the crowd.

"What are you doing here? Where is Mr. Darcy?" Elizabeth whispered.

"He is not here." Miss Darcy's voice was almost too weak to hear.

"You have come without him?" Elizabeth looked up at Sir Alexander.

"Oh, do not be so stodgy." He sneered. "You are the one who ran away to London. You cannot blame us for thinking it was a good idea."

Hateful man! "How did your work come to be performed at the Lyceum while we thought it had been finished for the house party at Pemberley?"

"My friends here had been waiting for it. I sent a copy of it to them as soon as it was finished so they could begin work on it."

"And you did not think to tell us?"

"What difference would it have made? It was exhilarating working on it with two different companies, as it were. Did you not notice many of your ideas were incorporated into the production tonight? I often shared your notions with the company here. You were an excellent assistant." A hint of suggestion quirked his eyebrow.

"How is it that no one here seems to know you by your real name?"

"There are times it is convenient not to be a baronet."

No, he would not bait her into that conversation. "Who else is traveling with you? I must speak with them."

He leaned down and whispered into her ear, "None from Pemberley are with us."

"Have you no sense of what you have done?" She hissed the words like an angry goose. If he crossed her again, she might just peck him like one, too.

"What are you talking about? We are merely acting in a play of our own. You know our roles, Samuel Lester, amateur playwright and his half-sister, Miss Davis."

"Your half-sister?" Bile burned her throat until she

could taste it at the back of her tongue. Half-sister indeed. "And this is how you have presented yourself whilst you have been … traveling?"

"Entirely." Miss Darcy wrung her hands, her voice on the edge of tears.

"You well know I enjoy my sister's company." Sir Alexander lifted an eyebrow and laughed. "I fear, though, my sister does not like travel very well."

"That was all I needed to know." Elizabeth took Miss Darcy's arm and propelled her through the crowd.

Miss Darcy stumbled a mite, but managed to keep pace with Elizabeth to the brightly lit and mercifully empty entrance hall. Elizabeth called for the Gardiner coach to be summoned and sent a maid to fetch Aunt Gardiner and their wraps. Her heart thundered in her ears nearly loud enough to echo off the marble tiles.

Aunt Gardiner appeared along with the maid with their wraps. "Lizzy?"

"Pray, do not make me explain here and now, but trust me, it is imperative that my friend Miss … Davis come to Cheapside immediately and stay with us."

"Shall I return with you now?"

"No, I think it better you and Uncle stay and enjoy the evening. Pray excuse me to Mr. Cluett—you might tell him that I was taken with a sudden head-ache." That was entirely true.

"This is most irregular, but I trust you, Lizzy. You are welcome to stay with us, Miss Davis. I am certain this will all make sense soon enough." No doubt, Aunt would not rest until it made sense.

Miss Darcy curtsied, eyes on her slippers. "Thank you, madam."

The butler announced their coach. Aunt saw them

to the door, watching until the driver handed them up and closed the door behind them.

Lizzy sat beside Miss Darcy. "Do you wish to tell me?"

Miss Darcy trembled and burst into tears. All things considered, it was impressive that she had held on until now to do so.

Elizabeth slipped her arm around her shoulders and held her all the way to the Gardiner's house. Once there, she instructed the housekeeper to see a guestroom made up and guided Miss Darcy upstairs to Aunt Gardiner's little sitting room overlooking the mews.

They sat on the couch, a bright moonbeam streaming over their shoulders allaying the need for candles. With the windows inched open, the smells of the night drifted in—peaceful and soft as the flowers on the upholstery.

"How long ago did you leave Pemberley?" Elizabeth held Miss Darcy's hands in hers.

"Ten days, I think. We were several days in Newmarket to see a little theater there. But he was anxious to be in London for the performance tonight."

"Are you pleased with your journey?"

Miss Darcy stood and paced the length of the moonbeam and back. "I thought so. I was at first."

"And now?"

"I miss Pemberley. At first it was all new with him. I thought he liked me. But he spends all his time in the theaters, and I find myself alone. I do not understand this world he is in. I do not think I like it."

"Do you want to return home?"

"How can I? You are not saying it, but you are

thinking it. I have been ruined. My brother will never see me again. If I do not marry him, no one will have me. What have I done? What have I done?" She fell to her knees, sobbing.

Elizabeth moved to the floor beside her and held her tightly until the paroxysm ran its course. "You will stay here with me until we can sort all of this out. It is not impossible. There may yet be a way."

"You would help, even after what I have done? Why?"

"Because that is what it means to be a friend."

# Chapter 18

Darcy paced the length of his oak paneled study for at least the hundredth time. Richard slouched in the wingchair near the fireplace, watching him and muttering under his breath. The drawn curtains blocked the moonlight, leaving the room lit by only three candles on the mantle. Dark and gloomy, exactly how he felt.

Darcy snarled something under his breath.

"Stop acting as though you are the only one with a right to high dudgeon. I feel even more guilty than you—it was I who brought the Garlands to Pemberley in the first place. You cannot know how much I regret that decision and the way they have interfered with both of you." Richard climbed out of his chair and headed toward the liquor cabinet.

"I would rather not be reminded of that right now."

"She treated you wrongly from the beginning. It is a mercy that she decided to end it with the hopes of keeping it all quiet. I am certain we will be able to achieve that." He poured two glasses and handed one to Darcy.

"I said, I do not wish to talk about it. What about that is so difficult for you to understand?"

"No, I must speak. It was my fault that you made an offer for her in the first place. Had I not tried to behave like some foolish match-making woman, you would have not succumbed to her machinations."

"I was a fool to allow her to turn my head when the perfect woman—the perfect wife—has been under my nose, overlooked this entire time."

"What are you talking about? No, forget I asked. I do not want to know." Richard lifted an open hand and gulped his brandy.

"You already know."

"You cannot afford to marry a woman without a fortune. Georgiana's dowry must be replaced or what will you settle on your younger children?"

"It will not be necessary if she has already eloped. Besides, Pemberley has seen strong profits in the years since I have taken over. I will find a way."

"How can you think of anyone but Georgiana at such a time? Besides, Miss Elizabeth chose to leave Pemberley of her own volition, and you have been asked not to interfere with her. You do not even know where she is."

Darcy removed a scrap of paper from his pocket, with Bennet's handwriting. "I may know."

"She is not of our circle; no one would accept her."

"That changes nothing." Darcy sipped his glass

and set it aside. "If nothing else, I must make her an apology. I … I compromised her."

"What? When? How?"

Darcy related the night she had spent in the parlor with him. "It was entirely my fault. She came to aid me in my discomfort. I cannot fault her for that. I am certain that Mrs. Reynolds and my valet have squelched all talk of it. Never once did she try to use that against me, only insisting I avoid any further soothing syrups."

"My God, Darcy! I cannot believe you never told me."

"Would you have insisted that I make an offer to Miss Elizabeth rather than Miss Garland, considering it seems I importuned them both on the same evening? Or should Miss Garland have been preferred because she was the first to have been sullied by me, or because she was the richest?"

"I cannot sit by and allow you to do something stupid. Do not expect my assistance."

"I am asking neither your permission nor your assistance. But if you cannot stand behind me, perhaps you should continue searching for Georgiana on your own." Darcy pushed up from his chair and stalked out.

His boots rang out on the marble stairs—even now, his ankle still throbbed without them. Damn it all, just another reminder of his sorely disordered life. He slammed his chamber door behind him—what was one more impropriety at this point?

How could he possibly face her after neglecting her so? He fingered the scrap of paper in his pocket and sank down to sit on the bed.

Richard was wrong. He did not merely have feelings for her. He loved her.

Merciful heavens, he loved her.

That was why Pemberley never felt right in her absence. Why he had felt a hollow shell of himself without her nearby. He had taken it all for granted, always assuming she would be there another day.

Then she was not.

And she might never be again.

But at least he could ensure she knew of his repentance.

Elizabeth fell into the soft bergère that matched the flowers on the curtains in Aunt's cozy sitting room and pressed her temples. Gracious—how was it possible for any young woman, any person, to cry so much? Surely it had been nearly every waking hour for the last two days. Miss Darcy—Georgiana she insisted on being called now—had sniffled, sobbed, and wailed alternately from dawn until nearly midnight, pausing only to take enough sustenance to begin weeping again.

Thank heavens, dear Aunt Gardiner had taken over comforting Georgiana. They were outside now, in the garden taking a little fresh air with the children. If there was anything that might cheer Georgiana, or at least distract her, it was the Gardiner children.

Relief from Elizabeth's headache, though—that would be harder to find. She pressed the heels of her hands into her eyes. That helped a little. Just enough. Perhaps a quarter of an hour like this and—

"Miss Bennet?" Aunt Gardiner's housekeeper asked.

Elizabeth blinked the fuzziness from her eyes as she struggled to focus on the stout, white-haired housekeeper standing in the doorway.

"Mr. Gardiner says he needs you in his study right away, Miss. He apologizes for the inconvenience, but it cannot wait."

Elizabeth jumped up so fast her head swam. "What is wrong?"

"I cannot say, Miss. He has a caller with him and says you must come directly."

Great heavens, had Sir Alexander come? What for, to claim Georgiana? Why would Uncle have allowed him in the house? Perhaps he was only here to return Georgiana's trunk. Pray it were only that.

Elizabeth scurried downstairs, and paused at Uncle's study door. She squeezed her eyes shut, sucked in a deep breath, and knocked. Uncle opened the door and ushered her inside the tidy, if overcrowded, room. Books and journals filled the shelves that lined the two side walls. A fireplace, covered with a painted screen, took up most of the adjacent wall, with a clerk's desk tucked into the corner. Uncle's imposing desk resided between two windows opposite the fireplace and several smaller chairs, one occupied, took up the middle of the room.

"Miss Elizabeth?"

"Mr. Darcy?" Elizabeth stumbled. Uncle caught her elbow and steadied her.

"I suppose that is indeed proof you are who you say you are, sir." Uncle pointed Elizabeth to a chair and sat down behind his desk. "You see, Lizzy, this gentleman came to the door claiming to be your father's patron, but with no letter of introduction. I could not be sure. He wishes to speak to you."

Elizabeth stared at him, blinking half a dozen times before coherent words took shape. "Your sister?"

"Who told you?" Mr. Darcy leaned forward, clutching the edge of Uncle's oak desk.

"You are looking for her?"

"Richard and I had given up hope—none of the intelligence we were given has been of any use. Do you know something, anything?" Weary lines crossed his forehead and lined his eyes, making his expression very difficult to understand.

"If you find her, what will you do? You wish to bring her home?" Elizabeth chewed her bottom lip and glanced at Uncle Gardiner, heart squeezed to aching in her chest.

"I would like nothing more than to remove her from Garland's company. Georgiana made a very foolish choice, but I do not have enough family to cast off my nearest relation because she made a terrible decision. I doubt that her reputation can be salvaged. But I will do whatever I can to ensure she is happy and comfortable, whatever that may end up looking like."

Thank heavens! "Pray come with me. I have something to show you."

"Has she written to you—"

She raised her hand for silence. Uncle nodded and opened the door for them. She beckoned for him to follow her. With tightly pressed lips and clenched fists, the strain of silence left him shaking. They walked through the kitchen to the mews, their steps falling in an oddly syncopated rhythm.

She pushed the door open and paused in the doorway as their eyes adjusted to the bright sun. The children played battledore and shuttlecock with their nursery maid in one corner of the garden. In the other, Aunt Gardiner and Georgiana sat on a white iron bench, talking softly.

Darcy grabbed her hand. "You found her?" The hoarse words barely made it above a whisper. "How?"

"She has been with us two days now. Most of it spent sobbing and in dread of what she would say to you. It is complicated, and I will explain later, but it is just possible that her reputation might yet be salvaged."

He pulled her a little closer. "I cannot believe it. Richard and I have been to three separate cities with no trace of her to be found."

"An act of Providence, I suppose. Go to her, but be prepared, she will weep."

He gazed at her, jaw agape.

She squeezed his hand and pointed toward Georgiana.

His steps were slow at first, then he ran.

Georgiana squealed and jumped to her feet. "Brother?"

The two embraced, Georgiana sobbing into his shoulder. Elizabeth's eyes burned, and her vision blurred.

The breach was hardly healed, to be sure. But somehow Pemberley was whole again. She swallowed a sob. All would be well now—and she could, she would, move on just as Papa counseled her.

"Lizzy?" A soft hand touched her shoulder.

When had Aunt Gardiner approached?

"I have asked the nursery maid to take the children on a walk, a rather long walk. I think it would be good for you to go with them."

No! She needed to stay and ... and what? What more was there to do for them? "I will fetch my bonnet." Elizabeth chanced a final glimpse of Georgiana with Mr. Darcy holding her hands, speaking too softly for anyone else to hear, a fitting final image for her to treasure of Pemberley and the Darcys.

## ✦Chapter 19

The Gardiner children clung to her hands and chattered excitedly, skipping behind the nursery maid. How easy it was for them to lose themselves in the thrill of something unexpected. If only all unexpected events sparked such joy.

Was it not enough that she had run into Georgiana and Sir Alexander? Did it have to be Mr. Darcy, too? How was she supposed to recover her fragile equanimity and make sense out of her new life in London when her old life chased her down like a highwayman in the night?

"Are you all right, Lizzy?" Little Thomas looked up at her, big brown eyes blinking in the sun.

"I will be fine, dear." She squeezed his hand.

"You look sad. Do you want to run? Maybe we can run away from the sad."

Run indeed? Ladies did not run—according to

Mama's strict lectures on what a lady did and did not do. But neither did ladies find themselves in such situations. Perhaps the most sensible thing was to run.

She grabbed Thomas' hand, and they sprinted down the mews, past the nursery maid racing toward the outlet to the street. Unladylike, yes, but perhaps not all the rules she had been taught applied when one was making a new life.

The second day after Georgiana's departure was one of Aunt Gardiner's at-home days. Odd how that staying at home required every bit as much preparation as going out to make calls. With Jane, and sometimes even with Mary, Kitty, and Lydia, getting dressed up and feeling pretty could be pleasant, even fun. It never felt lonely as it did with Aunt Gardiner's lady's maid.

Silly, foolish thoughts.

Elizabeth swallowed back a sigh as the maid pinned up her hair. Once her hair was finished, she still had to decide what to wear, something her sisters would have helped her with at home. But grown-up ladies did not have a bevy of sisters to call upon for such trivial matters, and it was time for her to be grown-up.

Was it wrong to dread company on an at-home day? Why not invite a herd of pigs to run amok through the parlor? It would be just as appealing and would probably remain so until she recovered from the last caller she had received.

The maid stepped back and waited, assumedly for Elizabeth's approval. The styling still felt foreign, but appropriate for polite company. "I will wear the green ensemble today."

The dress was the color of the leaves in the garden below. Fresh and crisp—and fashionable, according to Aunt Gardiner.

She twirled in the mirror. The lawn skirt hung just right, and the embroidered ribbons she and Aunt Gardiner had added to the sleeves reminded her of the late Mrs. Darcy's cutting garden—a quiet little way to bring a bit of her old life here into the new.

Somehow that helped.

She joined Aunt Gardiner at the round morning room table that filled most of the space. The walls were papered with sprigs of pink and yellow spring flowers, and the white curtains floated like clouds upon the breeze through open windows. Lingering scents of coffee and baked goods hung on the air. It was difficult to be glum in this space. One of Uncle's shirts lay spread out on the table, positioned to catch the light as Aunt mended it.

"Would you care to help me, dear?" Aunt looked over the rim of her glasses. "Your uncle is so hard on his shirts. Always catching them on this or that at the warehouse. I want to make sure I find all the spots that need stitching before I start."

"Papa does the same thing, though he has no such good excuse. I have become quite good at spotting tiny tears." Elizabeth pulled a chair close and sat beside Aunt Gardiner, carefully avoiding casting a shadow on the white linen shirt. "Would you pass me some pins to mark—"

"Madam?" The stout housekeeper stood in the doorway, white curls peeking around her mobcap, a tray in her hand with a calling card in the center. "A Mr. Cluett has come to call. Shall I tell him you are in?"

Aunt Gardiner glanced at Elizabeth.

Butterflies danced in her chest and muddled her thoughts. He had come to see her? No young man had ever done that. What did one do on such an occasion? Words would have been a useful answer, but a nod proved all she could muster.

"We will receive him in the parlor." Aunt stood, and the housekeeper trundled off. "He is a very nice young man. I am glad he has come to call."

"Do young gentleman often call on you?"

"Hardly. The compliment is all for you, I am sure. Remember there is no pressure, I am no matchmaker. Just relax and enjoy your company."

Mr. Cluett greeted them with a bow as they entered the downstairs parlor. Aunt Gardiner had specifically designed the room to receive guests and stimulate conversation. Trinkets from their travels throughout England and to the continent filled a curiosity cabinet and decorated shelves near the windows. More than the books in the cases near the fireplace, that bric-a-brac revealed the Gardiners' open and curious characters. Done up in various shades of blue, the room was reminiscent of Pemberley's blue parlor, comfortable and homey, if not eminently fashionable.

"I am very glad to see you looking so healthy, Miss Elizabeth." He seated himself across from Elizabeth and Aunt Gardiner on the settee. Though not in his stylish evening attire, his open and friendly air added a great deal to his run-of-the-mill appearance. "And Miss Davis?"

"She is very well, thank you. It was very good of her to accompany me home." The less said on the matter, the better.

"I confess my surprise at discovering you were already acquainted. Were you previously acquainted with Mr. Lester as well?" His artless expression matched his tone.

Good. Otherwise, they would have to end this interview immediately.

"I met him in passing, at an event much like the party the other night." She forced a smile. He could not possibly know how much she regretted her acquaintance with Sir Alexander.

"I hope you will not be disappointed, but I am sorry to say we will not be able to enjoy his company any more this Season."

"Is that so?" Hopefully, Aunt Gardiner's relief was not as evident to him as it was to Elizabeth.

"Yes, as I understand, he took a notion to go to Bath. A mutual friend mentioned a theater company in search of a new work. He said something about having made changes to his new play and that he wanted to see it performed with those changes."

"It must be very pleasant to be so free to move about when and where one wants," Aunt Gardiner said.

"Indeed so. There are advantages to being a gentleman who does not have the entanglements of a professional life." Mr. Cluett's eyes held a question.

One she should probably answer. "My father rarely takes time away from the parish. Though he could, I secretly think he is afraid he might miss something important if he were to be away."

Was it her imagination, or did he seem to breathe a sigh of relief?

"Have you any further plans to attend the theater?" he asked.

No, not the theater, perhaps not ever again.

"I think, perhaps, our next outing will be a concert or to see the opera dancers. Too much of any one amusement can reduce one's enjoyment of it. Do you not think so, Elizabeth?"

"I have only seen the opera dancers once, and I look forward to seeing them soon. Are you fond of the opera?" Elizabeth asked.

The housekeeper slipped in and whispered something to Aunt Gardiner. "No, now is not the time."

A shadow in the door way cleared his throat.

The housekeeper gulped and stammered, "Mr. Darcy. Madam."

Elizabeth's face grew cold, and the room spun.

He stepped inside, still favoring his injured ankle. His face pale and his cheeks drawn, it seemed he had not allowed his valet to shave him recently either. Had he not slept? Probably not. No doubt he was worried about Georgiana. Had he come to seek advice about her situation?

"Pray, excuse me. I should go now. Good day, Mrs. Gardiner, Miss Bennet." Mr. Cluett rose and bowed, though his tone suggested a bit of disappointment.

Somehow Elizabeth managed to make it to her feet and curtsey.

Mr. Darcy stepped aside to permit Mr. Cluett's exit, then approached with slow heavy steps. His scent—sandalwood ... and was it musk?— filled the room. Oh, to be back in Derbyshire, in the shadow of Pemberley!

Why was he wearing riding boots—to support his ankle perhaps? He would never be so improper without a very good reason. It was the sort of thing Colonel Fitzwilliam might have suggested and something she should have thought of herself. At least he had someone to watch over him.

"You are most welcome, Mr. Darcy. Might I inquire after your sister?" Aunt Gardiner gestured him toward a chair. The tight lines on her face—she was being polite, but was not pleased.

"She is—no, I cannot say she is well, but she has improved. We will be returning to Derbyshire very soon." He sat on the edge of the chair and looked directly at Elizabeth. "She would very much like for you to travel with us."

Aunt Gardiner crossed her arms and shook her head. "No. That is kind of you, but Lizzy has no plans to return to the vicarage. She is living with her uncle and me now."

Mr. Darcy drew breath, furrows deepening in his brow. "Mr. Bennet explained that to me. Still, we had hoped—"

"No, sir. I must ask you to leave now. I will not entertain this conversation." Aunt Gardiner stood.

"Is that what you want?" Oh, the look, the longing—longing, is that what that was?—in his eyes.

Her heartbeat, her breath, the rush of blood in her ears drowned out all the voices in the room. What should she want? What did she want? Hang it all, they were not the same. She should obey her father's wishes. That was what was best for her, was it not? It always had been before.

Her eyes burned, and she shook her head. No, no—everything she wanted was wrong. But it was what every fiber of her soul longed for.

Uncle Gardiner's strident tones jolted her back to the conversation. Aunt, Uncle, and Mr. Darcy stood near the doorway, arguing in low, strained voices.

Elizabeth ran to them. "Pray stop! Have I no voice, no say in this?"

"Your father was very clear, and you agreed." Never had Elizabeth heard such reprimand in Aunt Gardiner's tone.

"Yes, yes, I know that is true. But I was not even able to say goodbye when I left Derbyshire. Do I not deserve at least the opportunity to do that now?"

"It is not a good idea, Lizzy." Uncle glowered at Mr. Darcy.

"Have I not done everything you asked since I have been here? I have asked nothing until now. Does that not count for something?"

The Gardiners exchanged a conversation in looks, raised eyebrows, pursed lips, and shrugs.

"You may have a quarter of an hour. We will be in the hallway just beyond the door." Uncle Gardiner led them out, pressing a doorstop under the door to keep it open as he passed.

Mr. Darcy beckoned her a few steps away from the door. How difficult to control her trembling to make those few paces.

"Pray, will you consider traveling with us?"

"Why does Georgiana wish me to travel with her? You have not had another misunderstanding with her, have you?"

"No, in fact, I think we have a greater understanding than we ever had before. We have been talking over the letters my mother left for us. The ones you directed Georgiana to in your letter to her."

She pressed her hand to her mouth, a chill slipping down her neck. "You saw that letter?"

"Mrs. Reynolds found it and gave it to me in hopes it would offer some information on Georgiana's whereabouts. You were very generous toward me in that letter, and you gave Georgiana excellent advice. We both regret that she did not read your letter before making her decision." Darcy bounced steepled hands off his chin. "I cannot believe that you have known my family secrets for so long and never once gave indication to any of it."

"A secret is a secret. I had to honor your mother's wishes."

"It seems as though you have known my family better than I have."

"No, not at all. I have simply known them differently."

"Pemberley is not the same without you. Nothing is right. Pray, come back with us." He caught her gaze, the ache in his voice palpable.

Elizabeth forced herself to walk to the other side of the room. How could she say what had to be said with him in close enough to touch? "I cannot."

"Is it your father?"

"It is best that I stay."

"Why?" The voice came from just behind her, so close she could feel his warmth against her back. Why did he have to stand so close, teasing her with what she should not want?

"Do not ask me that."

"Why not?"

"I do not wish to answer."

"You have always been honest with me. Why will you not be so now?"

"Pray stop. I cannot. Do not importune me further." She wrapped her arms around her waist. Perhaps that would slow her thundering heart.

"Are you not my friend any longer?"

"I … I will always be your friend."

"Then come back to where you belong."

She whirled on him. How dare he continue to push her when she had clearly said—merciful heavens! She had never seen such a look on his face. But Papa …. "No, you must go, now. I pray you, do not persist in this. It cannot be."

"And that is your final answer?"

"It has to be." Why did it have to be?

"I see." Slow heavy steps withdrew towards the door.

She held her breath until they faded away.

There, she had done it, exactly what she was required to do, exactly what Papa insisted she needed to do. It was not right for her to leave the sphere to which she was born. And yet, was not coming to London doing just that? This was not her world, the city with all its wonders.

There was nowhere she belonged now, not after turning away the one single person she could not do without. She clenched her jaw and pressed her lips together, eyes squeezed shut.

Hot trails coursed down her cheeks. Foolish girl, only children cried— what purpose would there be in breaking down now? It would change nothing—and nothing would ever be right again.

"I have tried, and I cannot …."

She whirled and stumbled.

He caught her elbow and pulled her close. "I cannot function at all knowing you will not be there." He caught her gaze with a near physical force. "Nothing has ever felt so right as having you stay at Pemberley—and nothing, nothing at all, has been right since you left me."

"I did not leave you," she whispered into his chest.

"I suppose not. I was the one who became betrothed to another." He rubbed the back of his neck. "It was the worst mistake of my life. I regretted it almost as soon as it happened—and I am relieved it is over."

"Over?" No, that could not be what he said. She leaned back to look into his face.

"She is on her way to Sicily. She dare not be associated with Georgiana's indiscretions."

"I do not know what to say."

"Richard insisted that offering for her was the right thing to do after the way I behaved toward her under the influence of that bloody—forgive me—tonic of hers. He did not know I had behaved much more improperly toward you."

"I told you, it is forgotten. You owe me nothing. Pray do not—"

"I owe you a great deal." He held her shoulders. "For returning my sister to me." And closer still. "For showing me what an honorable woman does in the face of a difficult situation."

"I told you—"

"For your patience and friendship and sound advice for so many years now. For your love—"

"Pray stop this! I do not want you indebted to me."

He stepped nearer. "Pray then, what do you want?"

"I want you to stop!" She covered her face with her hands. "I cannot continue this conversation."

"Elizabeth, I am so sorry."

She peeked over her fingers. Such tenderness in his eyes.

"I have taken your friendship, your very presence, for granted, acting as though you would always be a part of Pemberley, with no consideration for … for anything."

"What are you saying?"

"The perfect mistress of Pemberley has been in its shadow all this time. I have been too thick to see it."

"No." She pushed his chest.

"What do you mean, no?"

"You are exhausted. You feel guilty. You have no clear answers and that always makes you anxious. I will not see you make another decision you will regret."

"I love you."

"Pardon me?"

"I expect you understand the concept." He cocked his brow, lips turning up a mite. Why did he have to look so handsome, so very dear, in this moment? "And while there are a great many things of which I am uncertain right now, I am unshakably certain—"

"No, I cannot—"

"Pray, allow me to tell you how ardently I admire and love you."

"No, stop, lest you come to regret what you are saying."

He tipped her face up and stared into her eyes. Was that fear in his furrowed brow? "You do not love me?"

She gulped deep breaths and squeezed her eyes shut, but she trembled hard in his hands. "Yes ... no ... I ...."

"You might say those words, but I will not believe you." He pulled her to his chest, his arms around her, safety enveloping her, taking her back to Pemberley.

"I should not love you. I should never have permitted it." She pressed her fist into his strong shoulder.

"So, you do love me." His arms tightened, so strong, so safe.

"It is not fair, not to any of us. I must not." She should pull away, leave before he spoke those words again, and her strength failed.

"But you do."

No, no, she dare not confess to it. She choked back a sob.

"If you love me, I will not leave here without you. I promise I shall never fail you again."

"But you cannot. You need so much more—"

"You see, you do not deny it. You cannot." Creases faded from his brow. "I do not need to marry a fortune. I need to be whole. I need to marry you."

"I cannot bear to be a decision you regret."

He pulled back a to look down into her eyes. "I am more worried that you might regret me. Is there someone else? Are you interested in that man who was here when I arrived?"

"Mr. Cluett is a good man."

"But you are interested in his company?"

"He is not you."

His lips twitched, the way they did when he was trying not to smile. He struggled a moment more, then surrendered to the expression, so compellingly handsome, happy. "So, you do love me."

"I am sorry. I should not. I have always been taught that I should not."

"But you do, and I am glad for it. More than I can say. If I am wrong, then tell me now, for if you do not, I shall kiss you. If you allow that, then I shall take that as your answer. You will accept my offer of marriage and come home with me to be Mrs. Darcy."

"There are so many who will disapprove my quitting the sphere to which I was born."

"None whose opinion matters to me." He leaned down and pressed his lips to hers.

Warm and soft at first, but then powerful and insistent. How could she not respond in kind?

"You have made me the happiest of men. I insist you permit me to do the same for you, my dearest, loveliest Elizabeth." He cupped her cheek with his hand.

"You already have."

Darcy's heart raced as the woods of Pemberley rose on the horizon, peeking between the half-drawn curtains on the coach's side glass. After a week in London, and another five days more in travel—could he be more ready to be home? He relished each creak of the carriage springs, each jolt and jostle through the ruts and rises in the road, signs the journey was nearly over.

So much remained unresolved, but with Elizabeth

beside him, all would be well. He pulled her in just a mite closer to his side, drinking in the heady mix of her lavender perfume, the leather squabs, and the fresh fragrance of the fields. Yes, all would be well.

Richard had disapproved of Darcy's offer for her —loudly, with a great deal of stamping and shouting. His reasons were sound, even as his facts were right. But it did not mean Richard was right. And he did not like to be wrong.

But neither was Richard a fool. When Elizabeth and the Gardiners laid out suggestions on how to navigate the social waters to minimize the possibility of scandal, he admitted Elizabeth might be a far greater social asset to Darcy and perhaps the entire family, than he had ever considered possible. It was a beginning, and that was enough for now, a season of beginnings.

"You are still comfortable with our plan? I know how you feel about disguise." Elizabeth nestled her cheek into his shoulder.

"No, I am not, but I think you hardly expected me to be," he whispered, pressing his cheek to the top of her head. "She is very young to be going to the continent."

Across from them, Georgiana stirred in her sleep.

"Richard will keep good watch over her. I think even Anne will rise to the occasion, especially considering how often she has said that she wanted to see the continent."

"Do you really think a ball to celebrate her come-out is necessary?" Could he stomach entertaining guests again so soon?

"It does feel a bit like rewarding her for her mistakes, but it will help quell rumors of her having run off, not to mention that she could hardly travel with her cousins whilst not yet out."

"Will a four-month journey be enough to ensure we know … know if …." It was stupid to act as though saying the words would make them more likely to be true.

"It will be. But do not borrow trouble. We shall hope for the best, even if we do have a plan for the worst."

He covered her hands with his and squeezed, and she twined her fingers through his. "How is it you have not changed your mind?"

She slipped her arm around his waist. "Miss Garland hurt you deeply even if you did not truly care for her."

"I suppose she did. Foolish, is it not? Then again, it is not worse than I deserved for the way I overlooked and mistreated you." He kissed the top of her head.

"You are harder on yourself than I can ever be. The vicarage is not far. Are you certain you want to do this alone?"

"I went against your father's express wishes. He wanted me to leave you to your new life in London. I have no doubt he will be displeased with me. You do not need to witness that."

"Papa is not so awful when he is upset. I mean no disrespect, but he is nothing like your Father was when in high dudgeon."

"That might be the case, but he is also the only man who can deny me what I desire most. I cannot take that threat lightly." The coach rolled to a stop in front of the vicarage, and he pushed the door open. "I will be at the house as soon as I can. Pray inform

Mrs. Reynolds of whatever you see fit for her to know."

The sun hung just a handspan above the horizon, the sky turning gold with its descent. A fresh, cool breeze carrying the perfume of some unnamed flower and green grass welcomed him home. Home. Yes, he was home, and with Pemberley at his back and Elizabeth at his side, all would be well.

He stared at the oak paneled vicarage door. But that was not going to accomplish his purpose. No, for that he had to knock. That much he could do. The rest? Perhaps, as Elizabeth told him, one step at a time was all he needed to be concerned with.

The maid showed him to the vicar's study, cluttered but welcoming as it always was.

"Mr. Darcy!" Bennet scrambled to his feet, nearly dropping his cane in his haste to maneuver around his desk. "I pray it is not too forward of me to hope it is good news you are bringing. Pray, sit down." He pointed a shaking hand at a pair of simple wooden chairs near the front of the desk.

Darcy sat. "There is quite a bit of news to share, to be sure. In my opinion it is all good. I hope that you will share that opinion."

"I am quite intrigued. Do tell me all of this news." Bennet slowly lowered himself into the chair.

Darcy launched into a concise rendition of Georgiana's rescue at Elizabeth's hands.

Bennet nodded and blinked, but waited far too long to speak. "I am very glad that your sister has been found. That alone is surprising enough, but Elizabeth's part in it? If it were any other man telling me this, I would declare it all a fancy brought on by too much brandy."

Darcy pulled a letter from his pocket. "From Mr. Gardiner."

"There is no need, I am certain you could not invent any of this." Bennet took the letter and laid it aside on his desk. He rubbed his hands together as though considering what to say. "I appreciate that you have confessed the way you violated my wishes in seeing Elizabeth. I did not make that clear to you, I suppose, but you should have inferred if from what I told you. Still, I can understand desperation—"

"Pray, sir, before you finish forgiving me, there is more I need tell you."

"Is something amiss with Lizzy? She has not written to us this last week—"

Darcy swallowed back the cotton wool catching in his throat. "Miss Elizabeth is quite well. She is with Georgiana, probably at Pemberley Manor right now."

Bennet's eyes flashed with unmistakable anger as he rapped his cane on the floor. "Lizzy has come back? I explicitly told you she was gone to live in London with her aunt and uncle. How dare you—"

"I have made her an offer of marriage. And she accepted."

"You did what?" Bennet braced himself against the arms of the chair and slowly rose. "How could you do such a thing?"

"I love her very dearly."

"Balderdash! You were just jilted by a very suitable woman, one of your circle and status. You are in the throes of melancholy and seeking a quick way to ameliorate your feelings."

Darcy stood, towering over Bennet. "I assure you; I am not melancholy over her defection. If anything, I am relieved."

"Relieved at being jilted? Do not be ridiculous."

"Only too late did I discover she had kept a secret from me that, had I known, would have prevented me from ever making her an offer." That was all he needed to know on the matter.

"And now you feel guilty for what transpired with Lizzy the night you were injured. You are trying to make amends for it, despite her assurances that it is forgotten? There is no good to be served in that."

Bennet knew about that? Darcy squeezed his eyes shut. "Why do you keep trying to make me out as insincere?"

"Not insincere. Ill-considered, short-sighted—"

"Why do you refuse to believe I love and admire your daughter and want her to be my wife?"

"I have said it before: she is not suitable for a man of your station. In marrying you, she would be quitting the sphere to which she was born. Is that not enough? Her mother and I have taught her better than that."

"Is that not a mean estimation of your own daughter?"

"Be reasonable. She has not the education a woman of your sphere would have, nor the connections. Her manners, though genteel, are surely not up to the scrutiny of the *ton*, nor is her wardrobe. And I am in no position to be able to supply it. Then there is the matter of her very pert opinions—"

"Trust me, I know a great deal about those. I am under no illusion about that." Those opinions were her best feature.

"You know her dowry will do very little toward replacing what you will lose when your sister marries."

If she has not ruined herself with her foolishness—but now was not the time for that discussion.

"Close to nine thousand pounds is what she will
cost you. That is a very great deal of money."

"I am able to do maths. Elizabeth is entirely worth
it."

Bennet cradled his forehead in his hand. "Your
family will not approve."

"It may take some time for them to fully embrace
her, but they are already coming to see her value. And
consider for yourself, sir. Is there any other means by
which your favorite daughter might be installed at so
easy a distance to yourself?"

"My comfort should not come before her happiness."

"I will make her happy and do my best to protect
her from those in my sphere who would seek to do
otherwise."

Bennet sank back into his chair and scrubbed his
face with his hands. "She loves you, you know. She
has for a very long time. But love is such an ephemeral thing to back a marriage upon. I cannot approve."

"She has been my friend for a very long time. I believe that is what all manner of advice givers
recommend as the basis for marriage. In fact, I did
not know what I felt toward her was love until she
left Pemberley, and I was utterly lost without her."

Bennet stared off through the window, head bobbing just slightly.

Pray let him speak—soon!

"It is irregular. It is not what is done."

"I understand all of that. But do I have your consent?" Darcy clenched his teeth and held his breath.

"I could not part with her to a lesser man."

# ✣ Epilogue

A month later, Elizabeth strolled the vicarage garden with Georgiana. Beds of sweet peas, dahlias, and lilies bade them welcome, tempting them to linger with the sweet perfume floating on the sun-warmed summer breeze.

"I still cannot believe my come-out ball is the day before your wedding," Georgiana said.

"I admit the timing is a mite unusual, but in some ways, it is convenient. Many of the guests for the ball are also invited to the wedding breakfast. It is to their benefit to be able to attend both events while only having to travel once. You must admit, it is very ex-pedient."

"I know I do not deserve it."

"Pray do not begin that discussion again. Yes, you made a mistake, a very grave one of which we cannot yet know all the consequences. We all acknowledge that. But you have thoroughly repented of the matter, and I am certain will demonstrate far better judgment in the future. So then, let us be done with it. It is in the best interest for you and your entire family that you have a proper come-out celebration before you are away to the continent."

Georgiana kicked a small rock out of the path. "Would I be ungrateful to say that I do not look forward to spending all those months in Anne's company."

Who could blame her? "You might consider that your fair penance for all that has transpired."

"You mean that society would not believe Anne would travel with me if I have been ruined."

"Effectively, yes. While Aunt and Uncle Gardiner were able to quash the one murmur from the scandal sheets, it is important that we do what we can to make sure their explanation is as believable as possible."

"I owe your aunt and uncle a great deal." Georgina picked at her skirts. "I am sorry to be so much trouble to all of you."

Patience, she needed patience now. How many times had they repeated this conversation? "Do not wallow in self-pity. Stop talking about how bad you feel and demonstrate your dedication to learning from it by becoming the woman your mother wanted you to be."

Georgiana sniffled—pray let her not break into tears again!

Darcy approached from the manor, his strides long and sure, without his riding boots. Perhaps now he would finally be able to leave the woes of this spring behind him and move into a new season. "I had been told I would find you here. Mrs. Reynolds wishes to consult with you about some flower arrangements." He looked at Georgiana.

"I am certain she can manage them very well without me ...."

"She has specifically asked for you." He glowered.

She squeaked and hurried off to the house.

"That is a very effective look you have." Elizabeth chuckled as she slipped her hand in his arm. He laughed, too—how often he did that now. "I wonder that Mrs. Reynolds did not send a maid to fetch her."

"I might have intercepted that message." He set off toward a little bench in the shade of the trees that bordered the garden.

"You wanted to be out of the house."

"I wanted to be with you."

"Away from the bustle of preparations and guests arriving?" She leaned her head on his shoulder. "I imagine guests do not evoke happy memories just now."

"Hardly." They reached the bench, and he gestured for her to sit with him.

"It will not be the same as the house party."

"Of course not. You will be here, helping to manage it all."

He was teasing her! Actually teasing. "I rather thought something else might be foremost in your mind."

He caught her gaze and looked into her eyes. The corners of his lips pulled up in a tiny smile. "Of course, it is."

The fuzzy edges of his voice tickled the back of her neck, sending delightful shivers down her spine.

Heavens, he was handsome, and the way he looked at her—how could she not return his smile?

Musk and sandalwood and something uniquely him filled her senses—scents that fluttered her heart. Gentle fingers cupped her cheek and drew her closer, so close their lips touched. Gentle and playful at first, but, as though he could not bear any misunderstanding, urgency and need crept in, reminding her of the depth of his feelings, ones to which he was only just learning to give voice.

"That is much better. It is good to see you have not forgotten." She caressed his cheek, still smooth from his valet's careful attentions.

He pressed into her touch. "A houseful of guests come to attend our wedding breakfast tomorrow will not allow me to forget, I assure you."

"Our wedding breakfast? And I thought they were here to attend Georgiana's come out and Jane's wedding breakfast." She laughed. "Who would have thought they might also wish to come to ours?"

"You do not mind sharing the day with them?"

"I hardly want to be the focus of all our guests' attentions. I have heard tales. It is said that both of your aunts—"

"Indeed." He bit his lower lip and quirked his brow. "It appears I am the one who seems to be acquiring the better connections."

"I can only imagine Colonel Fitzwilliam's face when he hears you say such a thing."

"He is usually the one saying things designed to shock and astonish. It will be pleasing to turn the tables on him." Some of the smile left his eyes.

"I know he has been your good friend. I hope he is able to reconcile himself to our marriage."

"He is proud and prejudiced, like the rest of my family—as I was. But he, more than the rest, I expect to come around to my way of thinking."

She draped her arms around his neck. "So, if you were proud and prejudiced, what are you now?"

"Impatient to be married—I have wasted far too much time. I do not wish to wait a day longer than necessary to have you installed permanently at Pemberley." He stroked her cheek with his knuckles.

"In sixteen short hours, you shall have to wait no longer. My pert opinions will be your constant companions."

"Of that I shall not repine, for your fine eyes will be there to accompany them." He kissed her forehead.

"So, I am tolerable because you like my eyes?"

"You are far more than merely tolerable. I find I cannot do without either your opinions or your eyes. My dearest, loveliest Elizabeth, I must have all of you, always."

## Acknowledgments

So many people have helped me along the journey taking this from an idea to a reality.

Debbie, Diana, Anji, Julie, Ruth and Susanne thank you so much for cold reading and being honest!

My dear friend Cathy, my biggest cheerleader, you have kept me from chickening out more than once!

And my sweet sister Gerri who believed in even those first attempts that now live in the file drawer!

Thank you!

# Other Books by Maria Grace

**Fine Eyes and Pert Opinions**
**Remember the Past**
**The Darcy Brothers**

### A Jane Austen Regency Life Series:
*A Jane Austen Christmas: Regency Christmas Traditions*
*Courtship and Marriage in Jane Austen's World*
*How Jane Austen Kept her Cook: An A to Z History of*
*Georgian Ice Cream*

### Jane Austen's Dragons Series:
*A Proper Introduction to Dragons*
*Pemberley: Mr. Darcy's Dragon*
*Longbourn: Dragon Entail*
*Netherfield:Rogue Dragon*

### The Queen of Rosings Park Series:
*Mistaking Her Character*
*The Trouble to Check Her*
*A Less Agreeable Man*

### Sweet Tea Stories:
*A Spot of Sweet Tea: Hopes and Beginnings (short story*
*anthology)*
*Snowbound at Hartfield*
*A Most Affectionate Mother*
*Inspiration*

# On Line Exclusives at:

- **Bonus and deleted scenes**
- **Regency Life Series**

## Free e-books:

- *Rising Waters: Hurricane Harvey Memoirs*
- *Lady Catherine's Cat*
- *A Gift from Rosings Park*
- *Bits of Bobbin Lace*
- *Half Agony, Half Hope: New Reflections on Persuasion*
- *Four Days in April*

# ❧About the Author

 Maria Grace has her PhD in Educational Psychology and is a 16-year veteran of the university classroom where she taught courses in human growth and development, learning, test development and counseling. None of which have anything to do with her undergraduate studies in economics/sociology/managerial studies/ behavior sciences.

She has one husband, earned two graduate degrees and two black belts, raised three sons, danced English Country dance for four years, is aunt to five nieces, is designing a sixth Regency costume, blogged seven years on Random Bits of Fascination, has outlines for eight novels waiting to be written, attended nine English country dance balls, and shared her life with ten cats.

Her books, fiction and nonfiction, are available at all major online booksellers.

## She can be contacted at:

author.MariaGrace@gmail.com

**Facebook:**

http://facebook.com/AuthorMariaGrace

**On Amazon.com:**

http://amazon.com/author/mariagrace

**Random Bits of Fascination**
(http://RandomBitsofFascination.com)

**Austen Variations** (http://AustenVariations.com)

**English Historical Fiction Authors**
 (http://EnglshHistoryAuthors.blogspot.com)

**White Soup Press** (http://whitesouppress.com/)

**On Twitter** @WriteMariaGrace

**On Pinterest:** http://pinterest.com/mariagrace423/

www.ingramcontent.com/pod-product-compliance
Lightning Source LLC
Chambersburg PA
CBHW051335250626
47155CB00007B/2604